TIME THE AVENGER

TIME THE AVENGER

By Jason Marinko

Charleston, SC
www.PalmettoPublishing.com

Time The Avenger
Copyright © 2022 by Jason Marinko

Paperback ISBN: 978-1-7369508-0-7

This is a work of fiction. Names, characters, places, and incidents are products of the author's imagination or are used in a fictitious manner.

Cover design by Jason Marinko

Author home page (timetheavenger.com)

DEDICATED TO MICHELLE

In 2008 a place in North America once too small for the country to notice—yet too large for the states it borders to completely ignore—had the eyes of the nation cast upon it.

A mass of land lay south of New York, jammed inside Pennsylvania and New Jersey.

Inside that place lay Middleton, a city the nation no longer ignored as news of the tragedy that had befallen it dominated world news following the presidential election.

The media coined a new name for the town, forever referring to it as **MURDERTON** *thereafter.*

TIME THE AVENGER

avenger *n.* **1.** one who inflicts punishment in return for an injury or offense

avenge *v.* **1.** to punish in kind the wrongdoer responsible;

synonyms: requite, retaliate, ***revenge***

TABLE OF CONTENTS

PREFACE:
A MEANS TO AN END

Thursday, November 13, 2008, 7:45 p.m.

"**D**evil, stoke the hellfire—you're about to have company." The hooded figure spoke through the skeleton half mask from the dead man's maroon Chevy Blazer once the woman in the silver Mercedes had come into view. Pulling closer into a space behind the Benz, they observed her slumped further in the seat. The stalker sat low enough to maintain a visual and not be noticed as Deidre Lisbon's arms flailed back and forth in a demonstrative fashion.

Her aggressive movements puzzled her stalker, until the lit-up cell phone in her hand came into sight.

"First off, what did I say about taking the car without telling me?" Matt Bergman questioned Deidre. She couldn't tell if her sugar daddy's tone was one of anger or embarrassment, so she took the defensive approach.

"OK, I know you're like almost two decades older than me, Matt, but that doesn't make you my dad, so stop acting like it. What kind of relationship is this? I have to start asking you for permission for everything all of a sudden?"

"Don't try and avoid the issue. Where is it? You sound all skied up right now. Call me back on the video screen. I want to see your face."

"That video calling thing works like shit, and for the thousandth time, I don't know! You probably hid it from yourself like last time. Maybe you shouldn't do blow anymore; it makes you too paranoid."

"Dee, I had almost an ounce left in the cigarette pack on the nightstand in my room. You were the only other one in there last night."

"Yeah, I'm the one who met your scumbag friend and copped it for you, remember? Look, I'll stop over there on my way back and get more. Let me go—Tharington's closes in, like, an hour."

"Why are you at the mall anyway?"

"Matt! You're more annoying than texts I get from assholes I hardly know, still telling me to vote for Obama! I have to return the shirt you didn't like!"

"Oh yeah? Just making a return? That why your Myface—or whatever it is—update says, 'I'm going shopping, bitches'?"

"OK, Dad! Is it OK if I go pick myself up some necessities? Matter of fact, how 'bout I act like you when you ask me to do all the nasty shit you like, huh? How 'bout that?"

"Never mind. Just go see the guy and bring my car back."

"That's what I thought, bi-atch!" Deidre said, ending the call. She reached into the console, removed a pack of Benson & Hedges cigarettes, and pulled out the bag Matt had been asking about. She then opened the glove compartment, grabbed the car's manual, and poured a clump on it. She planned to do just a few key hits, but Matt had revved her up enough to go for the gusto.

"Yes, I did, muthafuckah!" she said, humoring herself, and pressed the manual flush against her nostril and snorted until the rush hit her.

"Old habits die hard, huh? And tonight so do you," the figure said as Deidre brushed her hair aside and wiped her nose clean in the overhead mirror. She gave herself a smile, exited the car, and paced toward the entrance.

Tharington's was a store Deidre had only been able to browse back in the day—her high school days. Browse and occasionally sneak into a fitting room to lift something she had to have but couldn't afford. Those days were long over, and she was overcome by shopper's euphoria courtesy of Matt's card. "Let-Me-Get-That-Matt" was what Deidre and her best girl, Lana, called Matt Bergman behind his back.

Bergman, fifteen years her senior, in her eyes was old, but he had what Deidre needed—disposable income that could be spent on her. She screwed around on him all she wanted, used him to get coke, embarrassed him, and if it so suited her, insulted him and laughed right in his face. She only put out occasionally—a self-proclaimed professional cocktease—rationing and holding out whenever she wanted something from him. Her plan had been to take it easy and only get a few things, but she felt like teaching him a lesson.

She picked up the contents of her online wish list in the store: Donna jeans, Dior perfume, Kors purse, Blahnik heels, Prada boots, Versace scarf and shades, Gucci dress—all of it.

Deidre didn't stop there. A pair of four-inch stilettos accentuated her figure in the dress she was wearing to her upcoming reunion. Then for good measure, she piled on a matching platinum necklace, earrings, and bracelet because, as she told the fine-jewelry salesman, who repeated the final price in amazement, she was worth every penny.

The escalator lowered Deidre back down to the first floor. She felt pleased with herself and her purchases. When she had bought the shirt, she had known he'd hate it. Her intention was to get back into the mall with his credit card to make the return and make additional purchases for herself. So what if he knew she had gotten what she wanted? An announcement interrupted the elevator music playing in the store.

"Valued Tharington's shoppers, please bring any final purchases to the nearest sales associate as it is nine p.m. and we are closed. Tharington's re-opens tomorrow at nine a.m. Enjoy an additional fifteen percent off when you use your Tharington's store card. Good evening, and thank you for choosing Tharington's."

"Oh well, Matt's stuck with the shirt—not enough time."

The music resumed, and the overhead lights dimmed. Feeling the weight of her haul in the spiraling red-roped Tharington's bags brought Deidre immense pleasure as she stepped onto the ground floor.

She scurried toward the exit like a bandit heading for the hideout, then was stopped dead in her tracks by the most adorable pink cashmere sweater. She rifled through the pile next to the display mannequin and found one two sizes too small. Just what she had wanted, nice and tight. The closest sales clerk was a pretty but mousy-looking young girl who was hunched over counting down her register. The sound of coins hitting the plastic register tray echoed as Deidre rushed up to the counter.

"Can I get this?" she said anxiously, causing the young girl behind the register to lose count.

"I'm sorry, the store is closed. They made the announcement. We open at nine tomorrow," the girl replied, startled by the threatening-looking pretty woman, whose hostile eyes betrayed the beauty of her face.

I'm not coming here tomorrow, bitch, Deidre thought, looking the clerk up and down, then she zeroed in on her Tharington's name tag, flipping her straight golden-blond hair over her right shoulder. Deidre continued in a tone that managed to be condescending, insulting, and threatening all at once, "OK, here's the thing, Ash-ley. I'm not coming back tomorrow. So…" Her eyes rolled, both shoulders hunched up, and she raised both hands as if the victim of a great injustice. The girl stood her ground, shaking her head no from side to side, making Deidre want to harm her physically.

"Can't you just ring me up real fast?" The sweater was now clutched over her head in a threatening manner.

"I'm sorry, we're closed."

Now this little twerp is pissing me off, snotty little bitch! Deidre thought as hot blood warmed her face.

"Well, I'm a good customer here, and I want to see the manager."

Ashley sighed and picked up the phone from the sales desk. "Manager for customer assistance in women's winter wear." Ashley put the phone down and studied Deidre, who continued to shop in the dimly lit store with defiance.

"How long are they going to be?" asked Deidre in agitation.

Ashley was on the brink of tears and choked up but responded. "I'm not, ah, sure. The store's closed, and the managers are closing as well," the meek girl replied, looking away.

Deidre wasn't satisfied. "You've got a real fucking attitude problem, you know that?" she yelled, pointing her index finger at Ashley through the clump of items draped over her arm.

"What's the problem here, Ashley?" asked the approaching manager, a suited man with a narrow mustache whose glasses moved with his annoyed facial expression.

"Clarence. I told her we were…"

"Hello, Ms. Bergman!" Clarence exclaimed, straightening his lapels. He recognized Deidre immediately and addressed her by the name he'd seen on the credit card she'd used so many times before.

"I just wanted to buy these scarves and this sweater, and she is giving me an attitude problem! I'm a good customer and don't deserve to be treated this way!"

"Of course not" Clarence continued in a pacifying tone while scowling at Ashley. "Allow me to ring you up. We will give you a complimentary gift card for this inconvenience, courtesy of Tharington's."

"Well, I don't know if I can continue as a customer if a rude little girl like her is working here," Deidre said, lumping merchandise upon the counter as Clarence scanned the items and looked up Matt Bergman's Tharington's store card so Deidre did not need to provide it. When he finished folding the scarves and sweater like a dedicated manservant catering to a master, he stepped around the register and handed Deidre another red-roped bag.

"I assure you, I'll counsel Ashley about her behavior and if it continues, she will be removed," Clarence said, glaring in the direction of the shy girl the same way a pimp looked at a prostitute who had come up short with his cash.

Ashley said nothing. Stepping away from the counter, she picked up items Deidre had flung on the floor as she had waited for the manager while shopping in near darkness.

"Well, I hope so." Deidre scoffed, gathering her many bags aggressively.

"Have a good evening, Ms. Bergman," Clarence said to Deidre's back.

Storming toward the exit, she shot a look in Ashley's direction, a sneering smile, a face that mimicked her thoughts perfectly, one that said, *Screw you, bitch. I win.*

As she made her way through the exit doors, her cell phone went off, and she smiled, seeing it was Lana and not Matt. She shifted the bags and answered, eager to tell Lana about her victorious evening with Let-Me-Get-That's credit card and her triumph over Ashley. She had gotten what she had wanted, and it put an extra bounce in her step as she strutted through the exit doors leading to where her car was parked.

"What's up, girl!" Deidre brimmed with excitement, locating her car easily in the near-empty parking lot.

"A bitch just hooked herself up big time, people in the store all pissed, cuz a bitch is buying so much shit after they closed and all…yeah he gave me his card. I told his dumb ass I was taking a shirt back for him; hold on a second, doll…"

She reached into her purse for her keys but dropped them. Crouching down to retrieve them, Deidre turned, feeling eyes on her. She scanned the vacant parking lot, seeing a small white-and-blue mall security SUV pass by her with amber lights flashing.

Satisfied no one was there, she rose back up and continued, "Hey, doll. Let me hit you back. I'm loading the car up and all. Later, love. Peace out."

The still-quiet outdoors was a drastic change from the upbeat music playing inside Tharington's. Being surrounded by nothing but a few sparsely scattered cars and the towering trees of Middleton Pines Shopping Mall made Deidre jittery.

The drip from the coke kicked in, and her nose began to trickle as the trees swayed and a nearby flagpole made a repetitive clanging noise that echoed through the lot as the wind kicked up. A chill came over her as she tossed her items in the rear of the luxury sedan, closed the door, jumped into the driver's seat, and locked the doors immediately.

Inside the car Deidre let out a deep breath. Staring at nothing except the security vehicle with the amber lights circling back in her direction, she chuckled regarding her misplaced intuition and paranoia. She looked at the console and thought about snorting another bump to straighten herself out, then decided against it.

"Getting yourself all worked up for no reason, girl. Wait—what the fuck?"

Deidre had not seen the Chevy that was now three parking spaces away. It hadn't been there when she had walked out. Perhaps it was that whiny little twat Ashley's ride.

Deidre adjusted her seat belt and started the engine, still focusing on the Blazer with its lights off and motor running. Part of her wanted to watch the little bitch schlep out of the parking lot. *Maybe she'll be crying, and I can wave at her from the Benz,* she mused to herself—but she saw no one in the driver's seat.

Feeling she was being watched again, she grabbed the shifter, then her phone went off again. She looked at the screen and saw it was Lana again. She answered.

"Tell me what you got," Lana demanded as Deidre activated the car's speakerphone.

"A dress, shoes, scarves, and a sweater! And jewelry! I blew his card out of the water, girl!" she squealed in excitement.

"You are one lucky ass hooker, Deidre! I'm raiding all your winter gear from last year…"

Tap, tap. Two gentle rapping sounds pressed into the body of the car, followed by a louder one.

Tap. Deidre thought the sound was from her phone but couldn't be sure and looked down. That wasn't it either. The clicking sound she had thought was coming from the rear speakers sounded again!

Clink, clink. This time it sounded hollow, like a metal ring slowly hitting against the glass behind the driver's side. She turned around, then gasped and reached to put the car in drive.

Clink.

Immediately, as Deidre turned back, the driver's side window exploded. *Cer-ashh.* Fragments of glass littered her collar, clung to her neckline, and trickled down her shirt.

She lunged backward. "Wha…wh…wh…a…t! No! Please, nuh-nu-no, ahh-noo!"

A black-gloved hand grabbed a clump of Deidre's hair and jerked it toward the broken window, pounding her face into the remaining shards of glass. Lana heard muffled screams.

"Dee Dee!" Lana yelled through the phone, hearing her friend's savage beating. "I'm calling for help, Deidre!"

Just then the security vehicle pulled up.

"Hey, you get off her! Hands up!" Lana held her breath as multiple pops of distant gunfire sounded, followed by a brief pause in the attack.

"Ugh, no, uhhh…oh God!" Deidre sobbed, struggling to pull away once again.

"Cops came, Deidre? Dee Dee?" Lana gasped as the open-door signal chimed.

"No-nuh-nooo!" Letting out a final gasp, Deidre had no fight left and after some seconds, offered no resistance as her assailant delivered the finishing blows.

All Lana could do was listen. The flurry ended with a crunch of bone. *Snap.*

A voice grunted, and the seat belt retracted as the lifeless body was flung out of the driver's seat. Deidre's blond hair, saturated in blood that seeped from her head onto the white painted lines of the parking space.

Lana listened with the small hope that perhaps Deidre had gotten out of the car alive. The attacker spoke.

"Deidre can't come to the phone, Lana, because she's dead! The rest of you are dead too. You just don't know it yet!" the hard-breathing person said, then exited the vehicle's cockpit and moments later was heard speeding off. Lana dropped her phone, paralyzed with fear.

Ashley, Clarence, and the other employees made their way out of the separate exit designated for workers. Ashley took out her phone to call for a ride. Her encounter with Deidre Lisbon had caused her to miss the last bus.

Seeing the security guard laid out alongside the two cars and Deidre's lifeless body opposite him, Paula Jensen from the perfume counter shouted, "He's been shot! That girl's hurt! She's bleeding!"

"So-somebody help!" Clarence screamed. Ashley ended the call with her dad and dialed emergency for the now-dead woman who moments ago had sought the pleasure of seeing her fired. November rain gently pelted the body and surrounding blacktop. The overhead sky quaked, sending notice of the oncoming storm.

News of the murder aired over the television in the Darby household the following morning. Edwin Darby had one eye trained on the reporter at the scene as he struggled with his daughter Olivia's zipper.

"The victim, a graduate of Middleton High School, was murdered moments after exiting Tharington's department store. A guard arrived on the scene to come to her aid. The attacker shot and injured twenty-nine-year-old Middleton Pines security guard Marvin Sargene. His wounds are described as nonfatal."

"Stand still, damn it." He scolded Olivia. This routine had become all too familiar to his wife, Paige. Aggravated again, Ed was taking it out on their little girl. Olivia was about to turn five and still had a tough time putting on her coat and shoes.

"Ed, don't be so rough with her; that coat only zips if you line it up right," Paige said from the corner in the living room designated as her home office. Ed ignored her, as he so often did.

"Say, didn't you go to school with this Deidre Lisbon girl?" he answered back. Paige was pissed off. She turned away from her desk, took off her glasses, and faced her husband, seeing him trying to shove a shoe onto little Olivia's feet.

"Didn't you listen to a word I said?" She got up and took the child's shoe from him. Still focused on the TV, Ed backed away with ease, happy to grab his coffee and relieve himself from the task. Paige overheard a portion of the news report in the uncomfortable silence.

"We will have more on this story as it develops later in this newscast, but again, the victim, thirty-six-year-old Deidre Lisbon—who we believe is from Preytin and a graduate of Middleton High—was discovered here last evening murdered by what injured security guard Marvin Sargene described as a man about six feet tall with a skeletal mask that covered the lower portion of his face. Middleton PD has asked any viewers with additional info to dial the number at the bottom of the screen. This is Astra O'Donnel, reporting live from The Pines Mall."

"She went to Middleton?" Paige asked, forgetting her anger toward Ed. "What was her name again?"

"Lisbon," Ed said, speaking through the donut in his mouth. "Deidre Lisbon. You mentioned this girl before—got some dudes to jump your friend or something." Ed was shielding his mouth away from Olivia. "Screwed the guidance counselor to get straight A's, you said."

"Oh yeah, Deidre. Dee Dee. A real piece of work," Paige replied, heading to the kitchen. "Damn, Ed, I was going to RSVP for that reunion. Now that you brought her up, I may reconsider."

Returning with Olivia's lunch, she placed it in her book bag, looked back to the television, and questioned Ed further, still not grasping the report. "What happened, now? What did she do at Middleton Pines?"

"Do?" Ed snorted. "I wouldn't worry about her doing anything, least of all showing up to your class reunion. She's dead. Punched to death in the mall parking lot by some psycho in a mask. Broke her neck and all."

Paige dropped Olivia's book bag, her face pale white, drained of color. She felt faint and uneasy as time moved in slow motion. A voice from the past rattled around in her head.

"OK, left to right—Ross, Deidre, Harold McCarmick, and Moretz, that lying decrepit fuck." The repressed memory repeated in Paige's head. She sat at her desk partially hearing Olivia's voice: "Mommy, are you OK?"

"Ross, Deidre, Dwayne." The voice looped in her mind as her memory relived the smell of the woods, pumpkin seeds, smoke, and warm beer from the lips of a boy she once loved, till she snapped out of her trance and smiled to comfort her panicked daughter. "I'm fine, honey. Mom's just tired. You have a good day at school."

Paige watched her daughter be shuffled off by Ed, who had no concern that she had almost passed out. Looking out her window, Paige reflected further on her past—a history that the recently deceased Deidre Lisbon had had a profound impact on.

PART I: INVENTION OF VENGEANCE

Thou hast counseled a better course—than thou hast permitted.
—Saint Augustine

Chapter 1:
WELCOME TO MIDDLETON HIGH

Monday, September 5, 1988

Rays of sunlight scorched the pavement at the entrance of Middleton High School, warming the rubber soles of Paige Edmundson's pink Converses. She felt overwhelmed with anticipation. It was the first day of junior year, and she smiled, rushing toward a captive audience of her girlfriends. They were listening to Deidre bragging about spending the summer in Hessian's Cliff, a ritzy town north of Middleton.

"My cousin lives there," Paige chimed in. Lana Karrington cracked her gum and smirked a snotty smile at Paige. Wendy Damon gave Paige a halfhearted wave hello with little effort and reached into the pocket of her denim Studebakers for a comb to tease her hair.

"Hey, Paige," Deidre replied, ignoring Paige's contribution to her story, and carried on. "Anyway, they lived next to the house we rented. His dad was like an inventor or something. They were, like, superrich."

"He looked like Jordan from New Kids—and don't say anything to Ross, or I'll kill you all! But at night I'd sneak out, and he'd fuck the shit out of me in the indoor hot tub his parents had downstairs. Totally the best summer vacation ever," Deidre declared. The other girls giggled in unison, then Diedre looked to Paige, waiting for a reaction. Paige had nothing; she just smiled.

Over the summer she hadn't seen any of the girls she made friends with in her second year at Middleton. Freshman year she didn't know anyone, except Deidre, whom she'd known since second grade. Glimpsing at the clumps of five or more surrounding the front of the school, Paige recognized she had joined a clique of her own. Lana, Wendy, and the other girls reveled in their status of being popular; Paige thought little of it. Her accepting nature had kept her and Deidre friends all these years, but in many ways, Paige had outgrown her attention-needy friend.

"Anyway, he's like in love with me, naturally. Wants me to come up to The Cliff when I get my car."

"Ross will kill you, Dee." Wendy cautioned her, making Deidre sneer with wicked satisfaction while nodding her head in agreement.

Just then a police car let out a beep-bop sound. Dwayne Bishop's father, Officer Alvin Bishop, dropped him off in his police cruiser and gave him the siren instead of a beep of the horn goodbye.

With a new box fade haircut, airbrushed jeans, purple-and-gold converse on his feet, Dwayne clutched his backpack and grinned, seeing his friends— mostly jocks. They all had gray Middleton Rams shirts on. Team Captain Ross Aberdeen demanded they all wear their practice shirts on the first day of school. Deidre told him that it was stupid, so he wore a polo instead.

"I thought we were wearing our practice Ts for first day?" Dwayne asked Ross.

"Game-time decision," Ross replied with his arms crisscrossed, massing his own biceps.

In 1986 the Middleton Rams Varsity team's starting quarterback and halfback had been arrested trying to rob Malden's Pharmacy and expelled from school. This had automatically put Ross and his best friend, Greg Chapman, on the senior squad.

If Deidre was the unofficial head of their clique, then Ross Aberdeen, Deidre's boyfriend since the end of freshman year, was the alpha male of the jocks for sure.

As Deidre carried on, Paige studied her environment until her lack of attention was noticed by Deidre.

"You're still wearing the black fishnet gloves, Paige? That was, like, forever ago," Deidre quipped in an obvious rebuttal to Paige for ignoring her story.

"Yep, and I'm still like a virgin. Dee, how about you?" Paige snapped back, observing a green rusty sedan pull up in the spot Dwayne's dad's patrol car had just vacated. She took notice of the Gran Torino's cargo, a middle-aged woman and a boy she had never seen before. From what she could make out, he appeared handsome, with shoulder-length, straight, dark hair and the most intense bluish-gray eyes, which were visible to her from a distance.

"This girl is so funny; that's why I love her." Deidre backed off. Paige knew Deidre better than any of the other girls, and while they were OK with taking shit from her, Paige always refused to, quick to dish back whatever Deidre threw at her.

"Only Paige brags about being a virgin in junior year." Deidre laughed. The bell rattled like a dying drill outside the Gothic-looking building as the herds came together like one large clump of cattle filing into the double-door entrance.

From his mother's Gran Torino, Max Garret saw the students entering Middleton High. He was embarrassed by the car for certain, a sentiment he'd never express to his mother. Manufactured in 1976, it looked worn beyond its twelve years of existence. The hood was longer than some boats, its color was a green he'd never seen anywhere else, and the vinyl roof, once black, was cracked and weather-beaten, resembling a dirty sponge with flecks of leather embedded in it. He told her he'd walk, but she insisted on at least dropping him off on his first day.

"Look, Mom, everyone's going in. I'm late. I told you I should have walked."

"It's only five of. I wanted to see you off on the first day. If you won't take the bus, you can walk the rest of the year. All I ask is that you give me a great big hug, and I'm done embarrassing you," Barbara Garret told her boy with sincerity.

Max hugged and kissed his mother, laced up his beat-up pair of black Chuck Taylors, and grabbed his book bag. He groaned, looking at his once-black denim jeans, which were now a dull gray. No part of him looked forward to starting a new school, but like his mom had said about Dad getting laid off from the auto plant, "Some things are just out of our hands."

Max believed it was within "their hands." If only his old man could keep a bottle out of "his hands." He slammed the Torino's door shut to get it closed. Then he lifted the door handle so it caught the hinge. His mother leaned over and pushed down the door lock. This routine was necessary every time he got out of the car. Otherwise the door flung open as she drove off.

Bill Garret, Max's father, had promised to fix the ejecting door but never did. It was no wonder he had gotten laid off from the auto plant, Max thought. His mother rolled down the window after securing the lock and spoke out to him.

"New school, fresh start. I know you will make new friends and stay on that honor roll! Have a great first day." Her voice was one of unwavering faith and optimism. The past few years had taken a toll on Barbara Garret, and it showed in her run-down appearance. No matter how hard things got, she always remained positive for her son's sake.

Inspired by his mother's encouragement, the boy rushed up the concrete walkway. Standing at the entrance, he waved back to her as she let go a sigh, followed by tears she'd been holding back. Tears of regret, sadness, and worry for her only child.

The Garrets had moved from the sprawling countryside of Hessian's Cliff to the decaying urban landscape of Middleton City. It was a once-thriving community that never recovered from the riots of the late sixties. Middleton's businesses had packed up and its factories shut down. The suburban outskirts of the city still maintained the look of its once prosperous past. A deteriorating green border surrounded a dull gray center that it could not hold. The area was kept on life support by Hillshire Hospital, erected by the federal government in 1985 out of necessity, once Middleton General closed down in '84.

The old hospital, which had once served as a town landmark, became a shooting gallery for heroin addicts, a refuge for derelicts and transients. Residents nicknamed it "General Crack" due to the freebase epidemic that had added to the town's woes. Middleton General's implosion in '87 scattered the destitute into the inner city.

A menagerie of vacant buildings, boarded-up homes, empty storefronts, side streets filled with too many liquor stores, pawnshops, and bars that plagued the city. Run-down roads with crumbling concrete curbs and cracked sidewalks that led to alleyways like Murderer's Row and College Court where unspeakable acts were committed. A place that was a shell of its past with not nearly enough grocery stores to sustain the city's hunger and not enough churches to forgive the sins its poverty created.

Tears continued to stream down Barbara Garret's cheeks as she pulled away from the school, which was centered between the township and the city. Barbara's job, at Flowers II Remember floral shop and nursery, was in Middleton Township. The home her family had downsized to was not.

Closing her locker, Paige saw the boy from the green clunker making his way into the hallway. He didn't have much meat on him, and while he was tall, his guarded posture aligned him with her five-seven frame. She made her way over to Wendy Damon, who was decorating her locker, to get a closer look. Wendy and Paige had had homeroom together the last two years and always walked in together.

Wendy placed a small mirror inside the locker and fussed with her hair. Paige waited on her, patiently watching the new kid while Wendy brushed her hair and filled the air with Aqua Net hairspray.

Max Garret was making observations of his own. The place was a zoo compared to the order of his last school. A brutish boy in a striped shirt, with acne so severe he could have been a before model in a Clearasil commercial, slammed a smaller boy into a door. Balled-up clumps of paper were being thrown everywhere, accompanied by screaming and yelling in every direction. He looked for a teacher but saw none.

"Come on, Wendy—you look great." Paige encouraged her, eager to get to homeroom and escape the cloud of Aqua Net. Wendy was pretty but nowhere near as good-looking as Deidre and Paige, or the rest of their group, for that matter. Sophomore year Wendy had become close with Ross, which had led to Deidre pointing this out to her.

"Aren't you a little too ugly to be talking to my man all the time?" Wendy never forgot Deidre's spiteful question, which had made her permanently self-conscious. Paige had worked to build Wendy's confidence back ever since.

Two rows of lockers down from Paige's and Wendy's, Deidre Lisbon was soaking up the attention given to her by the flock gathered by her locker. This had become a morning ritual in the middle of last year. Ross Aberdeen, Greg Chapman, and Dwayne Bishop congregated around her, as well as her girlfriends, minus Paige and Allison Kyle. Ross wasn't there yet, and she looked around for him. Sure, he was an immature goofball at times, and he couldn't fuck half as good as superrich Ryan from The Cliff, but she liked his handsome face around her when she glided through the halls.

Scanning the hall, looking for her boyfriend, Deidre looked directly into the grayish-blue eyes of Max Garret. An attractive girl looking at him—Max smiled. She had a smile on her face as well, and when she whipped her hair back, he thought she resembled Kim Basinger. Max was about to ask her for help finding where he needed to be. Then she spoke.

"What are you looking at, fuck wad?" Deidre snarled, her smile gone, replaced by an angry open-mouthed scowl. The other girls near her broke out in laughter at the insult.

Max stammered. "Oh, I, uh, I'm sorry; I'm new here, and *ugh*—"

A shove in the back lifted Max off his feet. Looking up from the floor, he saw the force that had just thrown him.

"Hitting on my bitch, faggot?" questioned Ross Aberdeen with his fists balled up and his biceps stretching the sleeves of his polo shirt to their limit. "Huh? Are you?" Ross continued, threatening Max.

Overwhelmed by the ridiculousness of what had just occurred, Max began gathering his scattered belongings off the ground. Picking up his geometry compass, he thought about stabbing the goon with its needle but returned to his senses and responded.

"No, I was just saying hello. Besides, if I was a fag, why would I hit on her?" Dwayne and Greg joined in the commotion. Deidre laughed aloud at Max's reply, not finding it that funny but seeking to further instigate the confrontation. Greg Chapman's dumbfounded expression indicated to Max, who was slowly getting up, that he'd also like to pounce on him.

Deidre's laughter further infuriated Ross as Dwayne encouraged him. "He just called your mom a name under his breath; I heard him!" Greg joined in. "He was eye-fucking Deidre's butt; I seen him. Kick his fucking ass before I do, Ross." He slammed his fist into his other hand.

Before Max got back on his feet, Ross laid a kick into his chest with everything he had, knocking the wind out of him and sending him back to the floor. Max instinctively grabbed Ross's planted foot and yanked it toward him. Ross lost his balance and fell forward, exclaiming, "You're so dead, kid!"

They pulled and punched at one another in a frenzy.

"Ross, Ross! Mr. M!" Deidre alerted her boyfriend, who was about to gain the upper hand on Max and erupt.

Harold McCarmick blew his whistle twice to thin the herd, and the commotion ceased immediately. He pulled Ross up by the collar of his polo. "I don't know why we got all these people in the hall after second bell. I guess you all want detention on the first day of school? You got somewhere to be? I suggest you get there *now!*" Max decided by his relaxed dress this was a gym teacher or a coach.

All the students dispersed, save for Max and Ross, who McCarmick still had in his grasp.

"This punk tripped me as I was going to class, Mr. M!" Ross protested.

"That right?" McCarmick questioned Max.

"Hardly, he got all crazy because I said hi to that girl."

Harold McCarmick sucked his teeth, unsatisfied with Max's reply, then looked to Ross, released him, and continued. "Get to class, Aberdeen. I'd hate to drop you down on the depth chart before our first game of the season and demote you from team captain."

20

Ross silently mouthed the words "You're dead" behind his coach's back. McCarmick assisted Max to his feet while inspecting the boy's scattered items.

"Thanks, Mr. M," said the boy graciously.

"Athletes call me Mr. M; students call me Mr. McCarmick." He rolled up one of Max's comics and continued, "Aren't you a little old to be reading funny books?"

"Comics are a significant form of American myth and culture. Guess you don't teach history or English," Max joked.

McCarmick smirked in annoyance and moved into Max's face, looking down on him, poking at his chest with the rolled-up book.

"You see, here's the thing, Jughead."

"I'm Max."

"OK, Max, that athlete you just assaulted could have been injured. You could have put his future in jeopardy. So I don't care if you dropped your funny books or what, you understand? I'm only giving you detention for being late to class. You have it signed and return it first thing tomorrow." He held two fingers centimeters away from Max's nose and continued, "Two more, and it's suspension. Are we clear?"

Having been shoved, kicked, punched, and now punished for it, Max remained mute in hostile defiance. The fingers were taken out of his face as McCarmick stared into Max's eyes, his face flushed in a mixture of pale and red irritation. He chomped gum, causing the veins on the sides of his bald head to pulsate. He slowed his chewing and repeated, "I said, are we clear?" only with more anger.

"Yes," Max responded, eager for the repetitive cycle of confrontation to end.

McCarmick dressed him down further. "Yes, Mr. McCarmick! Whew, boy! You got yourself an attitude problem. You best fix it before somebody else decides to tune it up for you." McCarmick took out a pad and pen from the pockets of his warm-up jacket. He marked up the pink slip. While tearing the slip from the perforation, he stared at Max, dangled it before him, grinned, and said, "Here ya go!"

Max moved in the opposite direction of McCarmick with the strides of a speed walker. Seeing the school office ahead, he considered getting a copy of his schedule. Then his adrenaline wore off, and it hit: excruciating pain from his rib cage. His elbows and knees were bothering him as well, a result of Ross's initial shove. The pain there was almost welcome compared to the damage the punting kick had done to his midsection. Max saw a wooden door with a chrome handle with a placard that read, "Restroom" and entered.

A row of sinks faced the left wall, with stalls on the right. Max looked at one of the mirrors above the sink. "Damn it!" he said, seeing his ripped-up Def Leppard Hysteria Tour shirt. The only decent article of clothing he owned, ruined the first time he wore it, stretched and torn along the neckline from his struggle on the floor with Ross. Pulling the ripped shirt aside, Max inspected his ribs.

"Son of a bitch," he exclaimed, foolishly touching his injured ribs. The hallway bell rang out, signaling the end of the homeroom period. As the PA system signaled, he decided he should take a leak before going to the office. He looked over and was puzzled to see only stalls with no urinals. One of the stalls flushed loudly, and the door swung open.

What Max saw next had him conjuring up visions of Van Halen's video. A woman came out of the stall with her knee-length skirt up to her waist. She was attempting to remedy a runner in her stockings. She had long legs and had assumed herself alone. Max put two and two together slowly, realizing why there were no urinals.

"You're not supposed to be in here," a calm but concerned feminine voice called out to him. She quickly pulled her skirt back down to its original length.

"I'm sorry. There was no sign. I didn't know this was the ladies' room. This is my first day here."

"This is the teachers' restroom. You want to be upstairs, first door on the right," she replied, giving a kind smile.

"Thank you—sorry again," he stammered, making his way out of the door.

"No worries," she replied as he heard her turn on the faucet to wash her hands.

Flustered even further, Max made his way to the office. A grouchy man named Mr. Moretz begrudgingly gave him a copy of his schedule. "Don't lose it. You won't be getting another one," Moretz told him multiple times. "You should have gotten this schedule in the mail along with your locker number." Max knew it was common practice for his father to throw out any mail not addressed to William Garret and figured this was the case here.

The rest of the morning was uneventful, even boring, which was fine by Max. He had had enough excitement for the entire junior year this morning. He remained quiet in morning classes and only spoke when called upon by instructors. Looking at his schedule, he saw next up was fifth-period lunch in the cafeteria. Up to this point, he had had no classes with the new enemies he had made that morning. Avoiding them at lunch would be an impossibility.

Every teacher had had to add his name when taking attendance, and since no one was expecting him to be there, Max improvised. A kind elderly woman spoke to him as he entered the school library.

"What kind of book are you looking for, young man?"

"I'm new here, and if it's OK, I'd like to have a look around."

"Suit yourself. I'm Mrs. Evalum, if you have any questions."

"Thank you, Mrs. Evalum."

He took one of the many empty chairs, grabbed the first book he saw, titled *Philosophy in the Modern World*, and couldn't help snicker, seeing the 1964 copyright date. He took out his lunch and enjoyed what he could from the smashed-up brown bag. He thanked Mrs. Evalum on his way out after the bell sounded and glanced at his schedule: period six, chemistry. Finally, a class he liked!

At the doorway to lab room 237, he felt anxious. When he opened the door, his anxiety turned to elation.

"Are you sure you're supposed to be in this room?" joked the attractive teacher he had intruded upon in the teacher's restroom earlier.

"Yes, no confusion, miss?"

"Jalorean, and you are?"

"I'm Max, Max Garret."

"OK, Max, since you're first in the door, take whatever seat you like." He scanned the room and opted for the back, forfeiting the chance of a close-up of Ms. Jalorean for camouflage should any of his antagonists file in after him.

Paige strolled in a few moments after Max had settled. She began speaking to Ms. Jalorean; he noticed her contagious smile, bright blue eyes, and long blond hair that swayed from side to side as she spoke with great enthusiasm. Although he couldn't hear them from the back, it was apparent they had a friendly rapport as one's conversation and body language mimicked the other. Max wondered what the pretty girl and the chemistry teacher had in common that made them so candid with each other.

The day was hectic for Paige Edmundson. It felt like a back-and-forth struggle trying to pacify teachers with attention while wanting to catch up and make plans with her friends. Deidre had gotten her screamed at twice by their English teacher in a futile attempt to get Paige to go out for cheerleading. They had been friends since second grade, sure, but Paige refused to subject herself to the wrath of Captain Deidre. Nor did she wish to prop Deidre atop a human pyramid. Her old friend did that fine all on her own.

"How about you, Ms. J? How is the first day going for you thus far?"

"No one yelling at me or asking me to join their cheer squad. I did have a handsome young man walk in on me in the restroom next to the teachers' lounge, though," she said kiddingly but loud enough for Max to hear.

"Who?" Paige leaned over the chemistry teacher's desk in excitement, causing her jean skirt to reveal the bottom of her heart-shaped backside to Max, who was in the back of the class. His eyes marveled at the rainbow of colors in the skintight tie-dye tights under the skirt, which matched her shirt.

"I am not at liberty to say. I may be a chemistry teacher, but as an administrator of the school, I cannot gossip with you!"

"Come on. Was it that redheaded senior who has the hots for you?" Paige pressed as other students filed into the classroom right on schedule with the bell.

Ms. Jalorean smiled mischievously and told Paige firmly, "Take your seat, Ms. Edmundson" and leaped up and addressed the class from her lectern.

In addition to being easy on the eyes, the chemistry teacher was lively and energetic. She told them they would be pairing up in groups of two.

"Me and Paige are partners!" Lana Karrington piped up, interrupting Ms. Jalorean.

Lana was cool for the most part, yet Paige took Lana for what she was, a follower. Deidre's freshman year fixer-upper (her words) had turned from meek to migraine as she had cloned Dee's every move. From the rear of the class, Max studied Paige's surprised reaction and tried not to stare at her pronounced breasts, which could not be hidden by the baggy multicolor shirt. Max spent his next classes daydreaming about Paige Edmundson.

The bell sounded at the end of eighth period, and a stampede ensued. Upperclassmen wheeled out of the parking lot; the sound of growling engines and stereos blasting filled the air. The last herd pushed through the exit doors, and Max Garret trailed them all.

Katherine Jalorean saw his glacial pace out of the window of the teachers' lounge. *What kid isn't in a rush to fly out of here at the final bell?* she thought as her tea bubbled over. She hustled quickly to the sizzling cup. Looking back out the window, she saw Max moving even slower down the concrete sidewalk away from Middleton High.

Walking along a side street, Max observed graffiti littering an abandoned building that once had been a jewelry store. As he tried to decipher the various spray-painted words, he replayed the events of the day in his head. A stray dog nosing through the garbage on the side of the run-down building reminded Max that the hard part of his day was nowhere near over. He still had to go home.

Chapter 2:
SHELTERS OF HARMONY AND HORROR

Two blocks from his house, sore thoughts became an afterthought. A lump filled up Max's throat as he noticed the Gran Torino missing from in front of the Garrets' ramshackle, single-story rancher. His dad didn't have a job, and his mom rarely left the house in the late afternoon. Unlatching the gate of the rusted chain fence, he proceeded up the walkway and took a deep breath.

Catching his reflection in the screen door's glass window, he paused. Observing his ripped shirt and the marks all over his neck, he tucked in his shirt, put on a windbreaker that was stuffed in his bookbag, and pulled up the collar. Max didn't want his mother worrying any more than she already did.

The front door was locked, so he went into his bag's side pouch to retrieve the key. Reaching around inside, Max saw the bright-pink detention slip, which had conveniently escaped his mind. If his old man was out, he could count on his mom to sign it, sparing himself the wrath of Bill Garret's hair-trigger temper. He said a silent prayer, hoping it was not his mother who was out with the car, slid the key into the lock, and held his breath.

Max's concerns evaporated the moment the succulent aroma invaded his nostrils. He knew it was his mother's magnificent cooking. An oven door sprang open and shuddered closed again, and her soft, passive voice bellowed out to the living room, "Max, honey, is that you? I'm making your favorite!"

"Good. I'm starving," he answered, eager to supplement the contents of the smashed-up brown bag he had digested in the library. He slid out of his beat-up black sneakers in anticipation. Max had planned to go straight to his room and hook up his Atari to the black-and-white TV set to evade any questions about school. But as the smell of fresh garlic simmering in white clam sauce put him in a state of sensory overload, that plan was scrapped.

"Get washed up—we're eating in an hour," his mother announced. Even if he was absent, William Garret insisted on "dinner being on the table" no later than four thirty.

A meal in the Edmundson home was far less structured. Paige joked that her parents lived on West Coast time, a crack she made when plans with friends had to be canceled in lieu of late suppers. When she arrived home from school, she eagerly flipped through the newest issue of *Nintendo Power* magazine, which had come in the mail. She rushed out of her room and down the steps with the magazine half-open to drop hints about upcoming games to her mother.

Reaching the bottom of the steps, she chuckled to herself at the sight of her mother. Lynn was planted in front of her television, on her exercise stepper, wearing a workout leotard and fluorescent-pink headband. Her feet were churning a hell of a two-step, but her upper body was hunched over the frame with a glass of red wine clutched in her right hand. Elvis, Paige's dog, looked at Lynn with his head cocked in confusion, a scene of great amusement to Paige.

The show her mother was engrossed in broke for commercial, and she took a break. Lynn grabbed a towel, wiped her brow, and looked at her daughter's bemused face. "What are you grinning at? Take Elvis out for a walk—he's driving me crazy. I need to grab a shower, then start getting dinner ready."

The terrier eagerly sprang up and ran to Paige, barking with anticipation of his long walk. In the mornings Paige walked him around the block before school. Later in the day, they hit the trail that led to the woods behind the Edmundsons' house. Elvis circled, making it difficult for Paige to attach the leash to his collar. "Elvis! Stay still if you want to go out!" The dog lowered his head apologetically. Paige struggled into her jean jacket, and through the backyard they went.

Once down the dirt path behind the fence of the Edmundsons' back-yard, Paige removed Elvis's collar and put the leash in her pocket. This was routine because the application of the collar and leash was only meant to appease her mother's concerns or for the short morning walk. Once they hit the fence, Elvis ran free.

Paige trotted down the hill on the dirt trail that cut through the grass and led to the woods. She may not have expressed her anticipation the way Elvis did, but they were heading somewhere she was equally excited to go. She spent hours on end in the small clearing in the woods, reading and taking in the natural wonders from a run-down picnic table planted in the center of the clearing. Her mother wanted to know where she was all the time when she walked Elvis, but Paige had only revealed the clearing to her cousin Avery, who had named the place "Paige's fortress of solitude."

She ran around with Elvis until his energy gave out, and the September sky darkened, the buzz of Cicadas blending with the rustling of leaves from the surrounding trees. Paige attached the leash to Elvis's collar and headed back toward home. A light wind at their back seemed to guide them.

While Paige and Elvis were departing the fortress, William Garret was pulling in the driveway on Florsheim Way, fifteen blocks away. Mrs. Garret had told Max that his father was out looking for work and would be joining them shortly. They had waited an additional half hour, then started without him. Mrs. Garret ate very little as she took pleasure in seeing her son enjoy the linguine and clams she had made.

"I hope you saved room—there's chocolate mousse for dessert," Barbara Garret said, revealing the chilled treat from the refrigerator.

They were halfway through dessert when Will Garret brought the beater to a screeching stop in front of the house. The car door slammed, and Max decided to act fast.

"Say, Mom, I was a few minutes late and got detention. Can you sign this?" he said, retrieving the pink slip and pushing it across the table. The drunken voice of his father interrupted his mother's response, informing Max of his poor timing.

"Detention! On the first day? What a fuck up you are, kid!" Bill Garret growled from the darkened hallway in his slurred voice.

Max's mother came to his defense. "Bill, I dropped him off late. It's my fault. Where do I sign this, Max?" The kitchen, which had been filled with laughter and conversation just minutes ago, was now filled with tension.

"On the line at the bottom," Max answered nervously.

"Well, you're a fuckup just as well," Bill Garret retorted, stomping into the kitchen and reaching into the refrigerator as his wife prepared his plate for him in cautioned silence.

"What is this? I thought we were having pot roast," the drunken agitator bellowed, looking at the plate in front of him. Max's leg shook with a life of its own under the table. The only thing his father had been out looking for was in his system and spewing out of his pores.

Compelled to come to the defense of his mom, Max spoke up. "It's, ah, really good, Dad!" His father paused from chugging his can of Schaefer to sneer at his son with a look of utter disgust. Then he directed his hostile stare at his wife and spoke as if she was not there.

"Good, huh? Last goddamned dago dish she made gave me heartburn for a week! A week, damn it!"

"Would you like me to fix you something else, Bill?" Mrs. Garret offered as he sprang back up, causing Max to flinch, while grabbing himself another can of Schaefer. Mrs. Garret continued gently, "Any luck looking today?"

Bill let out a deep breath, his cheeks ballooned, and his crimson red face exploded. "I just walk in the door, and you can't shut your cock hole for five fucking minutes?" he said, flinging the plate off the table, sending it crashing in his wife's direction. "Shitty dinner, and I can't even have a beer in peace?"

Mrs. Garret stepped back in fear and responded with words she instantly regretted. "Well, it would seem you have already had plenty of beer."

A man who lived next door to the Garrets was curious about the family, who had recently moved in. His curiosities were remedied by the sounds he heard coming from their kitchen that night. Sounds of destruction, cries of anguish, pain, and terror made their way into his own home.

"Fucking get fresh with me? I'll fucking kill you, bitch! I'll kill you both." Bill Garret's voice thundered over the screams of his family and glass being shattered. The neighbor put his phone back on the receiver as the sounds died down, justifying to himself that if he were to call 911 about the violence, it would already be too late once the police arrived.

William Garret eventually surrendered to the spirits and passed out on the living room floor, mumbling to himself about the Phillies pitching staff. His wife wept quietly to herself in the kitchen, sweeping broken glass off the floor as her son lay in bed with an ice pack on his skull. The injury to his head had come courtesy of his father, who had become further enraged when Max had attempted to stop him from beating his mother.

Max looked at the brightest star he could see outside his bedroom window and wished death on the man he called Dad.

Sunlight burst through the bedroom window as Max's wristwatch beeped. The Torino's engine turned over outside, and hearing it drive off, he let out a sigh of relief. In a hurry he grabbed a yellow-and-black checked button-down shirt and draped it over the ripped concert shirt. Forgetting the small egg on his head, he shrieked in pain while brushing his tangled black hair. He then grabbed his book bag and headed out the front door.

His mother called out to him behind the screen door in a strained voice, "Maxwell, your lunch."

Turning around, his heart sank, and seeing his mother's eye peppered with purple bruises, he accepted the bag and the signed detention slip from her. "Thanks, Mom." He paused and before setting off turned back around to the door. "Mom, we should leave. We should just get up and leave and stay with Aunt Ida in North Dakota before he kills us."

His mother put on a brave face and addressed her son's concerns. "Please, you think we have it bad? That drought out there has your poor aunt on the brink." Mrs. Garret opened the screen and took her son's arm.

"You can still have a good day at school after a bad night at home, right? He just needs work, Max. Don't you worry; things will get better soon enough. You shove off now so you don't get any more of these silly detentions. And be safe..." she said as Max made his way back down the steps.

While making his way across the street a few blocks from his house, a speeding car caused Max to jump back on the curb. The red convertible blew past him blasting "Naughty Girls Need Love Too," by Samantha Fox, and he could see two pretty girls in the back laughing at his return to the curb in fear. Max returned to the street, watching the Benz in the distance speed up the street. The car passed the Garrets' Torino, parked outside a local tavern. Bill Garret emerged from the beater as the owner opened up the bar. Max let out a sigh and pressed on.

Passing the abandoned jewelry store, Max looked for the dog he had seen yesterday and instead saw a bagman searching through the trash. He looked at his wristwatch and saw he was making good time. Almost getting run over by the girls in the Benz had put a spring in his step. He slowed his pace and looked at the school's entrance from the street.

The only thing that indicated Middleton High was a functioning school were the cars in the parking lot and the students clumped out front. The black paint job on the iron gate was chipped and faded, the concrete walkway cracked and split with weeds growing out of it. The only new thing on the exterior was some fresh graffiti that covered the ancient building. Max passed the various cliques and made his way to the door.

Stoners sat on the wet morning grass without a care, and a trio of kids huddled around a boombox break-dancing to "Rock Box" by Run-DMC. Seeing Ross, Greg, Dwayne, and Deidre, he lowered his head and attempted to move past them undetected. This was futile, and before the doors had been opened, he had come up on Deidre's radar. "Rock Box" faded into "Jam Master Jay," and Max heard Deidre talking about him directly behind his back.

"He's wearing the same shirt he had on yesterday," she announced just loud enough for Max to hear. He was cornered between his tormentors from yesterday and the locked double doors of the school.

"What a dirt neck!" Lana chimed in.

"Tragic," added Cindy Lawton.

Max's face turned red with embarrassment as he heard the girls' growing laughter. Paige found no humor in this and offered an apologetic smile with a slight wave hello. The drilling metallic bell outside the school sounded, and the mad dash into the building began.

Centered in the vacant hallway was Harold McCarmick.

"Turn that shit off!" he said to the boombox crew, then zeroed in on Max. "You got something for me, jughead?"

Digging in his book bag, Max produced the crumpled pink piece of paper that had inspired the violence his mother had suffered last night. McCarmick yanked it out of his hands and studied it as if it were a document of the utmost importance. "All right. See you at three in the room next to the library," McCarmick said, awaiting a "Yes, Mr. McCarmick" or even a "Yes, sir" that was not to be given. Max passed him and said nothing.

A smirk came over McCarmick's face while he watched Max's yellow-and-black shirt become engulfed in the crowded corridor. His expression indicated the pleasure he anticipated in harassing Max. His life had stopped moving forward decades ago, and the only thing he took pleasure in was coaching football and fucking with what he described as punks at the school. He often complained to his fellow faculty members about having to stay and proctor detention after school. That was just smoke and mirrors as he enjoyed overseeing detention. That and coaching allowed him to exercise authority and command respect in a world where he had very little of both, outside the walls of Middleton High.

Unable to follow his mother's advice about putting a bad night behind him, Max found it hard to concentrate. After morning classes he avoided the cafeteria once again and escaped with his comics to the empty library. Growing up in Hessian's Cliff, he would make trips to the local comic shop, Hessian's Heroes. He never missed a monthly issue of his favorite titles, and he read the previous month's books three times over. Middleton had no comic-book store. The disappointments were mounting at a frantic pace.

Following lunch, the afternoon blew by, then the bell rang out, signaling the end of the school day. As the mad dash began for the school's exit,

Max walked in the opposite direction of the moving crowd. He headed up the back stairwell to enter detention.

There were four other students in detention, separated with desks facing the walls. One of them was Greg, who had been so intent in urging Ross Aberdeen to "kick his ass" yesterday. Passing him, Max approached McCarmick, who sat reclined in a teacher's chair, his dirty sneakers on the desk.

"Max Headroom, ta-ta-take a seat." He motioned to the closest desk, then handed him a rolled-up magazine. "Take this *Sports Illustrated*, read it, and write me a summary of the feature story." Behind McCarmick's back, Greg was looking at Max while giving McCarmick the middle finger and mouthing the words, "Fuck you, pussy." Max flipped through the magazine, which was from two years ago, and skimmed the article. The story was on the designated hitter rule being detrimental to baseball.

Initially Max had planned to write that boredom was a larger problem than the DH to get under McCarmick's skin. His better judgment told him not to, though. The fact was, he might have actually enjoyed baseball if his father didn't like it so much. By the time the hour passed, Max had written a strong summary of the article and completed a second draft.

"OK, get lost. Give me your summaries, and don't make me babysit you again," McCarmick said, breaking the silence. Max handed his work in first and headed for the door. He wanted to get out fast and avoid a potential confrontation with Greg on the way out. Just as he placed his hand on the doorknob, McCarmick stopped him, barking out, "Hold up, Garret. I'm not done with you yet." Greg threw a shoulder into Max on his way out, laughing to himself. "Take this bucket, fill it with hot water, and wash the blackboards, then empty the water and clap the erasers outside the steps of the gymnasium exit."

"I'm new here. I don't even know where that is," Max protested.

"I'm well aware of that, jughead. I'm helping you familiarize yourself with the facilities. Have at it." McCarmick shoved the bucket in Max's direction, then tossed the detention assignments into a wastebasket. "Come tomorrow, I want to see that blackboard spotless," McCarmick concluded as he took his leave.

If there had been any doubt in Max's mind he was being singled out by Harold McCarmick, that doubt had been removed. He begrudgingly took the bucket to the bathroom at the end of the hall. As the hot water steamed into it, he came to the sad realization that he was in no hurry to get home anyway. After wiping down the chalkboard, he obtained the location of the gymnasium from Mrs. Evalum as she locked up the library.

The gym was a combination of dim artificial lighting and fading sunlight. As Max walked across the basketball court, he balanced the bucket in one hand and seven erasers tucked under his other arm. He walked toward the overhead white exit sign lit up with red lettering. He backed into the door alongside the bleachers and made his way outside. As the metal exit door closed itself, the entrance on the opposite side of the gym opened up.

"Come on," urged Deidre Lisbon, pulling a hesitant Dwayne Bishop into the gymnasium. Ross had claimed his shoulder was sore from having hit the ground in his skirmish with Max in the hallway and being out of practice. Deidre saw this as an opportunity. She had fooled around with Dwayne at a party over the summer when Ross had passed out, and she was feeling a euphoric rush after cheering practice. She had noticed Dwayne coming off the practice field carrying his helmet and shoulder pads and approached him.

"Meet me outside the gym after you get changed," she whispered seductively into his ear. Dwayne acted confused and went to change out of his pads with nervous anticipation.

Sure, Ross was his friend, but he was often a dick to Dwayne. Plus, Ross had to be aware that Deidre fooled around with other guys. He got along with Deidre, and she intimated this to him while complaining about Ross's immaturity. He found her bitchiness, as well as her aggressive attitude, attractive. He had had only one previous sexual encounter, and it had been uneventful. A nasty skeezer his brother Lester had gotten to "give him some."

Dwayne's raging hormones got the best of him as he took a condom that had been in his wallet all summer long and placed it in his gym shorts.

He made his way from the locker room upstairs, where she stood in front of the light from the trophy case at the entrance to the gym. Still in her uniform, she grinned a mischievous smile. He returned a smile, understanding her intentions. She ran her hands up her thighs underneath her pleated cheer skirt and nodded toward the gym. Dwayne looked around momentarily and threw caution to the wind, allowing her to pull him into the darkened gymnasium.

"Grab a chair over there. I'm not getting on the ground," Deidre commanded as she shimmied out of her cheer trunks underneath the wooden bleachers. Dwayne quickly produced the condom and tore it open. People were dying from AIDS left and right, and he wasn't about to catch a sexually transmitted disease from Deidre's crazy ass. The condom had broken his first time and he had been petrified ever since; plus, his father told him he would shoot him should he get a girl pregnant.

Deidre never asked if he had protection or not. As far as he knew, she had only been with Ross and blown a few college guys. He pulled the plastic armless chair under the bleachers; Deidre's nipples were perking up at the sight of the hard-on inside his gym shorts.

"Come on," she beckoned, bending over the chair while Dwayne fumbled in the dark with the condom. Finally, the condom slid over his erection. He placed his fingers over her sopping-wet vagina just as Lester had instructed him to. Deidre purred with pleasure. "C'mon, D, put it in; fuck me good and hard." She wiggled from side to side, causing her pleated skirt to shift and reveal her flesh to him. He grabbed her hips and entered her forcefully.

While Dwayne was slamming violently into his friend's girlfriend, Max was just a few feet away, outside the exit door, slamming erasers with equal force. He poured the filthy board water over the steps and watched it cascade onto the blacktop. He put the erasers in the bucket and made his way back indoors. He flung the metallic door open with more force than he had intended to as daylight invaded the darkened gym through the doorway.

Max stood motionless, seeing Dwayne and Deidre under the bleachers going at it in muffled and hushed grunts and moans. He attempted to cut back across the basketball court and go unnoticed. Then the metal door betrayed him. It slammed shut on its own accord and rang out, causing Deidre to snap at Dwayne, "Get off! Who is that?"

Catching a glimpse of Max's side profile and the yellow-and-black checked shirt, Dwayne said, "Shit, it's the new kid."

Dwayne exhaled and pulled his shorts back on, forgetting to take off the condom. Deidre barked at him, "Well, don't just stand there—go fucking get him!"

Dwayne sprinted out from under the bleachers, mumbling to himself, "What the fuck you want me to do?"

Max darted toward the doors; Dwayne easily cut him off and pinned him up against the cushions underneath the backboard. "Hold on, I just want to talk to you." While Max was struggling to break free of his grip, he could see Deidre casually walk up behind Dwayne, cracking her gum.

"I don't care what you do; leave me out of it," Max shouted honestly.

"You better develop a real short memory, Garret, or else you may get a concussion to help you forget," Deidre said with confidence. "You understand?" Dwayne pushed harder.

"Yes, I understand," Max replied, pulling free from Dwayne, who then delivered a gut punch that knocked the wind out of him.

Bracing himself against the canvas of the gym wall, Max slid down in pain. Dwayne's strike further irritated his bruised midsection. Deidre cracked her gum again and crouched down to Max's level. She smiled with pleasure as Max regretted having laid eyes upon the girl who had so much outer beauty that it disguised her inner ugliness.

"Say anything about this, and I'll have Ross beat the living shit out of you. Got it?" she threatened, then removed her gum and pressed it into Max's hair, flush on the lump his father had given him. Moving away from Deidre's outstretched hand, Max noticed a man enter behind Dwayne.

The sound of light switches echoed as additional fluorescent lighting beamed off the basketball court, revealing the grouchy old man Max had gotten his schedule from yesterday. Timothy Moretz set down his briefcase, fixed his glasses, and called out, "What's going on there? What the hell are you three still doing on the property after hours? Practice is over!"

"Sorry, Mr. Moretz. We were just showing the new guy here around the school is all," Dwayne answered.

"Is that so?" quizzed Moretz, still adjusting his bifocals. "What's he doing on the ground?" he continued, walking closer to them.

"We were just messing around is all, sir," Max answered, eager to avoid any further trouble.

Unconvinced, Moretz looked over the three of them. "I bet. Well, I have to set up for tomorrow's assembly, so you best get home." Max walked out of the gym faster than some people run as Dwayne walked behind him, with Deidre close on his heels.

Moretz enjoyed a long look at Deidre's backside and bit down on his lower lip with perversion. *Nice dumper that Lisbon girl has on her—very nice,* he thought while aligning plastic chairs next to the podium centered at half-court over the Middleton Rams logo. He had had Deidre in his state and local class last year, and while he thought her a moron, he never tired of seeing her open mouth chewing on a pen. Of course, that was before the fuckers demoted him to guidance counselor.

They dressed it up real nice to him, saying a member of the faculty with such experience could better serve the school in a role in the guidance office. All because some fat girl's mother had complained about him and said he had touched her inappropriately. He estimated he had done a good amount of what they called inappropriate touching in the past few decades. It was never a problem until he touched that hippo's waist. Now here he was, a man with a degree counting fucking chairs, of all things.

The counselor's mood became further irritated when he discovered he was missing one. He cursed as he perambulated the court in search of it until he discovered it underneath the bleacher. "Damn it! Cocksuckers!" he growled after hitting his head on the overhead metal support and crouched to retrieve it. As he pulled the chair, he noticed something that forced a smile to his face.

In the fold of the chair lay Deidre's cheer trunks, accompanied by an empty condom wrapper on the floor beside it. He picked up the wrapper and placed the trunks in the pocket of his tweed sports coat. "Showing him around the school, my ass." He pulled the chair out from underneath the bleachers, with the gears in his perverted mind working double time. His heart raced with excitement and he reached back in his sportscoat for another feel of Deidre's damp pussy juice before the cotton could dry up.

Elvis and Paige were returning from their evening stroll, and he raced ahead of Paige to greet her father, Phil, who was just getting out of his car. "Hey, Elvis, somebody took you off your leash, huh? Should we ground her? Should we?" He teased his daughter. "So how's Jane Fonda doing in there?" he asked Paige kiddingly, referring to Lynn.

"Burning up calories and burning through the wine with that monstrosity you made me put together in our living room," she replied.

"Leave her alone, Paige. She likes the stepper. Come on, let's get in. I'm sure Elvis is hungry."

Paige and her father could hear big band music blaring outside the back door. Paige offered a smile of amusement to her father's surprised reaction. "What happened to the Van Halen?" he asked. Lynn Edmundson was good-hearted and kind, but she constantly went through phases. This year she was a workout and wine connoisseur. It now seemed that the sounds of the Harry James Orchestra had been added to the mix.

"Did this start today, Paige?" he asked with the door half-open. Paige shrugged, and they made their way indoors.

The Edmundsons sat at the dinner table in their comfortable and spacious home. Harry James played on as Phil told his girls about his workday. He was the manager of Electro's, an electronics store in Middleton Pines Mall. He always had interesting tales to tell of the quirky customers and the staff who worked for him.

"So I told him it doesn't make a difference to me. If you want to wear an earring, that's your business, but male employees can't wear them on the sales floor." Phil went on as Lynn poured another glass of wine and held it in front of her nose. Paige looked to her father in amusement at the seriousness with which she approached her wine.

"Way to lay down the law, Phil," Paige said, instigating.

"Oh, I forgot to tell you, honey—Lana or Wendy called for you earlier," her mother said, taking in the aroma in deep breaths, then taking a long swallow from her glass.

"If Wendy's coming over, you tell her don't eat all my Klondike bars again," her father joked. Unlike some of her friends, Paige was allowed and even encouraged to have her friends over to the house.

"Never mind your ice cream, Phil. What's up at school, honey? Any cute boys?" her mother asked, swaying back in her chair as if Harry James's trumpet was actually moving her.

"Mom, please," Paige replied, dodging the question.

She was a bit of a tomboy and was aware of her mother's ridiculous concern that this might mean she was a lesbian. Lynn Edmundson had no prejudices against homosexuality. Her only outlet to the world outside of Middleton Township was her talk shows. Watching them day in, day out, she saw the indifference, judgment, and pain homosexuals went through, and when she saw Paige throwing a football or playing with electronics, it activated her anxieties. So every now and then, especially after a third or fourth glass of the red stuff, Paige would have to deal with some gentle probing to put her mother's concerns at ease.

"OK, well, how are classes this year? Any new teachers?" she countered.

"New? Please, Lynn! Tim Moretz is still teaching there. He was teaching government before I was a freshman," her father chimed in.

Paige took a bite of her asparagus and recalled, "Actually, there is a new kid. He's cute—long dark hair, gray-blue eyes. McCarmick gave him detention on the first day."

Phil spoke up over the sounds of the thumping drums and blaring trumpets in concern. "You stay away from the McCarmick—he seemed like a real prick at that back-to-school night they had. Shit, while you're at it, stay away from Moretz as well. Guy always gave me the creeps."

"Mr. M is nice to me because I'm always good at gymnastics in PE. You may be right about Mr. Moretz, though; word is they won't let him teach anymore and demoted him to the guidance office," Paige responded.

"Never mind," her mother interjected, moving the wine glass in a circular motion in Paige's direction and leaning in with interest. "Never mind," she repeated. "Dear, don't listen to your dad about your teachers. He thinks the whole world is made up of a bunch of lunatics who want to steal Walkmans and blank VHS tapes from his store."

"It is!" Phil interrupted, getting a laugh from Paige.

"You shut up," Lynn snapped at him with a loving smile on her face. "Paige, tell me more about this new boy."

"I don't know much about him. I have chemistry with him, and he's kind of quiet. A few of the girls were laughing at him this morning." Paige looked down at the steak her mother had overcooked.

"I hope you weren't. Your father and I didn't raise you to pick on people," her mother said with utmost sincerity. "I saw this girl on Donahue yesterday…"

"No, it was Deidre and them," Paige interrupted, eager to put her parents' concerns to rest and not hear about who was on Donahue. "They were saying he wore the same clothes as yesterday. Stupid, really. Him and Ross got in a fight the first day. I think his name is Mark or Mike."

"He doesn't have clothes? That's terrible," her father said in disgust. Phil Edmundson could relate, having had to wear the same two shirts day in, day out, in his parochial school days. He frowned, recalling the torment it had brought him long ago. Paige's mother offered a solution off the top of her head.

"Maybe you could give him some of your father's old clothes? Since he put on a few pounds, he won't be wearing them."

Paige looked at her mother and mocked her absurd suggestion, saying, "Hi, I'm Paige. Want some of my dad's old shorts? No, Mom. Besides, Daddy's going on a diet," she added, aiming a playful grin at her father.

"That's right, you are! Call Wendy, and tell her the Klondikes are all hers!"

The three of them broke out in laughter as Elvis barked in confusion.

Her father stood up and took the wine glass out of his wife's hand and set it down gently and said flirtatiously, "You know, woman, before the Klondikes, I used to have aspirations of being a band leader myself, and I can still boogie with the best of them." He began bopping to the blaring trumpets and pulled her out of her chair to dance.

"Who are you kidding? You were a damn hippie when we met!"

"Then sway with me, my flower child."

Paige loved watching her parents dance, but seeing her father affectionately twirling her mother and the way they stared deep into one another's eyes, she knew this was the time to make herself scarce. She picked up Elvis, who was still barking, and carried him up to her room to call back Lana or Wendy and possibly do some homework. Her mother's contagious laughter erupted over the music, and Paige smiled from ear to ear, pulling Elvis close to her chest as she headed into her room.

Chapter 3:
COMRADES AND CONSPIRATORS

The evening had gone better than the night before for Max and his mother. His father had passed out on the living room couch and stayed there until waking up with the urge the following morning. Max heard the Torino fire up and wheel away, same as yesterday. His walk to school gave him mixed emotions as he saw the car outside the tavern, in the same spot it had been parked in yesterday.

On the one hand, he knew Bill Garret was heading inside, continuing the downward spiral he had started years ago. While this upset him, he was hopeful that if he started boozing early, like he had yesterday, Max could find relief in him being passed out by the time he got home from school. That was just fine. Max didn't hear the person exiting the Middleton Social Club directly behind him.

"At least he's consistent," Max said aloud, observing his red-faced father get out of the Torino, unaware of the stranger behind him.

"That kind of consistency ain't good for nobody, kid. Most them guys waiting on that bar to open its doors are in a bad way, shakes and all," said the stranger to Max as the tavern owner opened up and Bill Garret and a few more rummies filed in with him. "A sad existence," the stranger continued.

The boy turned, startled by the close proximity of the stranger, and backed up a step. Cautiously he spoke back. "Don't I know it, mister—that's my old man."

"Damn, I'm sorry, kid. I meant nothing by it. Don't pay me no mind. I'm Dominic, and you might be?" he said, extending his right hand. Max studied Dominic and looked into his eyes and discovered kindness and sincerity in them.

He extended his hand back to him and continued, "I'm Max, and no offense taken. Besides, your right. It's not good for anyone. Especially my mom and me."

If they had been in Max's old town, he would have carried on and said good day mister and that would have been that. These were different circumstances, though. This was the first conversation he had had with anyone besides his mother and his hot-tempered father. He gazed at the ruby stone set in Dominic's gold ring.

"My old man was the same way," Dominic said, pulling a set of keys from his overcoat. "You go to MHS?" he quizzed, looking at Max's stuffed book bag. Having felt uncomfortable at his locker, Max had elected to carry every textbook he had; the surplus history book and loose comics he had in his hands.

"Uh, yeah, nice meeting you, Dominic. I need to get going, though," Max said, panicked after looking at his rubber wristwatch, which he had decided was a piece of junk after seeing Dominic's. He imagined the shit-eating grin on that jerk McCarmick's face as he walked in the hallway late and was overcome by anxiety.

"That's quite a hike!" Dominic interjected, putting on a pair of gold-rimmed dark-tinted sunglasses. "Come on"—he motioned—"I got some errands to run. I'll give you a lift." Max was thinking of a polite way to refuse his offer and then saw him walking alongside a midnight-blue Cadillac coupe accented with gold trim. The car was right in front of them. Over the years Max had picked up one thing from his dad, and that was a knowledge of automobiles.

Max estimated it was an '86, just a few years old. The untrained eye would have believed it had been driven right off the lot, given its pristine condition. Dominic popped the locks and rolled down the automatic windows.

"Nice car," Max said cautiously, opening the massive door. He sank into the leather seat and thought to himself, *I very well may be the first person to sit in the passenger side.* Dominic looked out for oncoming traffic and pulled away. Max braced himself as he was jerked forward, a direct result of the car's pickup as Dominic had hardly grazed the gas pedal. "I mean, this is a really nice car," Max continued.

"Eh, it gets me where I need to be. You should have seen the Caddy I had back in seventy-five. That was a car to be impressed by." They pulled up to the school's entrance, and Max picked up the loose books that had slid forward on the ride. Dominic noticed the books on his passenger-side floor were not school books.

"Say, what you got there?" he asked, leaning over and rifling through Max's comics. "These look good. What's this? *The Nam? Alf!* They got a comic for that crazy show? No *Superman?* They still have him, right?" Dominic peppered Max with questions and interest.

"You read comic books?" Max questioned with amazement.

"Read 'em? Hell, I used to work at a newsstand. I would get to work early and read every single one of them before people bought 'em up. You got no idea—I used to read detective comics when they still had plain old detectives in them."

Max responded excitedly, "I know, before they had Ba—"

"Listen, kid," Dominic interjected, cutting him off in seriousness. "On my way back, I'm going to stop in the Candlelight Bar. I have to go there regardless, and I'm going to try and get your old man off that bar stool and get him some work. Sometimes a man just needs a purpose—so long as you don't protest."

"I appreciate it Dominic, but…" Max hesitated, thinking of his father's volatile temperament.

"If he turns me down, don't worry. I'll have him cut off at the bar as an incentive. Now get in that asylum and learn something," Dominic encouraged.

He put down the automatic window once more as Max got out and shouted, "It's gonna be all right, Maximilian; don't you worry." A spring in his step, Max looked at the cracked concrete and the graffiti stone walls of the "asylum" and grinned. He had just made a friend—a friend many years his senior, but it felt great nonetheless.

Greg was showing off, balancing a Hacky Sack back and forth, looking especially goofy to Paige. She rolled her eyes and saw the subject of the Edmundsons' dinner conversation last night getting out of a blue-and-gold car. Lana whispered in Paige's ear, "You know Greg really likes you, Paige; he told me so. He was like, 'Your girlfriend Paige is like so hot,'" as she watched Max walking toward them with a big smile.

"Uh, that's great," she replied to Lana, distracted.

This was the first time she had seen Max walking upright and not hunched. Seeing the carefree grin on his face, Paige decided she could tell her mother there was a cute boy at school and he wouldn't be needing Phil's shorts as he did have another set of clothes. The ripped-up denim jeans looked dull compared to his electric eyes, which beamed with his smile as his long black hair shined off his well-worn white T-shirt.

She walked over to him to make small talk but was halted by a Hacky Sack kicked in the direction she was heading. The smile dropped from his face as he caught the object that had been kicked at his head.

Behind Paige, Dwayne and Ross let out an instigating "Ohhhh" aimed at Greg as if to say, "You tried to hit this kid by kicking the sack at him, and he caught it."

"It's a Hacky Sack, shithead. You're supposed to kick it, not catch it, dick." Greg seethed at Max, who drop-kicked the sack right over Greg's head. "Nice kick, ass face," Greg responded with more venom. The drilling sound of the bell rattled, and Max was saved for the moment.

"Next time he asks you, Lana, do me a favor and tell Greg I think of him as a friend but not like that. On second thought, just tell him I'm not interested," Paige said as they made their way inside.

"So you won't mind if I get with him then, Paige?" Lana probed.

"Lana, my girl, he's all yours. Be my guest," Paige said, holding the door open for her friend.

A food fight had broken out in the cafeteria during the lunch period, which Catherine Jalorean had been assigned to proctor. She spotted her blouse with club soda to remove a ketchup stain as her sixth-period chemistry class students were making their way into her room. Max walked in, greeted her, and took his seat in the back of the room. She noticed Max had been absent from the mayhem-filled lunch period. Her lesson plan for today would be thrown off as one of her students, Daniel Carinsen, was in the discipline office. He had thrown a clump of macaroni and cheese in retaliation in the cafeteria. He had then been promptly tackled and head locked by Harold McCarmick and then dragged to the disciplinarian's office. So Daniel was not pairing up with his lab partner in today's class.

Taking a deep breath, Ms. Jalorean approached her lectern and addressed her class. She had started teaching at Middleton last year. Middleton was an exciting, lively environment in comparison to the stiff prep school she had resigned from before coming here. While she no longer had to contend with a vice principal who couldn't keep his hands off her ass, she was getting weary of the discipline problems, and the pay cut she had taken was affecting her financially. Being pelted with French fries had never been part of her teaching plan, and she hated proctoring the lunch period with McCarmick, who had come on to her several times in spite of him being married.

"OK, guys, you all have your textbooks, which we will be using sparingly," she began, but halted her speech, noticing Lana Karrington poking Paige in the back with her pen to get her attention.

"Ms. Karrington, please let Ms. Edmundson be, thank you."

Before she could resume, Lana broke her concentration once more. "Sorry, Ms. J, can I go to the ladies'?"

Retrieving the hall pass, Ms. Jalorean handed it to Lana, saying, "Hurry back, please. We're going to pick lab partners and start our first lab."

"Yes, ma'am!" Lana replied sarcastically.

After giving the disruptive girl the pass, Ms. Jalorean looked at the clock and fretted. *Fifteen minutes in, and we haven't even gotten started*, she thought.

"OK, people, please pair up. I'm going to let you pick partners. As long as it doesn't take forever."

The students all got up and began pairing desks together. She began counting the number of worksheets she would need to pass out to the pairs and saw her favorite student, Paige, sitting idle.

"Paige?" she questioned.

"Yes?" Paige replied.

"Pick a lab partner," urged Ms. Jalorean.

"Oh, I'm going to pair up with Lana," Paige responded, prompting Ms. Jalorean to leave her lectern and approach the girl privately at her desk. She knew Paige and Lana planned to be partners, and she wasn't looking forward to competing with Lana for Paige's attention. She observed the girls Paige hung around with and felt they were a bad influence on her. She never overstepped her boundaries but couldn't help overhearing Lana in the cafeteria and knew that chasing boys and coasting through the school year were her only ambitions.

"Don't you spend enough time with your girlfriends outside of class, Paige?" she asked Paige, smiling.

"Yes, but we were...J

"It may benefit you to team up with someone you're not social with. just a suggestion." Paige understood her favorite teacher's intentions. Privately she felt like a last resort for Lana, anyway, as she scanned the room for a replacement partner.

"Quickly people. Mr. Garret, please pick a lab partner." Ms. Jalorean called out to the back of the class, where Max sat idle just as Paige had been doing.

He was panicking since all the other students were already in pairs. He approached his teacher. "Excuse me, if it's all the same, I'd like to work alone, if it's OK."

She knew this would not be a problem as she had already accounted for Daniel's absence. Flustered, with Lana roaming the halls, she called out to the class once more.

"Would someone please partner with Max here?" she encouraged. An uncomfortable silence filled the bustling classroom for what felt like an eternity to Max.

A boy shouted in a muffled voice, "Hell no," goading the classroom into laughter. Max stood next to Ms. Jalorean at the lectern, filled with embarrassment, feeling a lump in his throat.

"I'll do labs with you," Paige said, prompting a smile from Ms. Jalorean. Katherine's intuition told her that the pairing of the quiet Max and the spunky Paige was best for all parties involved. Overwhelmed with relief and excitement, Max moved an empty desk next to his own in the back of the class.

After smoking one of her Virginia Slims in the ladies' room, Lana casually strolled back into the chemistry class. She was aware that Ms. Jalorean was a smoker as well and less susceptible to the smell of smoke on her. The overpowering scent of Lana's Halston perfume alerted Paige to her presence next to her. Paige looked up to see her friend standing over her new desk. Lana outstretched her arms in confusion and snapped at her, "What the hell, Paige? Picking pigpen here over me for labs?"

"Lana. Stop it. Ms. J asked me to," Paige responded.

"Lana, up here. I need that hall pass back, and I will be your partner today, until Daniel rejoins the class tomorrow," Ms. Jalorean called out to her.

"If he returns tomorrow," Lana snarled back, pacing toward Ms. Jalorean and surrendering the hall pass.

"Sorry about her," Paige said to Max, giggling a bit at her friend's frustration. "She's cool but gets a little bitchy sometimes."

"No problem. She can join the growing club of people who are pissed off at me here," Max joked, happy beyond measure to be paired up with the sparkly eyed Paige. He was entranced by her as she laughed at his comment.

"Yeah, what is the deal with you, Mark? A few days in, and you're leading Middleton High's shit list?" She giggled.

"Well, at least I'm ahead at something." He went on soliciting more laughter from the girl, whose inner beauty illuminated an aura around her. They recovered from laughing and shared an uncomfortable silence, absorbing one another with their eyes. Paige, a firm believer in reincarnation, decided that she had known this boy in a past life. Overcome by nervous energy, she felt compelled to say something. Anything.

"Are you good at this? Mark?" He looked at her slightly puzzled. "I sucked at biology, and I'll probably suck at this too, so you better help me," Paige emphasized.

During sophomore year Paige had encountered difficulty with the previous science teacher. It had only been after Ms. Jalorean's arrival that she had been able to improve her bio grade.

"Well, I do not suck at this, and it'd be an honor and a privilege to help you, Paige, m'lady."

M'lady? Where did that come from? Did I seriously just say that? Max questioned himself in panicked thought. He had never called anyone m'lady in his life. *Could anything sound dorkier than saying, "M'lady" to someone you just met?* He shuddered in embarrassment.

His concerns were put at ease as Paige replied with a glowing, radiant grin back to him, "Graciously accepted, Mark, my liege."

He felt almost wrong in correcting such a remarkable reply. He did anyway. "Um, I'm Max, uh, Max Garret," he said, plainly ending their medieval dialogue.

So pleased that she had forgotten about the stubborn ketchup stain on her blouse, Katherine Jalorean observed the pairing of Max and Paige. She couldn't hear them but saw them carrying on. It was apparent they hadn't heard a damn thing she had just said to the class. She saw the instant chemistry between them. She almost felt guilty interrupting them, but she did anyway.

"No talking until you have your assignment back there! Don't make me regret pairing you two up." Unable to hold back a smirking smile at Paige, she continued, "Each of you will be given the following materials…" and began handing out worksheets.

As Katherine Jalorean was prepping for her lab, one floor down Timothy Moretz was making preparations of his own.

Diedre Lisbon sat on a bench outside the guidance office, one leg crossed over the other, swaying in anticipation. She had been told to report there from PE. Mr. M had told her he didn't know why she had been asked to go there, which she had figured was bullshit. She supposed they most likely wanted her to rat out Ross for starting the food fight in the cafeteria and wondered why she had not been asked to go to the discipline office instead. She took out a stick of Big Red and offered a piece to the frumpy secretary, who politely refused.

"Marilyn, may I speak to you?" Timothy Moretz summoned the plump woman from his open office door. Deidre amused herself, thinking perhaps Marilyn should be sent to the discipline office and beaten for the horrendous California Raisins sweatshirt she was wearing. "Nice shirt, Ms. McCreery," Deidre complimented falsely, taking a second piece of gum into her mouth.

"Thank you, dear," Marilyn replied, nervously passing the bench and entering Tim's office. "Did you finish the correspondence I asked you to type up?" he asked, well aware she had.

"Yes, Tim, it's all finished."

"Very well, then, I will see you tomorrow. Enjoy the rest of the afternoon." Surprised by being given the afternoon off, she waddled back out into the main office. Marilyn picked up her bulky purse, which Deidre decided was more tragic than the raisin sweatshirt, and exited.

"OK, Ms. Lisbon, come on in," Counselor Moretz spoke out to the defensive girl on the bench. She plodded into the office. "Sit down," he offered, extending his palm toward the chair beside her. The office within an office was so small, once she sat, she felt his bologna breath in her face as he continued. "I wanted to speak to you privately about this first to give you a chance to speak for your actions." Moretz leaned over his desk in anticipation of her reaction.

Confrontational as ever, Deidre decided she was going to resort to a technique that had served her well over the years. Whatever he was going to accuse her of, she was prepared to deny. Deny with aggression. "What am I even doing here? It's a little early in the year for guidance, isn't it?" she barked back.

Angered, he rose from his desk, peered out into the main office, and once satisfied, closed the door behind them. "You are in a serious bit of trouble, young lady. Are you aware of that?" He questioned her like a prosecutor with irrefutable evidence.

"I didn't have anything to do with the stupid food fight, OK? Mr. M will be my witness. I was at the vending machine," she replied and cracked her gum. She pressed her hands on his desk, about to rise.

"Sit down!" he yelled sharply. "You are most certainly not here for the incident in the cafeteria. I can assure you of that." His voice calmed as

Deidre tried to figure out which of her acts she was going to have to defend herself against. She settled on the girl who had passed her in the hallway yesterday afternoon. Deidre yanked her shorts down to her ankles in the crowded hall, slapped her books out of her hand, and screamed, "Where are you going, sah-lut!"

The girl was a senior, for Chrissake, she thought, and what a baby. Nonetheless, she was nervous. There hadn't been any teachers around, she remembered, but she couldn't be positive. When Moretz threw her cheer trunks on the desk in front of her, she found herself wishing she was there for the hallway incident. "Missing part of your uniform, Deidre?"

"Those aren't mine," she automatically said as he held out the foil wrapper of the condom over her trunks.

"Oh no? Not yours either?" He went on, satisfied as concern filled her face. *I've got this little whore by the short-and-curlies,* he thought and went in for the kill. "You most likely will be expelled, and I'm going to have to phone your parents. They are probably going to want to have you take a pregnancy test, which I'm going to recommend. Do those you engage sexually always use a condom?" he asked as he picked up the phone receiver threateningly with an index card with her contact information held where she could see it.

"Yes! Always! I'm not pregnant," she cried in desperation. There it was. He fought hard not to smile as he had her and he knew it. He relished it as her eyes watered and her face was flushed in fear. All the confidence and cockiness he had observed in his government class last year was gone. "You can't expel me; you're not even a teacher anymore! You were demoted." Deidre lashed out in capitulation. She had nothing left in her arsenal except insults.

"That's true. I cannot. But another witness and I will inform Principal Volkem." He lied. "Engaging in sexual activity on school grounds? He most certainly will expel you." He began dialing numbers on the rotary phone rapidly until she crumbled.

"Please don't do this, please. I won't mess around anymore, I swear." Timothy Moretz then put the phone down and spoke the words that had served him so well in the decades of teaching at Middleton High.

"What do you suggest we do in order to keep your parents out of this? Perhaps you can convince me to do otherwise?" he said with a sick smile on his face as he got up and pulled down the zipper of his trousers and un-buckled his belt. "Do you want to help yourself out?" Deidre gasped and was taken aback by what was being asked of her. "Come now, we both know it's not the first time you've seen one of these. Spit that gum out." He ordered, taking her limp, lifeless arm and guiding it to his erection. Once she had accepted it in her hand, he guided her out of the chair and onto her knees.

"Do I have to? Isn't there suh-something?"

"Suck that cock, you dirty, little nigger fucking skank!" he growled, prying her closed lips open with his right thumb as he applied pressure to the back of her head. Overwhelmed, she succumbed, initially gagging, then slamming her head up and back with ferocity and anger as a combination of tears, mucus, and eventually Moretz's semen bubbled over her lips. "That wasn't so hard, now was it?" he said, concerned she was going to throw up in his office.

Moretz tucked in his shirt and closed his pants and belt. Deidre remained crouched on her knees in despair as one of his pubic hairs, stuck in her tooth, caused her to vomit in her mouth.

He took the trunks off his desk, helped her to her feet, and handed them to her. "I wasn't fooling you. No one else need know about you and those boys," he said, offering false consolation. "I can help you with your grades as well, provided you continue to help me. Understand?" Deidre nodded, unable to speak. "I'll have you on the honor roll with very little effort on your part so long as you keep your mouth shut, except when you come in here, of course. I want to see you at least once a week, understand?" He placed his hands on her shoulders, and she nodded again, her head hung low with embarrassment. "Good. Thatta girl. Now get back to class, and I'll forget about your indiscretions." Deidre went to leave the office so fast she almost walked right into the door. Moretz opened it and ushered her out. He observed the girl wiping the combination of tears and semen from her face and lips with her sleeve as she stormed out of the guidance office.

In the fifties Timothy Moretz had considered himself an idealist who wanted nothing more than to educate and mold young minds. Over the decades he had become increasingly bitter—so much so that his wife of twenty years had left him without so much as a goodbye while he was at a teacher's conference. He returned to his office and looked out the window with regret about how miserable and empty his life had become. A shudder ran down his back, snapping him out of his depressing reflection. He grabbed his briefcase and decided to leave for the day. He left his hole-in-the-wall office for his hole-in-the-wall apartment and drank himself unconscious, as he had done many a night before.

Chapter 4:

PLEASURE AND PAIN

The bell rang, ending Ms. Jalorean's chemistry lab. Students rushed out the door, but Paige and Max took their time. Lana Karrington watched them carrying on and grew tired of waiting on Paige and left in a huff. She saw Deidre in the hallway and went to catch up with her. Unable to match Deidre's rampant pace, she yelled ahead to her, "Dee, wait up." Lana juggled her handbag and book bag. Then Deidre turned around with daggers in her eyes.

"The fuck do you want, Karrington?" Deidre snapped at her.

"I just..." Lana stammered, at a loss for words, overwhelmed by Deidre's intense hostility. Deidre was about to offer Lana another insult, but her attention was redirected to Max and Paige walking the halls in laughter. She locked in on Max like a missile and proceeded to engage. Lana, perplexed at the conversation, or lack thereof, rushed to go talk to Greg, who was up ahead.

"I told you to keep your fucking mouth shut, you fucking scurf bag," Deidre growled at Max, ending his harmonious conversation with Paige. He faced Deidre and saw a familiar expression, one his father had had so many times before. Eyes wide open, upper lip simmering in anger, and face pulsating hot red.

"I didn't..." He attempted to respond. Deidre's rage-fueled look instantly transformed into a conniving grin. She was convinced of Max's guilt in compromising her with Moretz. Who else could the other witness he mentioned have been? It would have made no sense for Dwayne to have implicated himself.

Max had spent the previous evening trying to get the gum Deidre had pressed into his head out of his hair. Seeing the remaining pieces of Big Red on his scalp, she spoke her intentions.

"I'm gonna have Ross beat the living shit out of you. You fucking liar!" she said, making a fist and raising it in Max's direction

Paige had heard enough and stepped between them. "Dee, wait! What do you think he did?"

Paige's plea went ignored as Deidre extended her index finger from her closed fist in Max's face. "Spreading rumors about me because everybody hates you? You eat shit and die, Garret!" Deidre exclaimed, still nauseous from the permeating taste of Moretz's semen on her tongue and on both sides of her tonsils. The outburst was loud enough to get a teacher's attention down the hall. Deidre walked off before he could make his way there to access the situation.

"What was that all about?" The librarian, Ms. Evalum, questioned Max and Paige, who were still frozen in shock.

"I have no idea," Paige explained. She then grabbed Max by the arm, pulling him forward. Once clear from the inquisitive Ms. Evalum, she came to an abrupt stop as Max's momentum carried him forward. He forced himself to a stop but still collided with Paige. His lips accidentally pressed into her forehead. Momentarily befuddled by the physical contact with one another, they then recovered.

"OK, so what the hell was that about?" Paige asked.

"You stopped in front of me and turned. I didn't know you were going to—"

"No, not you headbutting me with your mouth. Deidre! What was she talking about?"

"Well, I guess it won't make a difference if I tell you now. Can you keep it to yourself?"

"Of course," Paige responded as the bell rang out. "Meet me outside after school and stay away from her until this blows over." Max nodded and set off to the foreign language room.

In the final class of the day, Paige estimated what could have caused Deidre's reaction. No stranger to Deidre going off over the years, Paige realized it could have been anything. Something was different, though. Whenever Dee had been about to confront someone in the past, she had had a wicked confidence. In the hallway she lacked any and all composure. Outside the school Max explained to Paige *why*.

Thinking her ears had just betrayed her, she repeatedly said to Max, "Shut up. No, really, shut up." Paige looked around, paranoid that students outside the school had been privy to what had been told to her. She leaned toward Max in disbelief and whispered loudly to him, "Deidre was doing it with Dwayne under the bleachers? Shut up!" she said once more. "Ross is going to kill them both," she said as if talking to herself.

"Or me," Max replied, interrupting her slight trance.

"Or kill you, exactly. Answer me, though. Why does she figure it was you who told?" In spite of being in hot water, Max was humored by Paige's posture. The prettiest girl his own age he'd ever seen stood in complete contemplation. She lit up the exterior of the gray building behind her in her vibrant tie-dyed shirt and gleaming white Guess jeans with one finger pointed to the sky and her head slanted back. Then, like a psychic who had come to a startling revelation, she lunged forward and exclaimed, "Oh my God, Max, what are you going to do? She's convinced it was you. You don't want to be on her bad side. She won't listen to reason about this, not even from me!"

As he was about to further protest his innocence to Paige, the duo was interrupted by a casually approaching Wendy Damon. "My sister's here. Paige, you coming with?"

"Uh yeah, sure," Paige answered, walking toward Wendy. Then she pivoted back in Max's direction. "Are you getting picked up, Max?" she asked, wondering if the rustic beater or luxury sedan was coming for her troubled new chem partner.

"No, I'm just walking home," he replied, hoping Paige wasn't going to ask him to ride with Wendy and her sister. He had gotten off on the wrong foot with Lana and didn't want to instigate Wendy by breaking up their routine.

"I'm actually going to walk today, hon; it's such a nice day," Paige told her friend, sounding apologetic.

"OK, babe, laters," Wendy responded, needing no further explanation, and headed toward the parking lot.

Paige rejoined Max in excitement and pulled him in the opposite direction. "Come on, there's a shortcut this way,"

"You don't even know where I live."

Paige made a pouting face, laughed, and said, "Trust me."

It had been a day filled with ups and downs for Max Garret. For Paige Edmundson, every day was up as she never let much of anything get her down. Today was especially exciting for her, though. She had met someone who was a complete stand-alone. He belonged to no clubs or cliques, and she was eager to learn more about him. They walked for blocks, with Paige doing the questioning and Max doing his best to answer before the next inquiry was made.

Paige asked Max so many questions—everything from whether he liked roller coasters to what his favorite food was—he eventually just laughed. When he gave a generalized answer like "Chinese food," she demanded specifics. Max had no idea where they were walking, and he truly did not care. He'd never come across anyone like Paige. After Paige had moved on from the usual getting-to-know-you questions, in amateur detective fashion, she made more personal inquiries.

"Do you have a girlfriend? "Did you have one before you moved here, and if so, did you have to break up with her because you moved?" followed by the slyest of all her probing questions, "So who do you think the prettiest girl in school is?"

He grinned at the loaded question. When her eyelashes batted in anticipation, he spoke his mind. "You, easily," he answered.

"Oh, wow. Thanks, Max," Paige meekly responded, giving him a rare demonstration of her shyness.

"Or you're at least a close second to Ms. Jalorean," he said in humor. Paige nodded her head in agreement. They ran from the sidewalk and were facing a wooded area when Max took control of the conversation.

"I have no idea where I am. What kind of shortcut is this?"

"Well, it's a shortcut through the woods to my house. Sorry if I asked you a lot of questions, but I had to make sure."

"Sure of what?" Max retorted, happy to play along.

"I wanted to make sure I could bring you to my sanctuary."

For a fleeting moment, Max wondered if Paige was setting him up, perhaps to get jumped in the woods by the crowd she hung around with? After all, she was friends with them. The notion evaporated instantly with one look at her beaming smile and honest face.

"Are you coming?" she asked, bracing the single strap of her backpack.

Following a few more questions about horror movies and what his favorite video on MTV was, they approached a clearing in the woods. In the center stood a red, white, and black picnic table. Paige explained that every time her father had paint left over from a project, she would add some to the distressed table. Wildflowers surrounded the table, and the birds chirped harmoniously from the trees overhead. The fading sun shone through to the center of the clearing. They sat alongside one another, talking while squirrels gave chase to one another up the tree in front of them.

"Only my cousin Avery knows about this place. Well, him and Elvis, my dog. He's from up north and comes here in the summer when he visits."

"Where far north? Like New York north?"

"No, my aunt and uncle live in Preytin, just outside of Hessian's Cliff on the New York side. He's totally rich, and his house is so rad! Yet for some reason, this is his favorite place, or so he tells me."

"That's where I'm from,"

"You're from Preytin?"

"No, Hessian's Cliff—I'm from there."

"What made you move here, if you don't mind my asking?" Paige questioned. Even the suburbs of Middleton Township were not a desirable destination for anyone north of the Diamond Strike District, in the center of Preytin.

Max didn't mind her asking, not one bit. He was glad she had. He told Paige about how his family had lived with his grandfather before his death. "He was on his way home from church and got run into by a drunk snowplow driver whose only excuse was that he was drinking blackberry brandy for a cold. He died instantly."

"Oh, I'm so sorry, Max. That's terrible." Paige comforted him as he let the lump in his throat settle. He withheld telling her that his father had crawled into a bottle after and never came out.

He explained that his family moved after his father was laid off from the auto plant. "Not that it helps anything, but I'm glad you moved here and I met you," Paige added with sincerity.

She had no idea how much her kind words meant to him, how immeasurably good it felt to get things off his chest, completely unaware that before he had been offered a ride by a sharply dressed older gentleman that morning, part of him had been debating throwing himself in front of the largest truck coming his way. Blissfully unaware, Paige Edmundson put her arms around a motionless Max Garret and hugged him. It had been the best day of his life in recent memory.

The overhead sunlight vanished from the darkening clearing as he returned her embrace. She buried her head in his chest, and they hugged in a moment they'd both remember for the rest of their lives. He felt her heart pulsate; pressed against him, she could feel his. Concerned the hug had gone on a bit too long for people who had just met one another, Max considered slowly letting go but chose not to.

As Paige lifted her head and looked at him, he nervously spouted out, "Thanks for being so nice to me, but it's late, and I'm worried about my mom."

"Is she sick?" Paige asked, letting go in concern.

"Yeah. I mean, no, sort of. It's complicated," he stammered.

"You can come to my house and call her, and if you want, you can stay for dinner," Paige said. Then she held out her hand and said, "But first…"

"What are we shaking on?"

"A secret oath about my little place here, which you can never tell anyone about, unless we both agree on it. I made Avery do the same thing."

Max took her hand, and she pulled away, clasping his forearm. "Not like this. Like knights in ancient times would do." Paige thought to herself, she had never felt comfortable talking this way with her friends.

"I'm pretty sure that's called a forearm shake." Max teased.

"Just do it," Paige ordered.

They locked arms, and upon releasing the grip, Paige noticed a prominent bruise on Max's forearm. He saw her reaction to it as she looked at him. Determined to keep things upbeat, Paige started toward the dirt trail in the center of the grass leading to her house.

"I hope you're not starving; my family eats on West Coast time. Are you good at playing Contra? I could really use a second player assist," she shouted back to him as he followed her.

"You have Nintendo?" he called out in excitement while fighting the urge to stare at the panty lines surrounding the back pocket and the Guess logo on her white jeans as Paige climbed in front of him.

"Yeah, we can play before dinner, after we take Elvis for a walk." As they reached her house through the backyard, Paige hoped her mother wasn't in the exercise leotard. Elvis greeted them, and she breathed a sigh of relief, seeing Lynn Edmundson curled up in the family room engrossed in a talk show about obsessive-compulsive disorder. Then her mother did a double take after she said hello to her. Max looked around the Edmundsons' home and couldn't help but be reminded of his grandfather's house.

"This is my friend Max. Is it OK if he stays for dinner?"

Lynn smiled, exchanged greetings with Max, and showed him to the kitchen, where he could phone his mother. Paige took out Elvis, who was excited over their guest as well.

It had been an equally good day for Max's mother. She hung up the wall phone in the kitchen in relief. Bill had gotten a job at the Italian produce market up the street, and her son was eating dinner over at a friend's house. She fixed herself a salad and decided to join her spouse in the living room and take advantage of his unusually pleasant temperament. She poured each of them a glass of Schaefer and sat alongside Bill as he watched baseball. She watched him smiling intently with great optimism. In her heart she wished for a part of the man who had swept her off her feet so long ago to return. Even a small part would have been just fine with her.

The line at Ross's house had been busy the last two times Deidre had called. She slammed the phone on the nightstand beside her bed down in frustration. Her dad was home, which meant Ross wouldn't be coming over. She was glad he wasn't; after her nightmare experience at the school that afternoon, she was definitely not in the mood. She had skipped practice and come straight home, gotten into bed, and let her anger fester. Normally when her father was home, her room was off limits to Ross and she spent the late afternoons after practice playing with herself, but didn't much feel like that either.

She did, though, want to talk to Ross about how the fucker was spreading rumors about her before someone else did. She bit her nails and thought about calling Dwayne but decided against it. One of her favorite films, *The Bad Seed,* was on. She enjoyed watching Rhoda take revenge on those who opposed her. Deidre amused herself, thinking of Counselor Moretz and Max Garret burning alive in a basement as the gardener did in the movie. In her excitement, her hands found their way into her sweats, and she carried on as she normally would. A fond reminiscence of summer nights in the hot tub in Hessian's Cliff got her out of her own head and got her off. She climaxed as Rhoda slammed on the piano keys while Leroy burned in the basement. She exhaled, slid out of her sweatpants, threw her underwear on the floor, and got back into her sweats. Once the movie was finished, she dialed up Lana, who was always so loyal to her, to get the ball rolling. Sure, she had told her to fuck off in the hall earlier today, but Lana'd get over it, the same way Deidre was over what had happened to her. She'd get what she needed from the prick's extortion and use him and Ross to get back at Max.

Following a pleasant dinner at the Edmundson residence, Max and Paige went up to her room to play Nintendo while Phil and Lynn cleaned up. Max was surprised at Paige's bedroom. He had expected it to be wallpapered pink with an assortment of girlie artifacts. He was wrong. Pittsburgh Steelers and New Jersey Devils posters were tacked up on the wall; between the two was a Guns N' Roses poster. Her bedroom looked as if it could have been shared by a brother and sister. The television in her room was larger than the one in the Garrets' family room. The disconnected Atari next to Paige's Nintendo was a reminder that, although he didn't want to, he would be going home soon.

"This is the furthest I've ever gotten in this game," Paige said, marveling at how Max was able to assist her. Then her mother called up the steps.

"Paige, you need to do homework. Does Max want a ride home? It's late. Paige?" Lynn said in between sips of chardonnay. Paige paused the game and sighed.

"My dad will drop you off. I told you it was a shortcut," she said with a grin. While he didn't want to leave, Max was relieved. At dinner Mr. Edmundson had told him that his street, Florsheim Way, was, by his count, "Fifteen blocks away or so."

"Do you have your own phone line at home, Max?" Paige asked as Max answered by way of a frown. "No sweat, neither do I," she said reassuringly. Max scribbled his phone number on a sheet of notebook paper, tore it out, gave it to Paige, and grabbed his book bag.

Following Max downstairs, Paige pleaded in vain to join the ride to drop Max off. Her father ordered her to finish helping her mother clean up and then do her homework. Due to her parents' hospitality toward her new friend who happened to be a boy, she did not protest. When Phil Edmundson returned and was greeted by Elvis at the door, Paige thanked him for taking her friend home.

"He's a nice kid, Paige. I waited for him to go inside, but he just stayed on the porch," her father remarked.

"He was so polite. I'm glad you made friends with him," her mother added. Paige nodded and smiled in agreement and headed back upstairs then paused midway as her mother called up, "I think Lana called when you were out with Elvis. You call her back after your homework."

"OK, Mom, thanks," Paige answered, continuing to run up the stairs. She jumped onto her bed and grabbed her clear Swatch-style phone and dialed Lana.

"Karrington Residence," Lana, answered chomping away at what sounded like celery. "What's up? My mom said you called," Paige said, a bit out of breath from her dash up the upstairs.

"Uh, must have been Wendy, but I wanted to talk to you anyway. Why did you blow me off for that dweeb in chem class?" Lana asked as the chewing over the phone intensified.

Looking at the paused game screen on her television, Paige let out a deep breath, regretting not calling Wendy instead, and responded, "I didn't blow you off, Lan. He didn't have a partner. Besides, he's really nice and cool."

"Yeah, sure. Well, he's not that nice; he's spreading fucked-up rumors about Deidre. She told me she caught him going through her locker trying to steal her trunks to her cheer uniform. What a perv! When she caught him, he made up some crazy story about her fucking Dwayne after practice and told Counselor Moretz," Lana said, chomping away.

Paige was flabbergasted and stopped her ill-informed friend from going further by interrupting her between chews. "That's not what happened, Lana. Max was over tonight, and he told me—"

Paige's rebuttal was cut off by a beeping tone on the line.

"Emergency breakthrough for Lana Karrington from a Greg Chapman? Do you accept?" an operator asked, ending Paige's defense of her new friend.

"Shit, Paige, that's Greg. Tell me tomorrow," Lana said, the urgent conversation now a distant afterthought.

After Lana got off the line, Paige's mother picked up the downstairs phone and scolded her. "Paige, get off the phone. You can see Lana in school tomorrow. Do your homework."

Paige thought about phoning Allison, who was more reasonable, to mount a defense for Max. Her mother was on the phone now, though, and would be for quite some time. She looked at her books, grabbed her Trapper Keeper, and was distracted by Max's phone number scribbled on the loose sheet of paper. "Can't call and warn him either," she said aloud while respooling her Peter Gabriel cassette tape with a pencil after her player had chewed it up. She opened her English-lit book and allowed her mind to escape the social turmoil of MHS. After ignoring the assigned reading, Paige read a few pages of *The Count of Monte Cristo*, then fell fast asleep.

Max woke to the upbeat, rhythmic humming of his mother in the hallway. This joyous expression was usually reserved for when she was disillusioned by some repetitive household task like laundry or dishes. Prying open his bedroom door, Max was greeted by the aroma of bacon frying. He tried the bathroom door, which was locked, an uncommon occurrence. Mrs. Garret approached her son with a wide smile and explained.

"Your father starts his new job today," she said in happiness.

"New job?" Max asked, somewhat stunned.

"He got a job at the produce market just up the street." She hummed on. Max had lain awake a good part of the night in excitement over Paige Edmundson. He was a bit sleep-deprived, so it took him a moment to re-member the scenario laid out to him by Dominic on the way to school the previous morning. The good-intentioned man with the blue caddy had made good on securing employment for Bill Garret. "Huh, OK, great, Mom."

"Better days are ahead." She went on. Her joyous tone shifted to serious-ness as she continued, "If you're not coming home after school, Max, please call me. I was worried sick before I heard from you."

"We didn't get to Paige's house until late yesterday. Sorry, Mom."

"Well, I'm glad to see you making new friends. Tell me, is this Paige pretty?" Her query had awakened Max completely now as his mother's question conjured an image of Paige in his mind. The toilet flushed as they stood midconversation in the hall.

"She's beautiful, Mom, inside and out," Max answered, causing his mother to smile even wider.

The bathroom door flung open, revealing a rushed Bill Garret. He had heard the whole rigmarole from the toilet and was agitated. There'd be no tavern trip for a liquid breakfast. Today he'd be reporting straight to some damn mini market. Yesterday afternoon an old-timer had bought him a shot at the bar and offered him a job across the street at a decent salary. At first he had thought the old suit was trying to come on to him, and he would normally tell a man who offered him a drink to fuck himself properly. His meager savings was nearly depleted, though, and William Garret found himself in the position to do no such thing. He begrudgingly accepted and was going to work today for the first time in a long time. As he exited the bathroom, he gazed upon his eager-faced wife and dimwit son smiling at him and added to their conversation. "You know what would be beautiful?" he offered rhetorically. "If a man could take a shit in silence before work!"

Mrs. Garret refused to let him dissuade her joy, ignoring his crude remark. She announced to him, "I made you eggs, Bill" while running her hand up and down his back in a comforting motion. "I need you strong and healthy for work! Max, you get ready for school." Never one to squander an opportunity to escape the presence of his father, Max crept into the bathroom while his parents went into the kitchen.

As Max was entering the bathroom, Deidre was leaving Moretz's office. She had made sure she got to school well ahead of schedule, telling her mother she had an early cheer meeting to attend and could not miss it. She took Moretz by surprise, the same way he had mentally disarmed her yesterday. Wearing her tightest pair of shredded stonewashed jeans and a top with a neckline that plunged into her cleavage, she rapped upon his office door, the mere sight of her bringing discomfort to the secretary Marilyn. Deidre laid out her terms to Moretz and gave way to his perversion provided he make good on his promise to alter her grades accordingly, as well as accommodating an additional request.

Embarrassed by his behavior and sexual misconduct, Moretz agreed. All the Lisbon girl wanted was for him to spread a rumor among the faculty. That wouldn't be difficult at all, and when she leaned close to him, his heartbeat raced and he forgot his self-disappointment, the same way he had yesterday afternoon. She understood that he desired her, and realizing this, she wanted to take advantage of him the same way he had her. She took hold of his genitals and massaged them aggressively and asked him to repeat what she intended him to report.

She groped furiously atop his trousers, forced him back in his chair, and went to work on him. In her head she pretended his dick was that of Dylan from Hessian's Cliff. She was in control now, and when she felt Moretz shudder, she backed away and let him come on himself. It took Moretz forty-five seconds.

The frat guys at Preytin U Phi Kappa had nicknamed her "The Cockgoblin" for her ability to scare come right out of a dick. She mentally prepared herself to whip up some tears for Ross, which wouldn't be hard after the scent of Moretz's rank breath. She left the office and gave a bitchy wince of a smile to the curious secretary and placed a stick of Big Red on her outstretched tongue.

Deidre still had at least a half hour before everyone would congregate in front of the school. She spent the time going through the desks of teachers in unlocked classrooms. She helped herself to some petty cash and amused herself by tossing out a pile of graded tests into the garbage bin in the ladies' room. The remainder of the time she spent in false self-admiration of herself in the restroom mirror.

The morning had turned overcast, but for the first time, Max was excited to go to school. He couldn't wait to see Paige again, and the hours that had passed since they had parted company yesterday had felt like an eternity to him. Perhaps his mother had been right and there were better days ahead. The incident with Deidre was a thing of the past, in his mind.

He arrived a few minutes late and didn't see Paige until after fourth period. He greeted her while she was talking to Wendy in the hall.

"Hey. Thanks for having me over yester—"

Paige stopped him midsentence and pulled him aside. "Max, did you say anything to Mr. Moretz about seeing Deidre and Dwayne? Tell me the truth."

"No. I told you, he came in after."

Paige turned to make sure Wendy had left and no one could overhear what she was going to say next.

"Look, I overheard Moretz and McCarmick in the teachers' lounge. Moretz was saying to McCarmick and the other teachers that you were in the girls' locker room after detention and that Deidre caught you going through her underwear or something and you made the whole thing about Dwayne up to spite her," Paige told Max with urgency. She became flustered as he seemed to be ignoring the serious accusations against him. He had a spaced-out look on his face. He was dumbfounded as to why Moretz would make such a ridiculous claim.

Indeed, Max had heard every word Paige had told him, but he was also focusing on the crowd at Deidre Lisbon's locker, behind Paige. Ross, Greg, Dwayne, Wendy, Lana, and Harold McCarmick were joking and laughing with one another.

"Max, are you even listening to me?" Paige yelled as the next bell sounded and the group dispersed from Deidre's locker.

"Yes. Look, Paige, no one's said anything to me, and if they do, I'll just tell the truth." He spoke with confidence. While his words to Paige were calm and collected, Max was equally concerned, and with good reason. He parted from Paige and went to put some books in his locker.

The hallway had cleared out, save for a few stragglers, and when Max shut his locker door, it revealed Ross Aberdeen. Max stepped away from Ross, whose face was covered in bad intentions. Ross sneered, drawing closer to Max, and shoved him backward, causing him to topple over Greg, who was crouched on all fours behind Max. As he fell, he heard Dwayne's voice. "Lyin' ass muthafuckah." The back of Max's head collided with the hard tile floor.

As if he were about to perform a scalping, Ross yanked Max's head upward. With a fistful of Max's hair in his left hand, he steadied him while delivering repeated punches to his face with his right. As Ross beat on Max's face, blood coursed out his nostrils. Max was slipping out of consciousness when Ross released him after the fourth punch. He fell back to the ground and felt his body vibrate in pain as a flurry of kicks was delivered from Dwayne and Greg, who laughed hysterically.

His head was pulsating as he instinctively covered his battered and bloodied face. A ringing in his ears was accompanied by an echo of Ross's voice.

"I hear you like girls' underwear and talking shit, Garret, huh?" Ross said while burying his knee into Max's chest, pinning him to the ground like an ant that had had a nail driven through its center. "If you wanted Dee's panties, you should have just asked me. I got something for you, though, from lost and found. Give it here, Greg!" Ross said, then tried to shove a yellowed jockstrap into Max's mouth with his other hand around his neck.

Max's nostrils were covered in blood, and he was gasping for air as Ross continued to shove the filthy jockstrap in his mouth. Having no alternative, Max bit down through the cloth into Ross's fingers.

"Fucking bite me?" Ross said, springing from his crouched position over Max. Greg looked around and saw Dwayne heading down the hall after getting his kicks in and urged Ross away.

"All right, Ross. He's good and fucked-up. Come on." Ross looked at his fingers, then delivered a final parting kick, then unzipped Max's backpack and dumped its contents on him. Curled in a partial fetal position, Max heard the echoed sound of casual whistling draw closer to him.

As he lay beaten and bloody, the still-whistling Harold McCarmick looked him over, squatted beside him, and said, "Well, you've made a fine mess of this hallway, Garret. A fine mess, indeed, while loitering in the halls and late to class again." McCarmick scribbled on his detention pad, tore a sheet, and carelessly tossed it over Max. "See you tomorrow at three," McCarmick said, walking away, continuing his casual whistling.

Looking from table to table in the cafeteria, Paige scanned the lunch-room for Max. She was anxious to pick up their conversation; plus, the girls at her table were being weird with her. This was no doubt attributable to Lana Karrington relaying what she had told her over the phone yesterday about Max being at her house. She looked over at the jock table and saw Ross performing a demonstration of how he had punched someone out. A pack of Skittles dropped to the bottom of the vending machine. Paige bent down to retrieve them and felt a pair of arms wrap around her when she got back up.

She pulled away and saw Greg's face. "What's up, sexy?" he asked, expecting some form of gratuity for his harassing gesture. He put one arm up on the vending machine, and Paige dipped under it to avoid being cornered.

"Nothing much, Greg," she said, moving beside him.

"I was thinking of cutting out of here early today, maybe go over to the bowling alley. You like bowling, right?"

"I do, Greg, but I have to complete a lab. Ask Lana; I know she will probably look forward to skipping chem class," Paige replied, walking away from him.

"Bitch," Greg muttered under his breath as she returned to her table.

"Trouble at the snack machine?" Ms. Jalorean asked Paige, having seen the exchange between her and Greg.

"Nothing I can't handle. Hey, did you hear anything about Max this morning?"

"Come see me a few minutes before class later. I wanted to ask you about that as well."

"Sure thing, Ms. J." Paige nodded as the bell sounded, ending lunch. Paige returned to her lunch table, which everyone but Lana had departed.

"Is Daniel back for you to partner with in chem class later, Lana?"

"I don't know and don't care, Edmundson. Greg asked me to cut and hang at his house."

"Not the bowling alley?" Paige slipped, confusing Lana.

"What are we going to do at a frickin' bowling alley?" Lana laughed while looking in her compact makeup mirror. Paige nodded and walked away.

"Hey, Paige, wait. If Ms. Jalorean asks where I'm at, just tell her I didn't feel good and went to the nurse's office—to lie down. Thanks, babe," Lana said, looking back to her mirror.

Deep down, Paige wanted to warn Lana of Greg's intentions, but she figured Lana already knew. If she intimated to her friend that he had asked her to hang out only moments ago, it'd only create conflict between them. She would not be telling Ms. Jalorean Lana's lie, but she also wouldn't rat her out either. By the time sixth period came, Paige had forgotten about the Greg and Lana drama after taking one look at Max.

Chapter 5:

INSTIGATION AND RETALIATION

Forgetting her plans to speak with Ms. Jalorean before class began, Paige rushed to the back of the classroom.

"Oh my God! What the hell happened to you?" Paige said in a nervous whisper, sitting beside Max. Both his nostrils were plugged up with blood-soaked tissues. As he turned to face her, she was horrified to see a trail of broken blood vessels on the side of his nose, leading to his swollen, purple eye socket.

"I'm OK. Just cover for me," Max answered weakly. Inspecting him further, she saw dried-up blood in his eardrum.

"I'm just going to put my head down." Max groaned.

"No, you can't do that; you're hurt bad," Paige protested to no avail as his head remained buried in his folded arms. She raised her hand, making Ms. Jalorean stop her lecture.

"I asked that you hold all questions. What is it, Paige?"

"May I be excused?"

"Paige, what's the matter?" The entire class turned to the back of the classroom, where Paige and Max were seated. This prompted Paige to get up and run to her teacher. She whispered into Ms. Jalorean's ear, and she in turn nodded from her lectern and quickly clapped her hands together and announced, "OK, people, I need to step out for a moment. Read pages forty-eight to fifty-one, and then answer the questions at the end of chapter four. I'll be right back."

Paige assisted her in helping Max out of the classroom through the back door. They hurried him to the nurse's station. The nurse retrieved an ice pack, which Ms. Jalorean gently placed on his head.

"This is all we can do for him here; he needs to go to the hospital. What's the last name? I'll call the parents," the nurse said.

In seeing the panic of those who had acted with haste to help him, Max was amazed. He had had his bell rung a good many times before at the hands of his father. Perhaps that's why he had been able to crawl off the floor and make his way to the bathroom. After some damage control, he had hidden out in the library, then gone to class more concerned about hiding his injuries than the wounds themselves. Ms. Jalorean cradled him in her arms as Paige held the ice on his head. The sweet scent of Ms. Jalorean's perfume mixed with the dry blood in his nostrils as she questioned him.

"Max, when did this happen? Never mind. Just keep your head upright." Her voice trailed off as he tilted his head back and faded out. Fortunately, the school had no emergency contact info for him other than the address since the Garrets' phone line had only been connected days ago. After some tests and treatments, he was discharged from Hillshire Medical's ER. Then he was taken home much later that evening by a concerned Phil Edmundson. Max explained to his mother the injury had occurred during a game of tackle football after school and had only intimated to Paige and Ms. Jalorean what had actually happened.

The detention was revoked after Ms. Jalorean ripped into Harold McCarmick. She was careful not to betray Max's wishes about silence in the matter. He had felt reporting his attackers would only compound his troubles rather than remedy them, and while she disagreed, she understood. She felt the least she could do was chastise Harold for penalizing an injured student for being late.

"I'm not doing that. Late is late. I'm sure you wouldn't give Aberdeen a break for being late cuz of his sprained shoulder as a result of that punk, Kath?" McCarmick opposed.

"Harold, you may not know this, but I know Evelyn. When you had the team away at football camp, she had your youngest here for the day camp program over the summer. Lovely woman. It'd break her heart if I had to tell her what I reported to Principal Volkem, about me not being able to wear a skirt and you not being able to keep your fucking hands to yourself. But if you don't lay off that kid, I'll do it." She threatened him.

"OK, fine. Have it your way." McCarmick relented.

Max's nose had been broken. The doctor at the ER had explained that it was good and bad. Bad in the fact that the high-impact blows to his nose could have resulted in death if the cartilage had slammed any farther into his head. Good that it was a clean, straight break. He was given a large needle containing antibiotics and treated for his bruised-but-not-broken ribs and discharged. After confiding only in Paige and Ms. Jalorean, Max refused to speak on the matter again.

After that day Paige drifted apart from her friends and closer to Max. In and out of school, they only hung around one another.

When Paige tried to talk to him about the harassment he was still receiving at school, Max changed the subject. While Ross and the others didn't lay hands on him again, the verbal abuse and pranks never stopped. As much as Max wished to put the vicious beating he had received in the hallway behind him, repercussions came in the form of an emergency room bill.

Since William Garret had found employment, his weekday drinking had tapered off significantly. Monday-through-Friday full shifts at J&J Produce left little time for him to get sauced. A pattern of him doubling down on the weekends quickly developed, and Max and his mother busied themselves away from the home every Saturday and Sunday. Mrs. Garret had become friendly with some women she had met at church, and Max began a tradition of spending entire weekends over at Paige's house. He packed what he needed and brought it to school on Friday, not returning home until late Sunday evening.

Having never been to Max's house except so that he could run in and grab something, Paige requested that they finish a class project at his house. Against his better judgment, Max agreed and quickly regretted it as his father barged into his bedroom holding an emergency room bill and announced, "Boy, send this little piece of tail home. I need to talk to you."

Paige was unnerved by his crudeness and looked at Max, who protested. "We're working on our chemistry project. It's a big part of our final grade!"

Bill Garret laughed at his response and figured since he couldn't send the girl home, he would have to embarrass him in front of her. "Is that so, missy? My son any good at this chemistry?"

"Yes, sir! Max is brilliant. I tell him all the time he's going to be an engineer or a chemist," Paige replied with enthusiasm.

"Engineer or a chemist," Bill Garret repeated, looking at the documents he held. "Well, answer me this, Mr. Chemistry: What is it in your chemistry that makes you a pussy?" he roared, holding the letter overhead.

"What are you talking about?" Max yelled back in frustration.

"Do you want to just finish up at my house?" Paige offered nervously.

Bill Garret left the doorway of Max's room and held the bill in front of Max's face and screamed out, "This is a bill from Hillshire Medical saying I have to pay five hundred dollars for you being a fucking pussy!" He erupted as saliva flew from his mouth.

"They jumped me; what could I do?" Max yelled back defensively.

His father's roaring tone turned into sarcastic mimicry as he carried on.

"Is that what happened? That's not the way I heard it. I overheard the football coach at the tavern. He said the Aberdeen boy pushed you over and you cried like a little pussy. He also said he hates you and all little sissy, fairy punks like you, and I don't blame him."

That was all Paige needed to hear. She gathered her materials off Max's bed in one motion and spoke to Max as if the hostile drunkard was not even there. "Come on, Max, let's go!" making her way to the door. Bill Garret blocked the doorway and shoved Paige back and continued his tirade in a booming voice.

"You mad, huh, boy? You got any idea how many cases of fucking lettuce and goddamned bananas I have to haul for that fucking guinea for five hundred dollars for you, little fuckin queer!" A silent rage came over Max, and a switch went off in his head. His hands trembled, and he looked down.

"Let her through, you drunk asshole!" Max shouted, prompting his father to rush at him. William Garret was strongly opposed to any backtalk when he was giving insults. His father ran to grab him as Max had expected. He picked up an ice skate off the ground and blasted his old man point blank in the face before he could take hold of him. Stunned, Bill Garret staggered backward with both hands covering his face.

"Go, go," Max shouted to Paige, who was in shock in the Garrets' hallway. They ran out of the house giggling like children much younger than they were. They jumped on their bikes, rode for a few blocks, and didn't stop. They gathered themselves at an intersection. Paige applied her hand-brakes, waiting for her accomplice. Max, who had no brakes on his blue, black, and rust bike, swung his foot around to the back tire using what he called "the Flintstones brake method."

They were still laughing and out of breath. Paige paused for a moment, thinking it rude to enjoy herself so much; then Max lost it and began cackling even harder. She joined in. Max wasn't happy, but he was proud—proud for finally standing up to his father and fighting back and proving in spite of his accusations that he most certainly was not a pussy. His real issue with the argument was he knew his father had no intention of paying a bill on his behalf to begin with. A car horn blared from the intersection, and someone yelled over to them.

"Hey, Edmundson! What's up, girl?" Greg called out from the passenger side of a new Mustang.

Paige let out a deep breath, looked to Max, and said in a low voice, "I'll be right back." Paige wheeled her bike up to the car; other drivers were pulling around in frustration as the light had turned green. Max saw Dwayne behind the wheel of the Mustang, revving the engine while parked as if this made him cooler. Max's excitement came to a crashing halt as he looked at the black gleaming 5.0, then at his rusted bike.

While Paige had only been talking to Greg for a few moments, Max felt like he had been standing there forever. He looked around aimlessly, then he saw Dominic across the street and moved from his stationary position and called out to him, "Mr. Gervallo!"

"Oh, Maximilian! How goes it?" Dominic called back while putting some boxes into his trunk as Max pedaled closer.

"Say, how come I don't see you in the mornings anymore? You didn't drop out or anything, did you?" Dominic quizzed.

"Oh no, I go to school with my friend Paige, so I head in the other direction to her house first," Max replied, motioning over to his friend, who was still being held captive by the duo in the Mustang.

"That her over there?" Dominic asked, seeing Greg hanging outside the passenger side window, with Paige backed up a good distance from him. Max nodded yes, causing Dominic to let out a high-pitched whistle of approval. "Pretty girl, Max. She got a good head on her shoulders?"

"She's great," Max answered, partially confused by the question but understanding enough to answer partially. "I was wondering if you could do my mom and me a favor?"

"Name it!" Dominic demanded as Paige joined them from the opposite curb.

"We're really grateful for you getting my dad the job at J and J, and he doesn't drink at all when he's working, but…" Max carried on as Paige approached from behind him, unbeknownst to him. This was visible to Dominic, who sensed the conversation might be awkward in front of his friend.

"Ah, here's the lovely Paige you been telling me about, right here." Dominic spoke up, then nodded to the smiling girl. "Say, Max, it sounds like you have a lot on your mind, so why don't you stop by here tomorrow about this time, and you can tell me about it over dinner if you want?"

"Are you serious?"

"Sure, and you're welcome to bring your friend here as well. I got to run," Dominic concluded, waving to Max and nodding to Paige.

Once Dominic had pulled off, Paige opened the conversation with a prolonged "Soooooo…Greg and Dwayne want us to come to a party at Greg's later tonight."

"Party with the guys who almost killed me? Yeah, Paige, it'll be a blast. Maybe they could finish me off this time. Can Ms. Jalorean come to take me to the hospital again? You know, so my dad doesn't get billed for the ambulance?"

"I told them no, so don't get mad," Paige returned, imitating Max's irritated tone. Eager to change the subject, Paige asked, "Who was that guy?"

"That's my only other friend besides you." His apologetic response was indicative of his anxiety at seeing Paige talking to his enemies in the Mustang. He looked up from his poorly aligned handlebars and continued, "He invited us to dinner tomorrow, but if you want to take a break from hanging out, I understand.

Paige was angry. She couldn't believe what he had just said to her. Rather than give into his sad-sack routine, she played along. "Well, I'd like to take a break from hanging out with you all the time." But her good-hearted nature would not allow her ruse to continue. "But since we still have to finish our project and I know you don't want to go home after hitting your dad in the face with an ice skate, of all things, you can stay over, and we will finish it tomorrow. Then we can take a break from hanging out," Paige teased, unable to keep the smile on her face from giving her away.

Max had once again begun looking down, facing his bike's crooked handlebars, and his heart had sunk into his chest until he had heard the girl he had come to love in such a short time finish her farce.

"And I'd love to go to dinner with you and your friend as long as you never, ever say or think that I would ever want to stop seeing you, Maxwell Garret."

Then Paige pedaled ahead of Max, whose emotions went from zero into overdrive as he stood up on the bike to gain speed and yelled ahead, "You want to order Chinese food tonight?"

"Definitely."

After an evening filled with games, movies, and General Tso's chicken, they cuddled in each other's arms in the Edmundsons' rec room. An unparalleled energy that neither of them had ever felt coursed back and forth between them inside Paige's Ghostbusters sleeping bag. Once comfortable, they reflected briefly on their argument and agreed to never fight with each other again. They fell asleep to reruns of *The Twilight Zone* until the static and white noise of the channel cutting off awakened Paige. She switched off the black-and-white-snow-filled screen and returned to her room. Before going back to sleep, she picked out an outfit to wear with Max and his mysterious "other friend" tomorrow.

The morning came and with it the sounds of Lynne Edmundson's blender and her newest interest—new wave music, which filled the Edmundsons' home. As she was busy getting breakfast together for Paige and her friend, Dominic Gervallo was leaving his house to meet a friend himself.

Before his wife, Maria, had passed away, Dominic had delayed making his rounds on the weekends. These days he had less running around to do and more time than he knew what to do with. Most of the guys he ran with were either dead, locked up, or too old to chase the action anymore. Maria had coaxed him to start going to church, but after she passed, that fell by the wayside. Weekends were just like any other day. After opening up the club, he went to Palmetto's diner and met his best friend, Carmine, for breakfast. They reminisced about the old days and talked about the bookmaking operation they still ran, mainly out of boredom. Neither of them needed the money anymore, but they considered themselves underworld elder statesmen. They were proud to pass on knowledge to the generation that did need the money and, like them, had little opportunity without cutting corners.

"I'm taking the kid I told you about over to Ray Gene's for a steak tonight," Dominic said.

"The one who's into you for a mint over March Madness? Is it going to be his last supper, killer?" Carmine asked in laughter, ribbing his old friend just a bit.

"No, you ball-breaker, the one whose old man I got working over at Johnnie's produce joint."

"Oh. Taking up an apprentice, Dom? You ready to groom a kid who's still in high school, and you say I'm still corrupt! Lotta nerve, Gervallo!"

"No, never, this kid's not like that. He's soft-spoken, and his whole demeanor and mannerisms make me think of Maria."

"I miss her too, Dom. She was a saint among sinners, but whatta ya mean, 'makes you think of her'? How so?"

"I mean, like, if she and I were to have ever had a son, this Max kid is what her…our son would be like, understand? Anyway, I like the kid, and he's got this cute little girlfriend who I told him he can bring along."

Hearing this, Carmine nearly coughed up his pancakes in laughter. Dominic got up from the booth, patted his friend's back, and gave him his untouched ice water. He panicked, thinking that if Carmine were to drop dead, he'd have no one to pal around with.

After sipping his water and getting his pancakes down the pipe, Carmine motioned upward with his right hand to signal he was fine. "Don't ever do that to me again."

"Do what? What did I do?" Dominic asked in confusion.

"Don't ever tell me that Dom Gladgem Gervallo is chaperoning a teen-age date while I'm swallowing food. I'm liable to choke to death in laughter if it happens again."

In what seemed to him a lifetime before he met Maria, when the drinking age was eighteen and Dominic was in good shape, he had once been worked over by a guy twice his size in a local tavern. The brute told the boy he wanted his gold ring, which had a crimson-red ruby set in it. While the ring was of little value, it had been a gift from his late grandmother, and he squawked at the notion of handing it over. After refusing, he was blindsided in the back of the head by a pool cue and the ring was taken forcefully from him. Bested but not beaten, Dominic left the bar, only to return when it was closing time.

The thief stumbled outside the tavern, and while he was taking a piss in the nearby alleyway, he was struck over the head with a piece of concrete and smothered to death by a Glad garbage bag. Dominic got his ring back, and the moniker "Gladgem" was coined by the tavern bartender who saw the attack unfold while taking out the trash. Fortunately for him, the bartender was equally agitated by the boisterous, annoying, thieving, wretch who spent hours irritating him and customers in the bar.

The bartender provided no part of the story to the police, who were not at all interested in finding the killer of a transient who was saturated in urine and blood. He did divulge the story, along with the nickname, which stuck over the years, to trusted regulars.

"Tell me, do these kids have any idea who they're going to be dining with this evening?" Carmine questioned, unable to stop harassing Dominic.

"Yes, the nice old guy he met on the way to school," Dominic said with a smile, pulling his overcoat from the hanger outside the booth.

"Nice guy my—hey, where are you going? It's your turn to pay for breakfast!"

"Nice try, Carm. See you tomorrow," he said, patting him on the shoulder while making for the exit.

"OK, well, when Mr. March Madness squares up with you, breakfast is on you for a month!" Carmine fired back, part joking and part serious. A waitress studied the aging man sitting alone in the booth, who appeared to be yelling to himself. Carmine saw her confused look and lashed out, "How about some more coffee and less staring, sweetheart?"

Carmine was a pain in the ass, but he was right, thought Dominic outside the diner, looking in at his friend, who he could see yelling. While he had no intention of grooming Max, he did have an urge to mentor someone or at least make a positive change in someone else's life. Maria had been in the ground almost five years, and he was over the grief stage. Back at the social club, he looked around in amazement.

He could remember a time when the place was packed wall to wall with anglers and hustlers dressed to the nines. Now there were only a few slouches in warm-up suits still recovering from last night's hangover. After kicking a stool out from some half-asleep cooch, he phoned Ray Gene's with specific requests and instructions. Dominic looked forward to breaking his routine and seeing how life was in the eyes of his young friend Max. In the few hours before dinner, the old man read the newspaper twice, then recaptured moments from his youth in the club's back office, reading the comics lent to him by Max. Time flew by, until a knock at the office door interrupted him. He removed his glasses and shouted, "What is it?" to the door.

"There's two kids say they were supposed to meet you here?" a confused voice said.

The voice belonged to Anthony Bartagglia. At least that was the name his mother had given him; everyone else just called him Tony Rhino. In the ring The Rhino had been a force to be reckoned with as a middleweight boxer in the late seventies. He had been impervious to opponents' blows, and he had scored a staggering number of knockouts for a fighter in his weight class. His mother had fallen ill in his prime, and he had had to take dives to keep up with her medical bills. Once his mother passed, he settled into the role of collector or adjuster for anyone who owed Middleton's outfit. Depression led to him nearly doubling his weight so that the only job he could get with his hunched six-two frame was darkening the door of the social club.

"Thanks, Rhino; let 'em in," Dominic yelled back. Then he paused for a moment, gazing at the various pinup girls who had been plastered on the office walls in the past six or seven decades and yelled back, "Never mind. I'm coming out there."

The kids wound up seeing the beer models and calendar girls as they needed to put their bikes inside. Paige giggled and nudged furiously at Max's arms after being properly introduced to Dominic, who was trying to position Rhino in front of the nude posters. They went to his car, and he prevented Max from entering the front seat by opening the car door for Paige first. After turning the ignition, he turned down the radio so they could talk on the ride over.

It was hard for Max to keep himself from laughing while witnessing Dominic being barraged by the Paige Edmundson line of questioning. He was elated that she had decided to come as Dominic deflected her questions with vague answers and grinning at the immediate follow-ups by Paige. He figured Dom would like her personality and as he observed the volley, decided his estimate had been correct.

"The man at the door was scary looking; is he mean?"

"He can be."

"What kind of restaurant are we going to?"

"A good restaurant."

"Will it be crowded?"

"It better not be."

"I see your wedding ring. Why isn't your wife coming with us?"

"She passed away."

Paige's cheeks turned rose red in embarrassment. "That was inconsiderate of me. I'm terribly sorry for mentioning her."

"Don't be, Paige," Dominic answered. "I loved my wife more than life itself, and I enjoy talking about her. Since you brought her up, I'll just tell you she was the light of my life and I'm a bit lost without her, which is why I'm so glad that you and Maximilian are joining me as I rarely go out for dinner anymore. If you ever wish to hear more, feel free to ask."

They pulled into a nearly vacant parking lot, and Max, taking a cue from Dominic, opened the door for Paige as she exited the sedan. Max and Paige were under the assumption that perhaps the place was closed. The exterior was covered in beige stucco with a modest neon red sign above the door that read, "Ray Gene's," accompanied by a small picture of a man in a striped shirt operating a gondola. A single red neon light in the window kept them from questioning Dominic.

Much to their surprise, they were immediately greeted by a host. "Good evening, Mr. Gervallo, and to your guests as well. I am Giorgio," he announced to Max and Paige. They all shook hands, and Giorgio hugged Dominic and continued, "It's so good to see you; it's been far too long."

"I guess it's been some time, huh, Giorgio? Place looks great, though. Gene left it in good hands with you. Ray's not in?" Dominic asked, bringing a grin to Giorgio's face.

"Oh, he was, but when I told him you were coming, he made himself scarce," Giorgio said, leading the trio to a cushioned circular table in the far corner of the dining room.

"What's wrong with him?" Dominic scoffed. "I don't even remember how much it was!"

"He's very proud, Mr. G, and I guess he was ashamed knowing he wouldn't have it for you. I can only speculate. Regardless, Ray instructed me to relay that your dinner is compliments of the house tonight, and he will square with you as soon as possible." Just then a duo of servers approached. "This is Adam and Carrie, your servers for the evening, and I thank your young friends for helping you find your way back to Ray Gene's. Enjoy your meal."

With that, Giorgio left them, went into the kitchen, and phoned Ray at home to inform him of Dominic's pleasant demeanor regarding the gambling debt owed to him. Only a few groups of diners entered after they had been seated and were denied seating anywhere near the table they occupied. Initially both Max and Paige felt a bit out of place and underdressed, but the relaxing tone of Dominic put them both at ease. They had a delicious dinner that consisted of multiple courses and excellent conversation and laughter. Paige noticed how Max opened up around Dominic and how carefree he was. It was a characteristic she only saw in Max when they were alone.

In the kitchen of Ray Gene's, Adam and Carrie peered out a small window in the kitchen door. Both were seniors at Middleton High and figured either Paige or Max to be relatives of the local legend. Prior to Dominic Gervallo's arrival that evening, there had been a great deal of discussion regarding Gladgem Gervallo—unbeknownst to him. Adam made his way to the table whose occupants were midconversation, cautious not to interrupt at the wrong time.

"So Max out of, like, nowhere just chucks a friggin' hockey skate at his head…" a most animated and demonstrative Paige explained to Dominic, who was hysterical with laughter. Slumping in the booth, he managed to question Paige in between his fits.

"Then what did you do?" Dominic asked.

"I booked out of the house faster than I think I have ever run. Then we saw you," she concluded, still giggling.

Adam sensed an opening and spoke up. "Would you or your guests like dessert, Mr. Gervallo?"

"Yes, let me have a few cannoli, some espresso for me, and, uh, how about hot chocolate for you two?" he asked his two companions.

"If it's all the same, I'd like to try an espresso as well," Max suggested.

"Me too," Paige added.

"There you have it." Dominic nodded in agreement to Adam, who took leave immediately. "So Johnny came into the club this afternoon and tells me old man Garret came into work today looking like he got face—pardon me,

Paige—face-fucked by a giant squid! I sez to him, 'He probably got worked over by my buddy Maximilian," he roared, massaging Max's shoulders as if Max were a boxer and Dominic his manager. Paige looked at Max, who was being a good sport, and laughing as well.

"Why do you even have skates?" Paige asked in confusion and amusement.

"Well, I'm glad you two can laugh. I'm going to have to go home tonight," Max said, still smiling, bringing an abrupt seriousness to the conversation and a stop to his friend's laughter.

But only for a moment. Paige replied, "Well, you can just throw the other skate right, Maximilian?"

"No, I only have the one for some reason."

The trio erupted in laughter once more as Adam brought their after-dinner drinks, assisted by Carrie, who had the desserts.

"OK, three espressos," he said, setting them on the table.

"You two are a couple of night owls, like me," Dominic commented. While he had not slept much at all, it had been some time since Dominic had prolonged an evening. He couldn't even remember the last time he was out more than two hours after sundown. Playing it cool, he casually said, "Say, you two want to go catch a movie with me?" unable to mask his anticipation.

"I'm in no rush to go home!" Max responded with equal enthusiasm. The wide-eyed look on Paige's face and her smile indicated she was in complete agreement with the idea.

Dominic offered, "I was looking at the paper today and read a good review of that Western picture *Young Guns*. It's playing at the Eric Twin close by here."

Unable to restrain her excitement, Paige blurted out, "*Elm Street Four* is playing there! My cousin told me it was so much scarier than the last one!"

They both looked to Max as Dominic said to him, "Well, Max, you're the tiebreaker. What'll it be?"

"Sorry, Dominic, but *Nightmare on Elm Street Four*, definitely."

Dominic took a long sip from his espresso cup, pulled a few large bills from his wallet, and placed them on the table.

"I thought Giorgio said dinner was compliments of the house? What are you paying for?"

Dominic nodded in agreement, taking a bite from his dessert pastry in a hurry. After chewing, he explained. "Yes, dinner was compliments of the house. But if you want them to shut down half of the house so you and your friends can dine in peace, you better leave a tip for at least half the house," he grumbled good-naturedly. "*Nightmare on Elm Street.* Come on you, sociopaths, we better scram if we're going to catch the previews."

They exited the booth and thanked Giorgio, who presented Dominic and Max with desserts to go and gave Paige a long-stem rose. Before handing it to her, he told her, "Be sure to come back before it wilts to get another one."

Max rushed through the exit doors of the Eric Theatre and shouted in excitement, "He's not dead! Right, Paige? I mean, he's definitely not dead. You saw him in the fountain, right, Dom?"

"All I know is I'm gonna have nightmares myself! Maddon! Next time I pick," Dominic joked.

"Thanks so much for taking us, Dominic. It was great. When can we go again?" Paige asked.

Dominic looked at them and realized this had also given him an overwhelming feeling of pleasure and excitement. The smile dropped from his face as they made their way to the parking lot, and he explained, "Mrs. Gervallo used to love to go to the movies, and since she passed, I stopped going myself. So as long as it's OK with you, Maximilian, we can go at least once a month if you and Paige are up for it." Paige looked at the widower with the utmost sincerity, as did Max, and they were both touched by his explanation, as well as his suggestion. They realized they had been the first people to sit in a darkened theater with him since his wife passed away. They both nodded in agreement, choked up by Dominic's expression and devotion to his deceased spouse. The silence was broken by an ignorant shout in the parking lot.

"Hey, Garret!" Ross Aberdeen's voice boomed in their direction. He was leaning on the trunk of Dwayne's Mustang.

Turning, Max gasped at the scene before him. Shortly after they had entered the theater, Ross and company had been thrown out. The group, which consisted of Ross, Greg, Dwayne, Deidre, Lana, Wendy, and Allison, had had to resort to hanging in the parking lot. They had intended on seeing the same film. When they had missed the start time and been forced to settle for the other movie, they had become irate. They had refused to leave, and then the manager had phoned the police. When a Middleton City cop had arrived, Dwayne had dropped his father's name to defuse the situation.

They had resorted to drinking a warm case of Pabst in the parking lot while passing around some Mad Dog 20/20 and Everclear. By the time Max, Paige, and Dominic exited, they were good and drunk. Greg circled past Max on a skateboard and said, "My boy Ross over there is talking to you, and he's been waiting to see you out of school." Greg tossed an empty can in Max's direction. As it skidded on the blacktop in front of him, Max ignored it and kept walking, until Paige was seen by both Greg and Deidre behind him.

"Oh shit! What's up, Paige?" Greg said, bringing the skateboard to a complete stop.

In a slurred voice, Deidre called out, "Yo, Paige, cah-co-come-here, slut! Where the fuck you been at!" For a moment Paige thought she could defuse the situation by saying hello. She found her solution to be useless as she saw Ross tilt the bottle up toward the lamppost's light and hurl it in Max's direction. Dominic pulled Max by his shirt away from the shattering bottle.

"Are these friends of yours?" Dominic questioned as a precaution.

"Not really," Paige said, seeing Allison Kyle walking away from the company she had kept in the past and feeling disappointed in herself.

"Not at all," Max added, staring at Ross, who ran toward the three of them in a sprint, only to stop a few paces away.

"Don't you hear me calling you?" Ross said, breathing heavy, his arms outstretched. Greg glided up behind him on the skateboard.

"Fuck off, Ross!" Paige yelled, offended at their behavior, especially with an adult as kind and pleasant as Dominic present.

"You going out with this dickhead, Paige?" Greg asked, pointing at Max.

"Get out of here, you punks. Leave these kids the hell alone," Dominic said, feeling some firm words would probably be sufficient; he placed his arms behind Max and Paige and led them toward his car.

"Fuck you, old man!" Dwayne said.

Dominic Gladgem Gervallo felt his blood boil in anger for the first time in a very long time. He turned away from Max and Paige and gave Greg a hard shove to his midsection to push him out of the way.

"What did you say to me, you little cocksucker!"

Still angered that Paige had told him to fuck off but too inebriated to reply, a confused Ross shouted to Max, "I'll kick yer grandpa's ass too, Garret!"

"Fuck him up, Ross!" Deidre shouted, stumbling over from the car.

Dominic had already decided. Whichever one of these assholes started at him, that person was going to get the brunt of the blast. He always found the jailhouse strategy of knock the first guy out so cliché, but here he was about to employ the same method. Ross picked up Greg's skateboard and swung it overhead, ready to hit Dom with it like a battle-ax as he inched closer. Dominic told himself, *Let him get that board high enough, and when he goes to bring it down, I'm gonna rip his little baby balls the fuck off.*

As Ross drew closer to the man who just a few decades ago had ended a man's life with some loose concrete, a garbage bag, and his bare hands, Dwayne egged him on. "Beat his old ass."

"I'm not even eighteen. You can't touch me. You shouldn't have pushed me." Greg copped out, seeing a glimmer of madness in Dominic's eyes, causing Ross to drop his guard.

"Yeah, old mother fucker, my dad is Officer Alvin Bishop. Middleton City PD—I'll have him arrest your old ass for hitting a minor, bitch." Dwayne threatened.

Hearing this, Dominic smiled, quickly turned to Max, and ordered him, "Here, take Paige to the car. I'll be there in a minute."

Max took the keys and started for the car, thinking to himself, *If any of these pricks hurt Dom, I'm running them over with the car.* He motioned Paige toward the car. She looked back nervously, afraid Dominic would face a similar fate to that of Max when he had been jumped in the hallway. Max opened the passenger side door, then he got in the driver's side. He and

Paige squirmed in the darkened Cadillac, trying to see what was going on. The only sounds were their heavy breathing and the rubbery sound coming from the car's leather upholstery.

Seconds passed, then Paige shouted, "He's coming back, Max! I think he's OK!"

As Max peered out the car windshield, he saw no sign of Dominic. "Where, Paige?" he asked in a panic, then the driver's door was ajar and the warning signal sounded and the interior lights came on.

"Who said you could drive? Move over," Dominic said, then got in the car, still agitated a good bit but composed.

"Well?" Paige questioned.

"Well what?" Dominic teased.

"What happened?" Max asked impatiently.

Dominic looked directly into Max's eyes, thinking about Carmine's comment to him over breakfast. "Oh, you won't be having any trouble from them anymore," he answered, being purposely vague.

"They ruin everything!" Paige said, slumped in the seat, so discouraged that such a wonderful evening had come to such a near-disastrous end. "So what did you do?" Paige followed up, slowing Dominic's skyrocketing blood pressure and putting a smile on his face.

He thought about lying to them, perhaps telling them that somebody said they were calling the cops. He may have, but after the one kid had threatened him, once he had dropped his father's name, Dominic had felt compelled to give his own, followed by some parting words of advice.

He took a deep breath and cursed Carmine in his mind. They argued about everything, but they both knew where the other stood on personal philosophy. *They were who they were* and had no romantic notions or disillusionment about growing up in the streets and what they did to make a life outside of them. He never lied unless it was for strategy or to keep a loved one from avoidable pain. He looked back in the rearview mirror and spoke honestly, "I told them that if they ever fuck with you again"—he paused—"their mommies and daddies were going to the cemetery." Dominic then put on the radio and did not speak again until he dropped them both off at Paige's house.

"Come by and grab your bikes tomorrow. Same time next month, right?" he asked the wide-eyed kids, who nodded in complete agreement. "Thanks for a most pleasant evening," he said, then drove off.

The following morning, during breakfast, rather than coughing up his pancakes, Carmine fell out of the booth in Palmetto's Diner in laughter.

Chapter 6:
SUMMER OF LOVE, AUTUMN OF ANGUISH

Word spread through Middleton High like wildfire. Adam and Carrie from Ray Gene's relayed juniors Max Garret and Paige Edmund were connected to the infamous Gladgem Gervallo. Deidre and the girls just scoffed at Paige and ignored her. Lunch in the library became a thing of the past for Max. He and Paige became friends with Adam and Carrie from the restaurant, both aspiring musicians who encouraged them to start a band.

The Edmundsons embraced Paige's new friends and allowed them to practice in the basement—much to Elvis's dismay. Aaron played the drums, Carrie was lead guitar with Paige on bass, and Max was backup lead guitar, as well as their lead singer. They covered songs from Guns N' Roses, Poison, Black Sabbath, Metallica, and when Dominic stopped by, Sinatra and the Stones, which he enjoyed. Phil Edmundson was initially concerned about his daughter hanging around with the aging gangster, but within moments of meeting Dom, he decided the older gentleman was nothing but sincere when it came to the kids.

Following wishes for a good summer from Ms. Jalorean, Max and Paige bolted out the doors of the school like condemned prisoners who had just found a means of escape; they ran free with no backpacks or books restraining their movements. Instead of going to the clearing and on to Paige's house, they passed the abandoned jewelry store and caught their breath at the end of the block. The school was out of sight, and they were heading to the social club to see Dominic.

He requested they drop by the club so he could give Max an early birthday present. As much as Dominic enjoyed having them around, seeing them at the club was something he avoided. They continued to see one another for dinner at Ray Gene's and a trip to the theater. Max and Paige agreed to include Dominic in the exclusive group that had seen Paige's fortress of solitude. Concerned that Dominic would find a misplaced picnic table in the middle of the woods stupid or boring, Paige was initially hesitant. When Dominic marveled at the tranquil and peaceful hangout and went on to tell them about his old clubhouse, her concerns were alleviated.

Dominic trekked on the path into the forest with them; he understood that while the clearing wasn't much, it was what they had. He appreciated the comradery shown to him by his young friends, despite the mosquito bites through his dress socks and his shoes being covered in mud. He was sworn to silence. This was something he had grown accustomed to over the years. Once he pledged secrecy, Dominic was given the customary oath handshake. He even told Carmine, despite his discouragement, "Hell, they showed me their hideout; why shouldn't I let them come by mine?"

No longer sprinting, Max and Paige were taking frantically long strides. They had only been admitted to the club once—to leave and retrieve their bikes in Dom's office. Every time thereafter they had had to ask Rhino for him at the door and wait outside until he emerged. The prospect of hanging out had them speed-walking like hunters pacing behind their quarry. Max rushed up to the entrance and rather than give the customary "Is Dominic there?" he told Rhino, "Mr. Gervallo is expecting us."

Tony Rhino looked up from his newspaper, glanced with humor at Max's formal request, and smiled. He had become familiar with the duo that had been dubbed by Carmine, "Gladgem's Gambits." It was nice seeing them instead of the usual mooks he saw in the joint. "Well, I shall notify him of your arrival at once. Follow me," he said kiddingly. He stood up from his perch and opened the second entranceway.

As the door opened, the sounds of harmonized tarantellas filled the darkened, smoke-filled room. One could deduce from a single look that the tables, chairs, bar, and surrounding fixtures were most certainly not from the eighties or even the seventies, for that matter. Paige feasted her eyes upon the various framed paintings that adorned the walls, which were painted blood red. There were reproductions of Roman frescoes, paintings of gladiators engaged in combat, and a black-and-white photograph of some men that seemed out of place with the framed paintings on the walls. "Do you know these guys in this picture?" Paige asked Rhino as he ushered them in.

"Who, the Rat Pack? Believe me, kid, if I did, I sure as hell wouldn't be hanging around here." He laughed. "Met Dino once; he saw me clobber Jake Fox. That one right there, that's me," Rhino said with pride, pointing to a black-and-white photo of himself in his prime, with closed fists in boxing trunks. Paige did a double take.

"You were very handsome."

"I still am." Rhino chuckled and pointed her in Dom's direction.

Max carefully eavesdropped on a conversation that he was too close to ignore. Two men seated on barstools were arguing with one another about the importance of the Olympics. "How the hell can you not like the Olympics?"

"Well, besides basketball, it's just a bunch of sports that ain't good enough to be played every year." The speaker saw Max and went on as if urging Max to side with his position. "I mean, they won't even let us have our best players in basketball. If they did, the US would win the gold every year. It's bullshit, right, kid?"

Max shrugged in neutrality. Dominic chastised the man at the bar. "Please don't go involving him in any of your ridiculous arguments, Artie. Besides, it's not so much the events; it's the one thing the entire world participates in."

"OK, Dom. Well, you enjoy the disc hurling or whatever they call it," Artie responded, feeling the need to get the last word.

"Let me tell you something, Art—if the Greeks from way back when had never started hurling them discs, you wouldn't have your football or basketball or any of that shit. So shut your mouth, have another drink, and let me talk to Maximilian here."

"Last day, huh? Don't mind these guys; they can argue about anything. Drive me nuts sometimes. It's a little early for espresso, so how about a soda or something from the bar?" Dominic asked, placing his hands on Max's shoulders as Paige remained nearby.

"I'll have a Coke, Dom," Max said.

"You sure? I only have this Coke Two shit."

"Cherry Coke, then."

Dominic walked behind the bar and crouched out of sight. A bit thirsty from the run over to the club, Paige was about to ask Dominic for a cold drink as well. Only, he seemed to be taking a while to retrieve the first one for Max. She stood on the partition under an empty barstool and saw him opening what looked like a trap door. He unlocked it and told them to come around the other side. They walked down the narrowest set of wooden steps either of them had ever seen. When they reached the floor, Dom pulled a string that was attached to an exposed light bulb that brightened the bricked basement.

"See that, Paige? I've got a hideout myself. Well, actually just a hiding place under my office where I'm at most of the time anyway. I want you guys to help me carry these supplies back upstairs." Unexcited, they made their way over to a few cases of cigarettes and candy. "Say, Max, grab a case of them Marlboros over there and the case behind them too. I have to restock. Vending machines are empty upstairs."

Max picked up the case of Marlboros in the far corner and immediately lit up seeing what was behind them. In an open case was a beautiful new liquid black-and-white electric guitar. "Is this for me?" he exclaimed in excitement.

"My friend at the music store said it's one of the best models they sell."

"It's awesome, Max!" Paige said with both hands over her mouth.

"This is a Gibson Explorer! Thank you so much, Dom! It's better than anything I could have wished for."

"Guy at the shop said there were only so many available, and the more I looked around, I felt like this one looked like you, I guess."

"A Gibson Three." Max carried on in disbelief, adjusting the shoulder strap.

Dominic smiled and continued, "Well, I know Carrie isn't playing with you guys anymore, and you've been sounding pretty good playing that red piece of junk you got, so I figured this could only help. I got something for you and your parents, Paige." Dominic teased, handing her a small metal ring with a single key on it.

"My parents and I want a key? I'm confused."

"I own a small block of garages close to your school. One of them is vacant, and your band can give your parents and that dog of yours a break by practicing there—should you want to," Dominic concluded as Paige lunged forward and embraced him in a hug.

They remained at the club a short while longer, had some sodas, and talked about upcoming movies. After the high schoolers had overheard one conversation too many, Dominic drove them to Paige's house and listened to Max test out his birthday present. Carrie, their former bandmate, had told them she had to quit the band due to her grades dropping. They figured she could resume playing once school was ending but never heard from her.

One afternoon Paige and her mother decided to surprise her dad at his work. On the escalator Paige came face-to-face with the real reason Carrie no longer played in the band or worked at the restaurant. Carrie made a futile attempt to avoid Paige, turning her head away, cornered on the descending escalator with Deidre Lisbon and her minions. Feeling bad for Carrie, who had naively centered herself in the viper's nest that was Deidre's inner circle, Paige decided not to tell Adam or Max the real reason she had defected from the band.

The band, Middleton's Crossing, found themselves a trio, with Max assuming lead vocals and guitar. They considered looking for a replacement for Carrie but felt it would disturb the chemistry and foundation they had already established. Plus, Max was truly playing inspired music with the new guitar, courtesy of Dom, who had plans for his young friends. He booked them multiple engagements at a few clubs where he had some pull, and the owners even let them play some of their original songs, which were well received.

The Edmundsons, Adam's mom and his brother, as well as Katherine Jalorean, all came to see them play, even at some of the rough-and-tumble clubs. Dominic saw to it that there was security—mostly guys from the Middleton Social Club, who were efficient and effective anytime someone got out of order. He personally waited for Max's mother outdoors before the start of each show and saw her to her car afterward. He had become quite fond of Barbara Garret, who referred to Dominic as "that remarkable man." William Garret became tired of hearing his wife sing the praises of

Dominic Gervallo and even more weary of her excitement over Max and his band. Whenever they played, it was a comfort to have the house to himself, a sentiment that was shared among all the Garrets.

Life was changing for Max, and he often reflected upon his mom's words the day he asked her to pack up and leave Middleton. Better days certainly had lain ahead, and they had started with a concerned stranger in the form of Dominic, who was experiencing a personal rejuvenation with Max and his band. And there was his energetic and pretty teacher Katherine Jalorean and most importantly, Paige, a lifeline when the ship that was his life had seemed to be capsizing.

Max and Paige spent nearly every day and night together that summer, often sneaking out of her house and lying on the picnic table in the clearing. They would gaze up at the stars and talk about anything and everything. No topic was too large or small, be it song ideas for the band, the fate of them meeting one another, the whereabouts of Rachel at the end of *Pet Sematary,* or Robin's death at the hands of the Joker. On the multicolored picnic table, they expressed their hopes, fears, dreams, and aspirations. Only one topic went unspoken of—the romantic feelings they harbored for one another. They were both too uncertain to reveal the obvious. Their moonlight chats lasted until evening ended its standoff with the daylight. They then retreated back to the rec room and fell asleep together.

That summer the hours went by like seconds. The band was gaining a good bit of local notoriety, thanks to their manager and backer. The summer was ending as the autumn wind rustled the leaves out in the clearing and the nights grew cooler. That August many of Max and Paige's discussions centered around returning to school. They both agreed nothing between them would change and hoped beyond hope they were correct. Unfortunately, hope can often be a deception that dreamers permit themselves, as change is inevitable and fate can be cruel beyond measure.

There were multiple visits to the Eric Twin theater that month by the trio. Max and Paige tried to convince Dominic to partake in *Nightmare on Elm*

Street 5: The Dream Child, which they referred to as their anniversary film. When Dominic objected, they argued that last year they had seen *Nightmare on Elm Street 4* and insisted on viewing the follow-up next.

Outnumbered on the matter, as he so often was, he agreed but with a stipulation: "If I'm going to endure another one of Freddy Kreuger's killing sprees, you two will have to come see *Uncle Buck*, a comedy with one of my favorites, John Candy, in the lead role." A compromise was reached, and it was two trips to Ray Gene's, as well as the theater. As the credits rolled and the lights in the theatre came on after *Nightmare 5*, Max and Paige were about to spring into their routine of critiquing on the way out of the exit with Dominic. They were halfway to the door when they realized he was still seated. Max raced up the steps, then into the aisle.

"How could you fall asleep during that, Dom?" The credits concluded, and the lights came on. Max nudged his friend's arm to awaken him. "Come on, Dominic." Max persisted, but Paige knew better.

In the back row, in his favorite seat just below the projector, sat Dominic Gladgem Gervallo. The kind eyes that Max felt at ease with appeared vacant and lost. "Get up, Domin—Paige?"

A half decade earlier, when he had lost Maria, the fire inside him was reduced to a flicker. Like a Lion in winter he pressed on, void of emotion, catering to survival instincts alone .In the face of a quiet kid named Max he regained a portion of the happiness he lost with his wife .His fire burned brighter than it had in years.. But now the fire was extinguished and the lion was dead.

Paige held on to the man who in such a short amount of time had become like a second father to her. She wept hysterically. Refusing to accept the reality of the situation, Max ran to the lobby faster than he had run out of the doors of Middleton High on the last day of school. He accidentally bowled over an usher in the lobby, then pulled the man to his feet and pleaded with urgency for him to call for help. He returned to Paige and with a second look, could no longer deny fact. His friend and mentor's once vibrant, life-filled face was covered in a pale mask of death.

When they got close to home, Paige felt compelled to say something. Anything. All she managed to get out was "Please stay at…" but her sobbing prevented her from finishing.

Max threw both hands upward like he intended to pull the sky down to earth. "I can't!" he explained, throwing his hands down in disgust and walking in the direction of his house, away from Paige's street.

The slamming of the screen door of the house woke Barbara Garret. She got out of bed and saw her son sitting in the living room with the lights out. The only indication that it was him was the streetlight that pierced through the window. In the dim light, she could see the blue of Max's eyes filled with tears. He gave her the bad news, and she wept aloud. Also awoken was William Garret, who was disturbed by the fracas, but when he heard his wife cry out, "He's dead?" he decided to relent and save his hostilities for another time.

The *Middleton Observer*'s headline read, "GENTLEMAN GANGSTER DEAD AT 76."

The *Observer* featured a multipage time line of Dominic's exploits, highlighting his checkered past, accompanied by a black-and-white mugshot from an early arrest for bootlegging in dry towns in the thirties. The accurate and fair article also pointed out his contributions to local charities and programs for the impoverished and included a color photo of Maria and him at a wedding anniversary.

The *Post* expressed less sophistication. The tabloid's headline wrapped around the front page: "SHOW WON'T GO ON! GANGLAND GRANDPA TAKES DIRTNAP IN THEATER." Rather than print an obituary, they manufactured a real hatchet job, the main focal point being his affiliation with crime families in neighboring states.

Carmine chomped on a cigar furiously with the rag paper spread out on the bar of the Middleton Social Club as a weepy-eyed Tony Rhino led Max in. "How long does he think I'm going to stay on hold here!" He spoke into the phone that was stretched around the bar, its cord straightened instead of coiled. Carmine paused from his anger to give a grimace to Max, then looked at the phone regrettably, and yelled at the man behind the bar, "Oh, hang it the fuck up!"

As the bartender made his way to take the receiver from Carmine, he threw it in anger. He then composed himself partially and pointed Max to the office. "Fucking *Post* don't have any respect for the dead," he grumbled, then opened the door and continued, "Fucking lawyers don't want to sue them for libel because it's too much damn litigation. Fungool!" he shouted, slamming the door behind Max. Once he was out of sight, Carmine's anger dissipated immediately.

"We've only met a few times before. I'm Max."

"You look around out there, kid? We don't have a lot of long-haired, gray-eyed Irish kids to confuse you with. I know who you are. Look, I know why you're here and all, and I understand that, OK?"

Looking at Max, he reached the first chair available to him, then, seeing it was Dom's chair, hung his head in sadness and opted to lean on the wall instead. "Look, I know you only knew him for a year or so. I also know he loved you and your girlfriend like his own kids." This caused Max to look at the ground in front of him and bite his tongue to keep from crying. "But the sad truth of the matter is Dom never had no will—too morbid for him. Plus, I think he was under the illusion he was never going to die. Shit, I suppose I was too. I mean, I never had any kids or anything, but he has a slew of nieces and nephews, so those are his heirs by default."

It took Max a moment to grasp the purpose of Carmine's explanation, and he spoke up to put the grieving man at ease. "Oh, I'm not here for that. I just wanted to ask about funeral arrangements. Mr. Gervallo was very good to Paige and me, and the papers made no mention of the service."

"They put the guy's whole life history in there and couldn't have the decency to...ahh! Look, kid, the wake is Thursday, and the service is Friday. I got to take a ride down there and make sure they print it in tomorrow's edition. I'm sorry for thinking you were here about money...it's just so many people are, and look, he'd want you to be a pallbearer, and the cute girl you pal around with—what's her name? Uh, Peg or..."

"Paige—you mean Paige. I haven't talked to her since, but—"

"Well, why the hell not? You know, every morning at Palmetto's, at breakfast, he told me how you two were perfect for each other?"

"It was just a bad night, and I haven't really spoken to anyone since is all. Are you OK?"

Carmine was bracing himself with the wall for support and in a calm voice spoke as if he were talking to himself. "You know, this morning I went to the diner thinking he was going to walk right in like always, and when he didn't it, it hurt real fucking bad."

Feeling himself about to break down at the mere sight of Carmine crying, Max made for the door, eager to exit. "I'll show myself out, and I'll stop over at Paige's and tell her about the wake and funeral." He then surprised Carmine by patting him on the shoulder and comforting him by saying, "It'd be an honor to be a pallbearer for him—and anything else I can do to help."

Overcome with emotion from Max's sincerity and his deceased friend's uncanny ability to be a great judge of character, Carmine gathered himself, tucked in his shirt, and summoned his strength. Exiting the office, he scanned the club, pointed to the two biggest bastards he could see, grabbed the keys to Dom's car, and waved them along. He was heading over to the *Post* to raise hell and bust some heads or at least threaten to if they didn't print a retraction.

Max pedaled his bike toward Paige's house and saw Carmine speed past with the massive goons in the back of Dominic's car driven by Tony Rhino. He paused momentarily, then resumed pedaling to the Edmundsons'. Paige met him at the door.

"The viewing's Thursday night, funeral's Friday," Max said to her through the screen door. Paige came outside and hugged Max on the porch.

"Carmine from the club…he said Dom told him we were perfect and…"

"And what?"

"And that we were perfect for one another."

"I suppose some things are just obvious, huh, Max?"

They parted from their embrace and looked directly into one another's eyes. Max leaned closer toward her as Paige moistened her upper lip with the tip of her tongue and held her breath. Her heart raced out of control as their lips gently touched.

"Paige! Elvis wants to go out again. He's driving me crazy in here!" Lynne Edmundson shouted from the living room, jolting them apart.

"Oh, hi, Max. I'm so sorry about Dominic, honey. Phil should be back soon. You want to stay for dinner?" she asked, handing Paige a leash as Elvis ran to Max out on the porch.

"Thanks, but I told my mom I'd be home tonight. Paige, I'll call you tomorrow."

Max got on his bike and started toward home, a whirlwind of emotions coursing through his mind and body.

Chapter 7:

A BONE TO PICK

Feeling the effects of a very long night of drinking, Ross Aberdeen awoke to a knock on his first-floor bedroom window. Pulling back the blinds revealed Dwayne and Deidre with huge grins on their faces. Ross opened the window as Dwayne displayed the *Post* like a newsy who was about to call out, "Read all about it!" Ross's head was ringing; he was dehydrated and in no mood for riddles. "Why the fuck are you showing me the newspaper, D? And better yet, what the fuck are you two doing without me around?"

"Garret's friend, the old mob dude, is dead; that's what we came over to tell you! Dwayne's dad said he was a dinosaur from way back and all the people he was running with or whatever are gone, so it's open season on Garret!" Deidre said, her every word uttered in annoyance at Ross's lack of understanding.

"Yeah, fuck that dude, telling me he would make my old man a grease spot; now his ass is going to the cemetery forever! Ha ha!" Dwayne cackled. Ross didn't care about Max or the old guy or anything. What he did care about was the rumor concerning his girlfriend and Dwayne. He felt like shit, and the sight of Dwayne laughing and carrying on was pissing him off, especially since he had shown up with Deidre.

"Well, for the record, he did say your old man was a bum-ass crooked cop who always had his hand out—like, forever," Ross said, leaning out the window, feeling the need to remind Dwayne of the conversation Dominic had had with them in the Eric parking lot the year before.

Dwayne only smiled, feeling a release of any guilt he felt over screwing Deidre behind Ross's back. "That was a lie anyway. My dad told us to stay

100

away from Gervallo, but he was never crooked. Anyway, man, we came by to see if you wanted to get something to eat. It's our last weekend before camp."

Ross refused, to Dwayne's delight, for that afternoon he drove the Mustang to Blackbeard's Seafood Shanty, but they didn't grab lunch. Dwayne parked in a spot farthest away from the Shanty. Deidre bent over in the trunk's interior and steadied herself, placing her palms flat. Dwayne pulled her Middleton sweatpants down, forgot about a condom, and relished in pounding away at Deidre. Ross's disrespectful comments about his old man made it that much more satisfying

The outdoor breeze blended with the new-car smell of the trunk. She'd never been fucked outdoors, and it was exhilarating. About to climax, she clenched both fists as the back of the car bounced up and down—Dwayne pulled out, took hold of her hair, and pulled her down to his midsection.

"What the fuck are you doing?" she asked, yanking her head back from Dwayne's grip as he attempted to ejaculate on her face. The ecstasy of the moment was over. Deidre went from being ready to have a thunderous orgasm to remembering Moretz shoving his shriveled-up cock in her face.

"Sorry," Dwayne said, embarrassed by Deidre's rejection.

"I was about to come, D! You fuck like a little boy getting his first piece of ass. Don't you have any dick control? Damn."

"You still want to eat Blackbeard's?"

"No. Take me the fuck home. I lost my appetite."

Neither her mother nor her father's car was in the driveway when the Mustang pulled up to Deidre's house. Inside, she handcuffed Dwayne's left wrist to the foot of her bed, then secured his right hand by knotting up one of her torn black stockings.

"Help me out of my shorts," Dwayne asked, expecting Deidre to mount him.

"No, your fine with them on," she replied, standing on the mattress. She reversed her body so it faced her headboard and straddled his face, focusing on the poster of *Miami Vice*'s Sonny Crockett over her bed. Dwayne murmured, struggling to breathe as she gyrated against his lips violently. This provided Deidre with pleasing vibrations until she burst all over his mouth, just as he intended to do to her.

"All right, you had your fun. Now pull my shorts off or untie me, you crazy bitch!" Dwayne said, ending Deidre's euphoric moment. She faced him and frowned. Dwayne was no Don Johnson. Hell, he wasn't even her summer love from Hessian's Cliff.

"I lost the key a while ago. Guess we'll have to wait until my dad comes home." She teased until Dwayne started pulling at the cuffs and marking up the finish of her bedframe. She went into her jewelry box and got the key to the handcuffs, then released him. After cutting the base of the knot with a pair of scissors, Dwayne reached for them to remove the stocking still wrapped around his wrist.

"No. Leave it on. It'll be, like, our friendship bracelet. Now get the fuck out of my house before my dad comes home and shoots you."

The following week Ross, Dwayne, and Greg went away with the rest of the Middleton Rams football team to camp. The practice field was a muddy mess, and the lodgings were a disappointment to the entire team. Public-school funding from Middleton taxpayers only funded the bare minimum of extras. Although they bunked together, Ross was standoffish with Dwayne the entire week. He gunned passes at him in warm-ups, criticized his performance on the practice field and in drills.

In an open scrimmage situation, Dwayne was the ball carrier tackled in a pileup. Ross seized an opportunity to act on his suspicions and jammed his cleat in the space between Dwayne's helmet and shoulder pads. Dwayne suffered an injured collarbone and for the remainder of camp, was forced to watch rather than participate.

On the bus home, Ross and Greg sat together and discussed the schools on the upcoming schedule they would be able to defeat. Dwayne sat behind them and didn't contribute for fear Ross would snap at him the way he had throughout camp. But then Greg included him when he questioned Dwayne on a subject Ross was not interested in—his crush on Paige Edmundson.

"Hey, D, what do you think about Paige and Garret?"

"I don't know. They must be pretty tight; they got that band and all," he responded while massaging his bruised neck, to Ross's amusement.

"What band?" asked Ross.

"Middleton's Crossroad or something. Supposed to be good. They had a write-up about them in the local section of the newspaper.'

"Well, she's way too hot to be going out with him, though. Right?" Greg stated, then thought twice when he didn't receive an answer from Dwayne or Ross. Irritated, Greg looked out the window as the bus passed the highway, until Ross decided to taunt him.

"What are you going to do? Join a band and grow your hair long like a fairy to get in Paige's pants?"

"No, dick. I was just wondering. Besides, I'm kind of with Lana anyhow," Greg said, regrettably seeing Ross's face light up.

Most of the class knew Lana had once blown Ross freshman year in the baseball dugout in Maidens Mist Park. After swearing secrecy to her, he told everyone. Earning her the name "Juggz and Chugz Karrington." Greg hated this.

"Exactly, Greg. Look, Lana the Chugger is taking care of you. You wind up with Edmundson, you'll probably have to buy a wedding ring before she'll even give you a hand job." Ross laughed, bringing a grin to Dwayne's face as well. Greg shifted his insults in Dwayne's direction.

"You better hope I don't quit and join a band because without me to run the ball, you'll be in piss-poor shape throwing passes to Dwayne. Stupid boon can't even run a route or catch a cold," he said, laughing and teasing as Ross joined him.

"Coach, do I'z run a post or a hitch on dis play?" Ross mocked, impersonating Dwayne.

"Go fuck yourselves, you two faggots," Dwayne said, then sunk into the seat of the bus. Frequently he found himself the subject of insults and black jokes from Ross and Greg, who, he felt, used him because of his car. He often contemplated hanging out with some other guys, but whom? They were the only "cool" people on the team in the eyes of the school, and it wasn't like he could quit the team. He only played because his dad insisted.

The bus took the exit toward Middleton, and Dwayne thought to himself in anger, *Keep it up, Greg, and it won't just be Ross's girl I'm screwing. I want to see how good Lana chugs myself.* The remainder of the ride back to the school, he sat in anger as the assholes he called friends brainstormed ways to torment Max so Greg could get with Paige. When the bus came to a stop, his father was waiting in his squad car. He couldn't believe it: even though he had driven his car and left it in the parking lot before they had made off for camp, his dad was so damn gung ho about football he had actually sat and waited on the bus to pull in. It had been a terrible camp experience for Dwayne. He would have much rather stayed home and taken advantage of Ross not being around, but Sergeant Bishop would never have had that.

Once off the bus, Ross and Greg chatted up his pop.

"How was camp, Ross? Got that arm oiled up and ready to go?"

"Is Sarge Bishop the best on the whole Middleton PD force?" Ross joked back.

"Suck-ass," Dwayne muttered, loud enough for Greg to hear. His father glanced at him and said nothing. He continued joking with Ross and Greg about how time after time he had gotten them out of trouble.

"Greg, you bulked up this year. Looking lean and mean. This boy's gonna be trucking over fools like Riggins "The Diesel" on the Washington Redskins, right?"

"No, I want to be more like Dickerson."

"Yeah, that's good and well for him on his level, but here the Middleton Rams and Coach McCarmick need you to pound the rock like Diesel. You keep all that finesse running for your Tecmo Bowl BS, you hear?"

Dwayne wondered what his dad would have thought of Greg's description of him earlier on the bus. He imagined the man, who had met his mother in the Black Panther Party, may have felt differently if he had bothered to believe him. Once he was finished yucking it up with Ross and Greg, he looked at Dwayne in disappointment and finally spoke to him.

"Well, what do we have here? I tell him all the time he needs to be doing strength conditioning and training like his friends on the team. But nah, he's goofin' off, driving around in that car I got him. How long?" Alvin

Bishop asked in his sternest voice, indicating to Ross and Greg it was time to get lost.

They joined the rest of the team, and Dwayne muttered back to his father, "Few days, maybe a week—just a deep bruise," he answered, seeing his own reflection in his father's mirrored aviators.

"Well, there's no reason you can't be in the garage doing squats and building more leg muscle. You need a better burst off the line. I'm going to talk to McCarmick. You and that car better be home by the time I am. After all, you are injured."

Dwayne said nothing; he just stared at his cleats on the blacktop and nodded. Once his father was a good distance away, he headed for the pay phone to call Deidre but got no answer.

Last year Deidre had been mortified at Timothy Moretz blackmailing her for sexual favors, but she had quickly made the best of the situation. Her grades had never been better than they had been last year. Moretz had boosted them significantly but not enough for anyone to notice. A D on an exam was improved to a C+, and so on. Then she had realized, why should his favors for her end there? She had been bored with Dwayne and Ross away at football camp, so she had phoned Moretz, who was at the school. Teachers were required to come in a week before school started, and Deidre wanted to go shopping. She phoned his office, and after some initial hesitation on the counselor's part, he conceded once Deidre offered to "make it worth it." While the receiver at the Lisbon residence rang, in the seedy Paradise Motel across town, Deidre was rewarding Timothy Moretz for contributions made to her wardrobe at Tharington's department store.

The Edmundson household was in a panic. When Paige returned from Dominic's service, her mother announced that she had let Elvis out in the yard and he had been missing all morning. Since Paige had been at the funeral, she had been unable to take him out, so her mother had let Elvis run around in the yard as she always did. After a short time, she had gone to check on him, and he was gone. Still dressed in her funeral attire, Paige and her father went to his store to make copies of flyers with the family's pet terrier's picture. Max was inconsolable, but Paige called him for help in finding her pet anyway.

The death of Dominic not only affected Max, Paige, and the guys over at Middleton Social but also Max's father. Frequently, Johnny from J&J Produce complained about William Garret, whom he had been told to hire. Customers griped about his demeanor and the fact that many times he reeked of booze. Johnny asked Dominic if he could let go of the hindrance to his business. Every time Dominic refused and later sent some form of appreciation to Johnny for dealing with Bill Garret. Sometimes it was a nice bottle of wine or a piece of fine jewelry to gift to his wife.

Returning to his store after the funeral, Johnny saw Garret sleeping in the back room. He smelled the booze coming out of his pores; the back room reeked. *That's it. Dom's gone, and so is this bum. I've had to carry his ass in this place for the last year.* He kicked at him, snapping him out of his deep snoring. "Get lost; Garret; I'm shitcanning you. I'm cashing you out for this week, then I never want to see you here again. Not even as a customer."

Johnny rang no sale on the register and slammed a handful of crumpled-up greenbacks and three quarters into Bill Garret's palm. He smiled and held one of the quarters in Johnny's direction like a priest presenting a parishioner with communion and said, "Here's a tip for ya, Johnny. Take this here coin and pound it up yer mother's filthy twuat, ya greasy dey-goh. Fuck ya!"

Johnny took hold of the baseball bat he kept behind the counter and started toward Bill, who threw the coin at him and made off toward the door. On his way out, he yelled to the few customers occupying the market, "This scurfy fuckin place has got banana crates with fucking spiders in 'em and cockroaches the size of yer foot upstairs!" Bill Garret slammed the door of J&J as hard as he could on the way out, sending items crashing off the shelf, causing Johnny to give up his pursuit of him. Feeling liberated, he stumbled across the street to the Candlelight Tavern, where he stayed until closing.

The walk to MHS on the first day of school was much different than Paige and Max had imagined. They were still mourning the loss of Dominic, and Paige was losing hope of finding Elvis, who remained missing. Paige and her father had driven down every side street in Middleton City and the township, to no avail.

Max's father, now unemployed, regressed to his previous routine and told Max he had better find a job because he wanted him to start paying board. With both their households in turmoil, they only made small talk. Paige, normally so attentive, was barely participating as she looked around every corner and alley they passed for her lost dog. If recent events had done a number on them, when they faced the entrance of Middleton High and saw those they had been able to ignore all summer long, they truly had the wind knocked out of their sails.

Before the opening bell sounded, Paige found herself the target of cat-calls. Barbara Garret had gotten her son a new ball cap that he wished she had not. Dwayne swiped at the brim of the hat, knocking it off his head, then Deidre picked it up and threw it around to Greg. Part of Paige wanted to knock Deidre to the ground and punch her until her arms gave out, but she was so disheartened she just marched up the steps with Max beside her. Max was also too defeated for a game of monkey in the middle and surrendered the new hat without care.

Something had worked out in their favor, though. Comparing schedules, they saw they had more classes together this year and once again had Ms. Jalorean. Max tried to keep things upbeat for Paige, who could think of little else except whether her dog was safe or had been hit by a car. A variety of scenarios ran wild in her head—mostly bad. Even Paige's worst thoughts could not compare with the reality of Elvis's fate. He had been picked up out of her yard by a passing Greg Chapman, who had instructed Dwayne to pull over on their way home from the school after camp.

As the day went on, Paige was becoming more and more unglued. When classes changed, some of the girls, informed of her missing pet by the multitude of flyers hung throughout the town, taunted her by making dog sounds in the halls. The day was almost over, and the end couldn't have come sooner. She had Ms. Jalorean for the final class of the day. She told Paige she had a friend who worked in animal control and that she would give him one of Paige's flyers. She also told Paige and Max she had petitioned Principal Volkem to have their band play at the pep rally next week, and they agreed to do so.

On the walk home, they made plans to get back in touch with Adam. Their group hadn't played together since Dominic's passing, and Adam was out of school. Paige agreed since Carmine had told Max he could use the garage space they had practiced in all summer until the end of the month. After the funeral Carmine had informed Max the estate was selling all Dominic's property except the social club, which wasn't in his name anyway. Carmine had also explained that once all of Dominic's affairs were in order, he was leaving Middleton and relocating to New Jersey. He offered Max Dominic's car, which he refused. Max had no license, nor the means to insure the car, and he'd be damned if he was going to let his father do what he did to the Torino.

"Kid, I don't need it, and I want you to have something to remember him by," Carmine protested.

"I have the guitar, which is more than enough."

Carmine looked him over, as if an ongoing debate was occurring in his mind, then he said, "Ah, the hell with it! Here." He dug into the inside pocket of his coat and produced the gold ring with the red ruby. Carmine held out the ring Max had seen gleaming on Dominic's hand the first time they met.

Carmine placed it in Max's hand, then closed it and said, "There's no way I can explain to you how important this was to our friend—just understand that it was. Never sell it, and never give it away; that way you can remember him. He would have liked you to have it; I'm sure of it. Besides, what am I going to do with it? I got these damn sausage fingers," he joked while pinching Max on the cheek.

They hugged and parted company. Walking away, Carmine called out, "You take care of yourself, Maximilian!"

As he relayed the events from after the funeral, Max saw tears streaming down Paige's cheeks. When they got to the clearing before her house, Max handed the ring to her and clutched her forearm. They swore an oath to one another that they'd share it by taking turns wearing it.

"This way we will never forget him or lose touch with one another," Max explained. This prompted the sad girl to kiss him softly on his lips before taking the ring and placing it on her necklace.

They reconnected with Adam, who wasn't too keen on the idea of returning to play for a pep rally at the school he had just graduated from. But Max was able to convince him. They had not played together since summer, and the pep rally was a good warm-up before their next show. Adam also agreed to play since his brother was to be a freshman and he knew he enjoyed setting up with them. Middleton's crossing was permitted to practice in the gymnasium.

Paige got a ride to school, and Max stopped in Middleton Social to drop off the keys to Dominic's garage at the club. There was a slew of new faces, and Carmine was nowhere to be found. He wound up leaving the key with Tony Rhino. Making his way out, he noticed a picture of Dom centered above the bar. It was a comfort to know his friend was gone but not forgotten. As he walked, he noticed every telephone pole, streetlight, and store front had a colored piece of paper attached to it that read:

Loved Family Pet Missing

Generous Reward If Found

Terrier Mix Answers to Elvis

A photo of Elvis was anchored at the bottom of the flyer, along with the Edmundsons' phone and address. Weather had taken its toll on the once vibrant flyers Max had assisted in posting around town. It had been weeks since Paige's dog had gone missing, and Max couldn't ignore his gut feeling that this was not a random case of a dog chasing a car and not returning. He thought this but dare not speak it to Paige, who distracted herself with the band and the upcoming pep rally before homecoming.

The football team had already played its first game at Goulding High and gotten blown out. Ross had thrown two interceptions that had been run back for touchdowns and had had a fumble as well. The passes that had not been thrown to the other team had been dropped by Dwayne. Greg had had himself a decent game running the ball, but the scoreboard had read 49–0 at the final whistle. The Middleton Rams had never lost while Harold McCarmick was coaching, and the entire team felt his wrath after the game. When the team bus returned, rather than allow them to go home, he had them run laps in full pads for another two hours.

Exiting the locker room, Ross saw Adam, Max, and Paige in the middle of a weekend practice session in the gym. Dwayne and Greg had tried to talk to him when they were running off McCarmick's punishment, and he had said nothing. He was mad at Dwayne for the drops in the game, but what was really bothering him was his suspicions about Deidre and him. The band was just finishing up and having fun just jamming out. A furious Ross Aberdeen studied them from the opposite corner of the gym.

Seeing Max made Ross recall the rumor he supposedly spread last year about his girlfriend and his friend. This sent Ross's paranoia into overdrive. *What if Garret wasn't lying after all?* he thought, gritting his teeth as Max smiled, enjoying the music. Perhaps Garret was humping Deidre as well, and that's why she was so pissed at him. Greg made his way up the steps and joined Ross in observing Middleton's Crossing doing their best Hendrix impersonation.

"I fucking hate that kid!" Greg said, stopping the wheels from turning in Ross's head.

Bitter as ever, Ross offered fuel for his friend's hatred. "Paige seems to like him," he quipped and then decided to put Greg on the spot. "You ever think there's some truth to what he was saying about Dwayne and Dee?" he asked with his eyes locked into Greg's pupils. Before Greg could answer, he followed up with a counterquestion, "You think he may have been messing around with her as well?"

Relief came over Greg's face as he was much more eager to point Ross's suspicions toward the kid who was now back-to-back with Paige. "Definitely, man. He had the hots for your girl the first day of junior year, remember?

Dwayne told you he was eyeing her butt the day you kicked his ass in the hallway. I mean, he's a lousy receiver, but he isn't going behind your back, dude! If anybody did, it was Garret!" As they looked, they saw an enraged Harold McCarmick pull the plug on the amplifier and scream at the band.

"Practice is over! Pack it up, and go home! Is this what you're doing with your spare time, Paige?" McCarmick's voice seethed with condescension. Before she could answer, McCarmick shouted at Adam, "You! You don't go to school here anymore; you're not even supposed to be on the property!" Paige protested in vain as Ross and Greg exited the gym to avoid coming across their coach again.

On the way to the parking lot, where Dwayne was waiting in his Mustang, Ross read one of the flyers regarding Paige's missing pet. "The Edmundsons? Paige's dog is missing?" he said as he pulled the flier down from the Middleton banner that was attached to the chain-link fence.

"Dwayne didn't tell you?" Greg smiled.

"Tell me what?"

Greg pushed the passenger seat forward and jumped into the back. Ross turned to him, awaiting an answer to his question.

"On the way back from camp, I snatched the mutt out of their backyard. I got it locked up in the shed behind my garage!"

"Yeah, tell him your stupid idea." Dwayne frowned, pulling out of the parking lot.

"It's not stupid. It's been over a week. I see her crying in the hallway, her and Garret putting up fliers everywhere. Once I return the mutt to her, I'll be like Prince Charming, and I'm in her pants like that!"

"It's stupid because when you return it, she may figure it was your dumb ass who took it in the first place," Dwayne added.

Ross nodded in agreement with Dwayne for the first time in a long time. "It is stupid, but that's not what you're going to do. They're doing the music at the pep rally before homecoming next week, right? She can get her mutt back then."

"No, I mean her home address is right on the flyer; why would I return it at the school?"

"Why? I'll tell you why. Because she's not getting it back in one piece; that's why. Fuck those pussies." Ross glared.

Two days before the pep rally, Greg hosted a small keg party with Ross, Dwayne, and some other guys from the football team, as well as Deidre and her friends. The beloved terrier named Elvis, who had brought so much joy and love into the Edmundsons' home, was doused in tequila.

It was Deidre who took the matches out of Ross's hands and insisted on lighting up the starving dog herself. Elvis trembled and lowered his ears. As she approached the cowering dog behind the Chapmans' house, it seemed to plead for mercy with its terrified eyes. A cheer went up from the inebriated onlookers when he was set ablaze and let out whimpers and yelps of excruciating pain before collapsing. The following day Greg collected the charred remains of the Edmundsons' once spunky and love-filled terrier in a garbage bag. He brought it to the school the day of the pep rally, as Ross had instructed.

Adam's brother assisted him in taping down the speaker wire as Max and Paige came from behind the stage curtain to help set up equipment. They were just about done and thanked Adam's brother, who returned to his homeroom class. Max was performing a sound check of the microphone as students began to pack the gym. They were sectioned off by class in the bleachers.

"Hurry up. Give me the bag!" Ross called out to Greg in a loud whisper behind the curtain. He opened Max's guitar case and dumped the garbage bag's contents into it. Deidre was writing frantically with a marker. She then taped a sheet of notebook paper to the lid of the guitar case. "Gross," she said in disgust, inspecting the case's contents.

"Wait!" Greg called out to Ross and Deidre, who were making their escape.

"C'mon, hurry up; they're going to come back here!" Deidre called back to him.

"A little something for good measure," Greg replied, unbuckling his belt. Then he proceeded to urinate in the guitar case, prompting Deidre to shake her head in disapproval. Ross, however, did not share Deidre's sentiment and joined Greg. They slammed the case shut and ran to the backstage exit.

They walked around and took their seats with the rest of the senior class at the foot of the bleachers and giggled, telling Dwayne about the surprise they had left Middleton's Crossing.

"I think we should start with 'Rebel Yell' or 'Welcome to the Jungle,'" Paige said to Max, who nodded in agreement.

Adam took notice of the packed gymnasium and told Max, "We're good with sound? Ready?"

"Hell yeah!" Max rushed behind the curtain as Paige and Adam followed close behind. Max opened his guitar case and gagged, took a few steps backward, and stood motionless.

"Come on, Max, we have to…what's that smell?" Paige asked, then covered her mouth with both hands as Max grabbed the sheet of paper from the lid. Tears streamed down Paige's cheeks. Any doubt that the charred body in the case was her missing dog's was removed by the sight of Elvis's metal collar.

Max, blinded by rage, spoke aloud to himself. "I'm going to kill them. I'm going to fucking kill them!" he said repeatedly and tossed the sheet of paper, then stormed off.

Paige inspected the crude print that read, "Grandpa Gervallo's as dead as this dog and so are you, Garret." Unable to look at her tortured pet, Paige followed behind him, yelling, "Max, wait!" As Paige came from behind the curtain, she saw Max jump down from the stage, gripping the microphone stand in the direction of Ross, who was distracted, groping Deidre. The laughter-filled faces of Greg, Dwayne, and Deidre filled with terror as Max stood in front of them. As Ross had turned his head toward Max, he was coldcocked by the weighted metal base of the microphone stand. Max hoisted it up over his head a second time to take Ross's head off.

Before he could land the finishing blow, he was thrown off balance and tackled by Harold McCarmick as the gym erupted in pandemonium.

A sea of humanity parted around the injured body of Ross Aberdeen, who was curled up inside the bleachers with both hands covering his bloodied face. Max lunged toward Greg and Deidre like a man possessed to break out of McCarmick's bear hug. "Come on, Greg, I'll fuck you and that skank bitch up like big Ross there; get the fuck off me." Max seethed as Moretz and other faculty assisted McCarmick in wrestling Max to the ground.

Paige's legs gave out, and she collapsed, devastated by the state of her pet and the sight of Max being pinned to the ground by teachers and administrators. Principal Volkem ran past her and picked up the microphone, ending the ear-piercing distortion, which had added to the madness, and ordered, "All students return immediately to your homerooms."

Somehow Paige was in the nurse's station. She didn't remember anything until seeing Ross's bruised-up face and bloody lip. He was holding an ice pack on his head, and Paige immediately got up to add to the damage. She was restrained by Adam and Ms. Jalorean, who carried her there after she fainted. Injured and laughing, Ross gave her the finger as she spouted obscenities at him.

"He's not worth it, Paige. Come on, please," Katherine said, ushering the hysterical girl out of the office to take her home.

Paige, still crying, ran out of tears and energy. She gasped for air and in a mellow voice asked, "Ms. J, what happened to Max?"

In spite of her instinct to lie in order to comfort her favorite student, Katherine fought the urge and answered honestly, "I don't know, honey, but he's in a lot of trouble."

Chapter 8:
EXPIRED PUMPKINS AND PROPHYLACTICS

As she escorted Paige home, it fell on Katherine Jalorean to give the Edmundsons the bad news about their pet. Paige went straight to her room and remained there from Friday afternoon until Sunday evening. Phil Edmundson watched Paige wander down the path to the woods from his back porch.

The fresh air felt good, but Paige was gripped by emptiness—walking the trail Elvis was always so excited to take with her. Before going outside, she had phoned Max's house.

"He left, Paige—hours ago. He told me he was going to be with you. I don't know where he is. If you see him, tell him to call." Barbara Garret had said, the tension in her voice a clear indication of concern over the mayhem at the pep rally.

Paige made her way to the clearing and saw her intuition was correct. Max was throwing rocks aimlessly into the woods. Hearing Paige approach, he gave her an apologetic frown and continued flinging rocks without a target. She drew closer and placed her hand on his fist, which was clenching a rock.

"I'm so sorry, Paige," Max said, dropping the rock. "It's because of me. If it wasn't for me..." His voice trailed off as Paige hugged him and sobbed. She led him by the hand over to the multicolored picnic table. After a shared silence between them, Paige decided if she didn't say something, neither of them was going to.

"So? What's the verdict?" she asked Max. He hung his head and shrugged, "They didn't press charges, but I'm suspended indefinitely until some hearing with some superintendent."

"Wouldn't press charges against you? What about what they did to us? They killed my goddamnned dog! I'd be pressing the fucking charges if I could prove it!"

"After some suggestion from Counselor Moretz, the faculty concluded that it was most likely me who killed Elvis and pissed in my own guitar case because—"

"Because he said you lied about Deidre and Dwayne last year and went in her locker."

"'Lied' wouldn't have been so bad. I think they said 'dishonest, violent, and deviant behavior.' McCarmick added in he had had problems with me since day one. They also told me that even if I was the victim of a prank, it didn't excuse my reaction. Can you believe that?"

Unable to reply, Paige just stared at Max, who was staring back, wide-eyed. His lower lip trembled before he was able to continue. "Adam quit the band. Can't say I blame him. Guitar's destroyed—the only thing I have from Dom." Max despaired as Paige pulled her chain over her head and handed him Dominic's ring, which Max refused.

"No. You hang on to it for both of us. I'm sorry about Elvis, and I swear I'm going to get them back, mark my words. I've been thinking, and I wanted to ask you something, though," Max said, his tone dire with the blue in his eyes all but gone and replaced by a flat gray.

"Well, I hope you're not going to ask me to go to prom with you because your timing would really suck, and they most likely are not going to let you go to any school functions—that's if they ever let you back into the school to begin with,"

Unamused, Max looked at her, a stern scowl covering his face. He threw another rock and looking away from Paige, asked, "If I tell you to cut school on a particular day—I mean, not go in at all—will you listen to me?"

"I'm not going to stop hanging out with you, if that's what you're worried about," Paige replied, picking up a rock and joining Max. Before she could throw it, he took hold of her shoulders and repeated his request frantically.

"Paige, if I tell you not to go in, you won't, right? I'm dead serious," he exclaimed.

"Yes, OK. Fine, I won't" she responded, pulling free from Max's grasp, troubled by his hostile demeanor.

"Depart from me, you who are cursed into eternal fire for the devil and his angels," Max said turning into the darkening woods.

"What? Max, you're scaring me,"

"I'll be fine. Just remember what I said."

"Fine. Do you want to come over? We can get a pizza, maybe pick up our quest in *Zelda*? I think we could both use the distraction." Paige pleaded as the clearing became enveloped in darkness.

Max gave a regretful smile. "I can't. Since my dad got fired and I got suspended, he's become worse than usual. He's doubling down on the booze and is really on the warpath. I'm worried about my mom being alone with him too long."

"How about if I come over to your place?"

"You'd be better off if you didn't, believe me. Don't forget about what I said about staying home one day," Max concluded and headed home in the opposite direction.

"OK. See you tomorrow?" Paige whispered. Only the surrounding trees heard her before she rushed back home.

She was overcome by sadness when she mistakenly held the back door open for a pet that was not following behind her. When she made her way to the stairs, she was comforted by the sight of her parents, who were curled up together on the couch watching *Married with Children*. She made her way up the stairs, feeling bad for Max but thankful she did not have a similar homelife. Then comfort escaped her as she realized she had to return to school tomorrow without Max.

While Paige sat alone in the cafeteria reading *Catwoman: Her Sisters Keeper*, Max returned from a bike ride to the Satchel Mayes Library, where he had checked out a variety of books on explosives, compounds, and wiring. At home he helped himself to one of William Garret's beers before going into the basement. After a few hours of reading and tinkering at the workbench left by the previous owner, he took two more beers as well as a wap of the old man's whiskey. In the following days, this became a routine for Max, until he was beaten by the old man for dipping into his stock. The miserable bastard accused his mother of drinking up all his beer, compelling Max to admit to the act. The day after a most savage beating at the hands of his father, Max returned the books, making the librarian, who had seen him unmarked with bruises just days earlier, uncomfortable. Then Max headed off to Covington's Hardware.

Using the money from the gigs they had played in the summer. Max purchased the materials he had read so much about. Then got a homeless woman to buy him a six-pack and gave her the change. Once home, he took stock of his materials, put on his safety goggles, cracked open a beer, and got to work. He stopped sleeping in his bedroom mainly because the cellar was farther away from his father, who couldn't just barge in on him anytime. He became comfortable in the dimly lit dwelling, which drowned out any and all outside noise. Max brought down his tape player and only showed up on the ground floor when he had to go to the bathroom or when his mother insisted he eat something. Since the school was against him and was intent on giving justice to his enemies, Max Garret had decided to create justice of his own.

In school Paige made the best of her friend being gone, kept to herself, and was permitted to work alone in Ms. Jalorean's class. Paige hadn't seen Max since that Sunday night in the clearing, and in his absence, she hung out with Adam, who had joined another band. He asked Paige to join his new group, but she declined. Once in a while, she would talk to Max after his mother had gone downstairs and brought him to the phone. When he came to the line, she tried to strike up a conversation with him, but he was distant and always in a hurry to get off. The weekend before she couldn't even bait him with coming over for the WPIX 11 horror movie marathon.

She thought perhaps he might have met someone else and wasn't telling her. Paige went to a Halloween party hosted by Adam's new band and left soon after the party was crashed by Ross and Greg, both dressed in their Middleton Rams football uniforms. Since Max had mashed Ross's face in at the pep rally, he had been forced to miss games due to a cheekbone fracture and a separated jaw. While Ross had been sidelined, Greg had shined, setting single-game rushing records, leading the team to five consecutive wins. When Ross had been able to play, Harold McCarmick had benched him and only let him play defense, which had infuriated him.

Adam later told Paige, "It was a good thing you left early because somebody asked Ross why he wasn't starting quarterback anymore. He dropped the guy with one punch, got crazy, started shoving people around and trying to start a fight with anyone who looked at him." When all was said and done, the house that belonged to the drummer in Adam's new band was destroyed and money and jewelry were missing as well. When Paige saw Deidre with a gleaming gold charm necklace in the hallway the Wednesday after Halloween, it was obvious who had stolen it and given it to her. It took everything Paige had to keep from spitting in her face.

Since Max no longer walked home and Lana was no longer her friend, Paige was picked up by her mother after school. Frequently the trip home led to Paige accompanying her mother to the grocery store. The supermarket was closed for renovations, so they went to the J&J Produce Mart instead. On the way into the store, Paige stopped at the door and looked across the street where she had first met Dominic with Max. Her mother was already inside, and she nearly walked into a woman who was exiting. It was an overcast day, and she had large sunglasses on, and her hair was wrapped up in a scarf that covered most of her face. She excused herself to Paige and made her way over to a rusted old car. That made Paige call out to her. "Mrs. Garret! Barbara Garret was already near the driver's side of the Torino and without acknowledging Paige, got in and pulled off. Paige joined her mother inside and told her she was confused as to why Max's mother had ignored her. Then she heard Johnny the manager and another fellow gossiping at the counter.

"Did you see her eye?" Johnny questioned his worker.

"How could I miss it? It was so black and blue them big glasses couldn't cover the mark."

Johnny replied in disgust, "I swear part of me wants to hire the useless bastard back just to keep him from beating on the poor woman. To tell you the truth, I've got a good mind to go across the street and get one of them guerillas to go and break his fucking legs." He lowered his voice as he saw Lynne Edmundson approach the counter with some bread and broccoli rabe.

Johnny's coworker, however, did not see the customer as he was taking inventory and spouted back, "I'd agree with you one hundred percent, but what good's that goin' to do? Plus, you may do more harm than good, you know?"

The conversation overheard by Paige let her know Max was not avoiding her. Things were bad in his house, really bad. As soon as she got home, she went straight up to her room and called Max's number. After the phone had rung a bit, Max answered. Paige was surprised as his mother had answered all the times she called before. This time Max sounded excited to hear from her.

Before Paige could voice her concerns, Max said, "I'm sorry I've been ignoring you. Maybe we can hang out in the woods after school tomorrow?" Eagerly Paige agreed, but before she could get a word in, Max said, "Sorry—I have to go," and hung up. Her worry for Mrs. Garret was still there, but she was looking forward to seeing her friend for the first time in almost a month.

The next day, looking in the mirror, Paige fixed her hair, then put on her scarcely used cherry-red lipstick, spritzed on some perfume, then tied up the laces of her white Keds. She felt a little odd getting sexy to go hang in the woods but shrugged off her inhibition. She had known a short time after meeting him that it was Max whom she loved and would eventually want to lose her virginity to if the opportunity presented itself. Absence had made her heart grow fonder, and she was ready.

On her way out the back door, she was briefly teased by her father, who was just getting home, about being "all dolled up." She gave him a hug and went off skipping toward the clearing to meet Max.

She had it planned out in her head and went through it again as she made her way to the clearing. Paige thought to herself, *I'm going to get him to stay over; we will hang out in the rec room like normal.* She knew her folks were going out to eat. Her mother had invited her, and she had politely declined. As Paige went over her calculations of the average length of time an Edmundson evening out took, her thoughts perished at the sight before her.

The multicolored picnic table was turned on its side. Her skip was brought to a stop. There was a multitude of scattered rotting pumpkins set up across the table on the other side of the clearing. Max heard her and popped up from the other side of the upended table as if he were taking shelter behind it. He was very involved in whatever it was he was working on but was taken aback at how stunning she looked. Paige momentarily forgot about the rotting pumpkins and was amused as well as pleased with his reaction.

"Well, if you planned to start growing pumpkins here for next year, I'd hate to disappoint ya, Max, but it won't work. I already tried it." She held out her arm for their customary handshake, which turned into a hug. Soap and the amazing familiar scent of Paige's skin overpowered the flowery fragrance and danced wildly in Max's head. But Paige smelled something else—beer! Warm, of-the-mouth beer at that! While it wasn't as pleasant as his usual scent of Juicy Fruit, she disregarded it, overcome by the joy of seeing him.

"I'd never start a pumpkin patch without consulting you first. These I picked the day after Halloween behind the back of the supermarket that's closed down. Some of them are still in good shape."

Paige pulled one of the cans of Schlitz free, cracked it open, then stood back and leaned forward, sipping the foam from the top of the can. "OK, I have two questions for you. First, why do we want all these busted-up, near-rotten pumpkins on the first Friday in November? Second, how did you get them all here?" Paige asked, wiping the Schlitz foam from her mouth with caution to prevent smudging her lipstick.

"Why don't you turn around, Mike Hammer?" Max replied.

"You stole a shopping cart?"

"No, it was damaged and out back where they threw out the pumpkins. If anything, I fixed it!" he said in defense.

"Fine, but you still didn't answer the first question. What do we want with rotten pumpkins that you stole and gathered with a repaired shopping cart?"

"I was just going to show you but decided to let you start a line of questioning first, Detective Edmundson. All right, left to right—Ross, Deidre, Harold McCarmick, and Moretz, that lying, decrepit fuck." Max pointed and then retrieved another beer for himself and Paige. He was about to go on but was interrupted by Paige, who was curious about the wires attached to the pumpkins with poorly drawn black-marker caricatures of their high school nemeses' faces.

"OK, so what are we going to do? Conjure a fairy godmother to appear with the power to turn assholes into pumpkins?" she asked.

Max handed her a device that looked like a controller for a toy car. "Yeah, something like that," he answered and proceeded to chug the rest of the beer, crush the can, and throw it near the rotten pumpkins.

"Pick that up! Since when did you start littering, dick?" Max went to pick up the can as Paige questioned, "OK, so what am I doing here with your *Rad Racer* controller?"

"You're going to stand back a bit and squeeze the trigger back all the way."

"Wait! Not yet!" Max, who was not back from getting the can, shouted.

It was too late. The pumpkins erupted all over the clearing as Paige ran back from her original position. "Holy shit! Max, are you OK? Max!" The air in front of her was thick. As it cleared, she exploded into laughter at the sight of Max. He was covered head to toe in a combination of kicked-up dirt and pumpkin guts. Paige set down the controller and began removing seeds from his hair.

Too dirty to mind, Max laughed and said, "That was a much bigger blast than I expected!"

A low rumble of thunder echoed in the distance. It seemed to come from inside the clearing. It stopped for a moment, then quaked again. The sound of the wind traveling through the remaining leaves whistled in the trees high above them. "You may want to check your calculations again, there, pumpkin head," Paige joked as Max saw droplets of rain pelting her white shirt. She continued to pull pumpkin guts from his lowered head. Paige stood on her tippy-toes as the pace of the rain increased on and around them.

Max gently took hold of her wrists and looked directly at her and placed his lips on hers. They took hold of each other violently and continued kissing each other ferociously, each kiss more intense than the last, until they were completely saturated from the teeming downpour.

A smile widened across Paige's face as she leaned back from Max, patted him on the chest, and said, "Come on." They both took off running out of the clearing and through the trail in the woods that led to her house. Drenched from head to toe, they stepped into the kitchen. Max stood shivering in the Edmundsons' kitchen for minutes while Paige ran upstairs to get him a towel to dry off. Upstairs Paige also grabbed a pair of her dad's sweats and a Bud Light Spuds MacKenzie shirt.

She then ran into her parents' room to snatch a box of condoms she had noticed once, when her mom had asked her to get something from her nightstand.

She started down the steps but feeling too obvious, ran back upstairs and returned the box after taking out two condoms. She placed the rubbers inside the hooded sweatshirt she had thrown on. "You can get changed in the downstairs bathroom," she told Max, pulling him by the hand. Paige studied her family's old couch in the rec room with the *Ghostbusters* sleeping bag atop it and thought to herself, *I always thought this would happen in a bed, when it did.* Her thought was interrupted by the sound of Max, who was drying his hair vigorously. He was saying something to her, but she heard nothing. Instead she looked at the unavoidable erection poking out of her father's sweatpants.

"You have to use these!" she blurted out to him, forcing the condoms toward him in nervousness. Max accepted the condoms from her and inspected them. "I'd be happy to, Paige, except this says these expired in June of 1987."

They made out together on the couch, only to be stopped by the sounds of a slightly intoxicated Lynn Edmundson upstairs. "Paige?" The scourge of the electronics store has indigestion. We're home!" Lynn called up to her room and then was surprised to see her daughter come upstairs with Max.

Her parents were happy to see Max and warmed up some dinner for them. Max knew his mom was leaving tomorrow for a weekend retreat with her church group, but he still called to notify her he'd be spending the weekend at the Edmundsons'.

The following morning Max rode Paige's bike with her on the handlebars to Malden's pharmacy, then back to Paige's house, and returned to the clearing. On a sunlit Saturday afternoon, they gave themselves to one another atop the multicolored picnic table in the clearing that was covered by the *Ghostbuster* sleeping bag from the rec room.

It hurt. Paige had expected it to, but as her legs pressed against the metallic zipper of the sleeping bag, Max's movements ceased. She felt as relieved as did he. While it may have been painful at first, that didn't stop them from trying again. Each time was more amazing than the last. In the rec room late that Saturday night, then in Paige's bedroom all of Sunday afternoon while Paige's parents were at a local bazaar. As the daylight faded on the most exciting weekend in both of their young lives, Max looked out the living room window at the snow careening down in large flakes.

Paige, who was covered in nothing but the comforter from her bed, joined him. He wrapped his arms around her; they shared a kiss and a beautiful quiet moment gazing at the snowfall.

After retrieving Max's clothes from the laundry room, Paige handed them to him, along with a mug of hot chocolate. As he sipped cautiously at the steaming liquid, she said to him, "You know you're my boyfriend now, right?"

She posed the question more like a statement. He set the mug down, smiled, and said to the anxious girl whom he loved beyond measure, "Paige, nothing would make me happier."

Max put on his clothes, but he'd remove them once more. Paige carefully discarded the empty condom box in the bottom of the outside trash bin. They did not want to leave each other, but the magical weekend was over.

After Paige's parents returned home, Phil Edmundson put his coat back on and asked Max if he was ready for him to drop him off at home.

"That's alright, Mr. E, I'd rather walk." He hugged Paige and said, "I'll call you as soon as I get home."

As the fallen snow crunched under his shoes, Max Garret felt as though he were walking on air. He didn't want to be driven home; he wanted to walk to extend the weekend as long as possible. The roads were empty due to the snowfall, and he played back the events of the weekend. He had forgotten all about explosives and revenge. He just wanted tomorrow to go by as quickly as possible so he could see his girlfriend again. "Girlfriend," he said aloud. "Imagine that."

The euphoric feeling came to a screeching halt in the form of Dwayne Bishop's Mustang wheeling out in the snow and racing toward him.

Chapter 9:
VENDETTA RESUMED

The Mustang's engine growled in his direction as Max took off to avoid it. He ran into an alleyway as the car's headlights beamed behind him. There was little to no traction on the snow-covered ground, so Max ran for a nearby fence.

"Come on. He ran through here," Ross shouted to Greg and Dwayne, running hard from the car at the mouth of the alley. Max gripped the top of the fence and was about to lift his leg over to the other side.

His foot was suddenly caught in a vice group in the form of Ross's right hand. Max straddled back and kicked at him with his free foot. The effort proved futile as Ross yanked him off the fence, causing him to fall backward. Max felt dizzy from hitting the pavement. His ears rang with the sound of Dwayne trudging in the snow as he caught up to them. Ross leaped down from the middle of the fence as Max groaned

"I'm not even closed to finished with you!" Ross said, pinning his knee into Max's chest.

His skull felt like it was on fire, and Ross's weight bearing down on his chest wasn't helping. Max grunted in pain as his hands grasped at the ground below him. Maybe there was a loose piece of rock or gravel he could club Ross with, he thought, but he only came up with a small handful of snow. Dwayne laid into him with a kick, laughed, and spoke, giving insult to injury. "Say, Garret, my man, Greg here is gonna take your honey Paige to prom and tear her ass up!" Dwayne then high-fived Greg as they swarmed him, Ross still pinning him to the ground.

Max forced his body from side to side to break free, to no avail. He couldn't move. So he spoke instead. "Well, I guess Greg is going to need to Wayne," Max said in a weakened voice, his response piquing his attacker's interest. Max mustered up his strength and continued louder, "I mean, it's not like Deidre can fuck all three of you. Can she, Ross?" He wheezed under the increasing pressure being applied to his chest. Momentarily stunned, Dwayne turned away from Ross, who was now staring at him, and kicked Max again. Greg, too, then kicked Max so hard he thought his foot was sprained.

Ross pulled Max upward and punched him in the throat, then dropped him back to the ground and screamed, "I missed three fucking games because of you and your cheap shot, Garret. It's your turn to take a stand to the face."

Ross stepped on Max's head with his right foot and pressed his weight down on him. Then, dissatisfied with the amount of damage it had caused, he threw off his ski gloves and began punching away at Max. The first four punches hurt like hell but not enough to keep Max from clutching his Adam's apple, which felt like it was caved in from the shot to his throat. Then everything became numb before Max passed out.

A flashlight beamed out from one of the backyards in the alley. An older man in a flannel jacket had been alerted by the sound of blows being landed and grunting. He shined the light out into the alley and shouted out, "What are you boys doing back here?" then turned the light down to see Max beaten and bloody. He began to make his way over to see if someone was hurt. Then his suspicions turned to worry.

"Shut the fuck up, and go back in your fucking house." Ross threatened him.

"You get off him and get the hell out of here, or I'm gonna call the cops!" the man replied, refusing to adhere to Ross's warning. As he got closer, the man was tripped by Greg.

Max came to momentarily but was going in and out. Everything was dark, except for the blur of the streetlight overhead. He could hear the sounds of the man who had tried to help him being beaten as well. Once the old man was dropped, Ross yelled out to his flunkies, "C'mon, let's jet!" Greg held his hand to high-five Ross, and Dwayne yelled out, "Woo-hoo! Gimme some!" They retreated back to the end of the alley, all three of them laughing.

Simon Cartwright rose to his feet as Dwayne drove off. He'd seen his share of dustups in his youth, and while aching, the retired roofer shook off the pain and retrieved his flashlight. Simon looked on in horror at the beaten boy who lay before him. The snow where Max lay was blood-soaked. He ran to his shed and after using a wheelbarrow to bring Max's unconscious body from the alleyway to his back porch, carried him indoors. The smell of peroxide awakened Max, who panicked on the couch of his rescuer's living room. An ice pack fell from atop his head, and a black and white cat gazed at him curiously.

From across the room, a voice said to him, "Ambulance is on its way. It's good you're awake. You got a bad knot on your head." Simon restrained Max from rising. "You need to get to the hospital!" Simon explained as Max looked around the room's walls, which were covered in antique wall clocks. His head throbbing, he ignored the pain searing through his entire body and used the arm of the couch to pull himself to his feet.

"I can't go to the hospital, mister; another ER bill is not what I need."

"Give me your phone number; I'll call your parents if you won't listen to me. They should go to the hospital with you."

"You have no idea how bad of an idea that is. I have to go," Max said, stumbling and using the wall for balance and heading for the back door.

"Your father should make a report to the police," Simon replied, taking hold of his flannel coat as if he were going to follow Max outside.

Max stopped and again braced himself, this time on the countertop of Simon's kitchen.

"One of their fathers is the police, and my old man is the town drunk."

"I see. Well, I'm sure this isn't the first problem you have had with them, um—"

"I'm Max, and no, it's been nonstop."

"Name's Simon, and I hate to say this, Max, but I've seen this kind of thing get worse before better. Friend of mine killed himself when I was younger."

Max nodded in understanding as Simon tried to stall him before the ambulance arrived.

"If you can't get help, then help yourself. Might makes right. You might have to make this right for yourself, before it's too late, you know?" Max nodded a second time then faced the back door. "I'd drive you wherever it is your headed, but I don't see so good at night anymore, and with the snow…"

Exiting the doorway, Max took hold of the porch railing, looked back, and told Simon, "Thank you. I'm sorry you got hurt trying to help me. I'm glad you did help, though, and don't worry—I'll make it right." With that, he limped off through the alleyway, and Simon followed close behind watching him until he stepped out past the streetlight and was enveloped by the darkness that bordered it.

The "friend" that Simon Cartwright had spoken of was his own son, who had shot himself after years of torment. Relocating from New York to Middleton a decade ago had made all of that a repressed, painful memory that Simon relived seeing Max unresponsive and bloody in his alleyway.

Max made his way onto the street where he had first seen Dwayne's Mustang coming after him and saw the ambulance in front of Simon's house in the middle of the street. After seeing the street set aglow from the emergency vehicles lights, he collapsed, then fell two more times before making it into his house. He crept past his father, who was passed out on the living room couch. His mother was sobbing at the sink, drying dishes. He frightened her when she heard a thud in the living room, the sound of Max's legs giving out once more.

"Maxie, is that you? Are you OK?" she called out from the kitchen. Halfway into the cellar entrance, he shouted back, "I'm OK, Mom; I just tripped." His head was throbbing, and blood profusely ran from his nose.

When he reached his way to the bottom of the basement stairway, his mother called down, "Paige called, and Ms. Jalorean dropped off your assignments Friday for your classes. She doesn't want you to fall behind."

Barbara Garret waited for a response but heard nothing.

"Max? Are you sure you're all right?"

"Yeah, Mom. I'll work on it later. I'm going to do some stuff downstairs tonight."

Nothing mattered—not the throbbing in his skull, not the pain that pulsated through his entire face. Following his suspension from school, Max had taken notice of the school's calendar. It noted an assembly in the gymnasium. That assembly was tomorrow. The weekend with Paige had made him set aside his destructive plan against those who had beaten him, harassed him, destroyed what was his, and killed Paige's pet. Friday in the woods had just been a test. A small fraction of the blast he was prepared to set off underneath the bleachers, where he had become an unwilling witness to Deidre and Dwayne and become enraged enough to bury his microphone stand into Ross Aberdeen's face.

Every Monday morning the gym's door was propped open to air out the body odor from the contests held there over the weekend. He planned to sneak onto the grounds and set his charge underneath the bleachers. Once noon came and they were herded in for assembly, he would blow them all to high hell. Droplets of blood fell from his face and spotted up the workbench as he toiled away. He set his pliers down for a moment, concerned at the maddening thought that one of his intended victims might cut school tomorrow.

While Max worked feverishly on the black powder, cultivating and priming and testing his blast caps, Paige squeezed a pillow tightly in her arms. She thought, *He should have been home by now.* His mother had said she'd have him call back as soon as he got in. Normally it took him twenty minutes to a half hour tops to walk home from her house. It had been over an hour and a half. Growing more impatient by the second, Paige dialed the Garret house once more.

Getting up from his cluttered workbench in the basement, Max hurried to pick up the phone to prevent it from waking up his father. After answering, Paige questioned him as to why he had not phoned her upon returning home as he customarily did. Part of him wanted to describe to his compassionate friend the savage retaliatory beating that had delayed his arrival, but he felt ashamed and embarrassed. Instead he quickly apologized, claiming to have forgotten, and changed the conversation. "Are they still having that fall assembly tomorrow?" he questioned Paige.

"Yeah. What do you care? It's not like you have to worry about sitting through some boring lecture. Say, when do you have to meet with the superintendent?" she asked, eager for Max's suspension to be over.

Before he could answer, an agitated William Garret picked up the phone and barked. "Don't you be tying up this line talking to that little piece of tail all night. I'm waiting on an important phone call, boy," his father announced to Max's embarrassment.

"Yeah, I'm sure you are," Max replied, causing his father to hang up and end the disruption. "Say, remember what I said about not going into school a while ago?"

"Why? Do you want your little piece of tail to play hooky tomorrow? Maybe head over to Malden's pharmacy again?" Paige joked.

The stairs to the basement rumbled as Bill Garret flew down them as fast as he could. Flustered, Max rushed the conversation. "Just don't go in tomorrow, like you promised!" he exclaimed. He faced his father, who was at the opposite end of the darkened basement and coming toward him at his workbench.

"Why?" Paige questioned, unaware of the threat standing before Max on the other end of the phone.

"Just don't go to school tomorrow. Promise?" he said with urgency.

"Fine, I won't. Call me..." Paige stopped midsentence as the line cut off.

Snapping the belt he had removed from his pants, Bill Garret waited for Max, who slammed down the phone. "When I tell you I'm waiting for a call, you listen, boy!" he yelled, gripping his belt tightly. There was a baseball bat on his workbench with a few crisscrossed nails in it. It had been left there by Max in preparation for a future confrontation with his father.

Before Max could take hold of the bat, his father took hold of him and shoved him onto the workbench, rattling the powders and materials he had been testing and bumping the phone off the receiver. As he shoved his son backward, William Garret sneered in disgust at the sight of Max's injuries.

"Get off me, you fucking asshole!" the boy yelled as tears streamed into the dried-up blood on his face.

The outburst brought a rare chuckle and grin from his father, who after shoving him once more, turned away, saying, "Looks like someone already beat your ass for me, he-he." As he turned to make his way back up the stairs, he concluded, "You tell 'em your father said thank you!" and staggered back up the stairs, laughing in amusement to himself.

Planning to play sick the night before, Paige decided to put off her homework and played *Double Dragon* to keep herself distracted. After realizing how hard the game was without Max's assistance as player two, she played *Zelda II* with the volume off until daylight. It felt like she had just fallen asleep when her mother woke her in an alarmed voice.

"Paige, honey, wake up; you fell back asleep after I woke you up. You're going to be late." This was a time for vigilance, Paige thought. If she was going to have a fun-filled day with Max, she had to remove any doubt from her mother's mind that she could go to school. It was what she and her former girlfriends referred to as *Ferris Bueller* time.

"I don't feel so good, Mom," she answered weakly, then regretted it feeling a bit over the top.

Lynne Edmundson immediately placed her palm on Paige's forehead, checking her temperature. Before she could give an estimate, her father called out to them from the hallway, wrestling with his necktie, "How's my favorite girl this morning?" Her father entered her room, his curiosity piqued by her mother sitting at her bedside. This was critical, Paige thought. She had to have them both in agreement that there was no plausible way she could manage going in.

"She doesn't have a fever," her mother said, expressing doubt of any serious illness.

"It's my stomach!" Paige responded in urgency. She could tell her parents were skeptical once they looked at one another and smiled.

The situation had turned desperate, and she was contemplating making an emergency dash for the bathroom to convince them when her father said, "I'll tell you what. You tough it out and go in. Maybe I'll come home from work tonight with that boombox you've been eyeing in the store," Phil said, offering a most tempting bribe.

Her mother added, "And you keep your perfect attendance, which you and I have a bargain about," referring to the prize money she was offered every marking period she went without missing a day.

The boombox was supposed to be a Christmas gift, and the extra cash could buy a few new tapes.

"OK, fine. Just let me call Max first, then I'll get ready fast as possible,"

"Are you two walking?" her mother asked, concerned about the time.

"Did those jerks let him back to school yet?" her father asked. The subjects of the torture of Elvis and Max's reaction were never discussed.

"No, I just have to tell him something he wanted me to find out about the assembly today," Paige said, leaning toward the clear phone on her nightstand.

"Assembly? Oh, that's why you're not feeling well." Her mother teased. "Hustle up; I'm driving you in. I'm going to make you a Pop-Tart so you have something to eat." She exited the room just as the busy signal sounded as she tried Max's house.

Her father smiled, finally getting an acceptable knot in the tie. He had tried several times since entering her room. He told Paige, "If you still don't feel good, I'll come by and pick you up on my lunch hour." He followed Lynn downstairs to make sure he got his share of Pop-Tarts as well.

Light shone through the glass of the dual windows in the basement of the Garrets' home. About twenty minutes after the confrontation with his father last night, Max had begun feeling lightheaded. He had lain down on the floor with a Cutty Shark Whiskey towel he had converted to a pillow and fallen asleep. The old towel was used for wiping moisture from leaking overhead pipes that dripped onto his work space. Overnight the droplets of water settled atop the desk into fuses and batteries.

Dampness crept into the blasting caps on the workbench, alongside a broken pickle jar of black powder, as well as loose traces of ammonium nitrate that were scattered everywhere. There was further disruption to the work space brought on by the multiple shoves into the desk Max had received from his father. The phone had been jarred loose from the receiver, preventing Paige's or any other calls from getting through to the house.

The Mustang's horn sounded outside the Aberdeen residence. Ross came out slowly and directed a bit of a scowl toward Dwayne. After making Greg get into the back seat of the car, Ross held out his right hand and displayed it after closing the car door. He shouted with pride, "That freak's face did a number on my hand—check it out!" and proceeded to high-five Dwayne and Greg with his other hand.

In the crammed back seat of the car, Greg contemplated telling them how he had hurt his foot kicking Max but decided against it, the same way he chose not to protest staying in the front seat even though he was bigger than Ross. He was in his glory, and when Ross was happy, everyone was happy. This was a sentiment shared by both Greg and Dwayne. Music blasted, and Ross kicked at Dwayne's dash to the rhythm, in spite of how many times he had asked Ross to refrain from doing so. Dwayne pressed harder on the accelerator, and the car sped off. He harbored feelings of resentment toward Ross; he also held back feelings of regret for them beating Max as badly as they had, as well as beating the old man.

"The answering party will need to accept the charges," the operator instructed Paige, who requested the emergency breakthrough to cut through the busy signal at Max's house. She had been expecting to see the delighted look on his face when she proudly set the boombox atop the picnic table in her fort later that day. But when the operator mentioned the charges, she pictured a disastrous scenario playing out, one in which it was Mr. Garret on the line, who not only refused the call from her but also gave Max hell because of it.

"Shit, his dad." Paige spoke her thoughts aloud by mistake.

"Miss the number?" the operator asked.

"I'm sorry—never mind," Paige said, then hung up. She met her mother downstairs. On the way to school, Paige figured that Max wouldn't be so disappointed in her not staying home sick and they could always hang out later.

Monday, November 6, 1989, began like any other day at Middleton High. Deidre Lisbon exited Timothy Moretz's office with a grin for herself and a snarl for his quiet yet curious frumpy secretary Marilyn. Greg Chapman obtained permission to get into the weight room early from Harold McCarmick, who was shining up his whistle like a prized possession. Ross and Greg injected one another with syringes before their workout, both of their backs peppered with red acne, which made the Gold's Gym tank tops they wore a poor choice. Their coach was well aware that they were on a steroid cycle and had been for some time. Paige kept to herself, and the morning was mundane as usual.

It was a tradition of Katherine Jalorean's to open Friday's mail on the following Monday. Bills made up the bulk of her mail, and this practice served her well as it allowed her to never dwell on them and enjoyed weekends much more. There was additional time at her disposal on Mondays since she didn't have to get to work until later for afternoon classes. In the pile of mail, between her American Express bill and bank statements, was an envelope with no postage or return address. She opened it with curiosity and from the wall phone in her kitchen, dialed 911 after reading the printed note written in marker, which said,

STAY AWAY FROM SCHOOL

SOMETHING BAD IS GOING TO HAPPEN

—A FRIEND

After she phoned emergency services, her next call was to the school. The phone rang off the hook at the main office as everyone was gathered in the gymnasium for the afternoon assembly. Paige took a seat on the bleachers with the rest of the class, unaware that she was atop a bulk of Max's planned explosion. Lana was seated away from her friends. She resorted to making small talk with Paige, who was seated in front of her.

"Hey, can you believe Deidre is on honor roll this year?" she said, attempting to strike up a conversation. Paige smiled back at her and said nothing. Lana looked at the foot of the bleachers she was seated atop and saw Deidre chewing her gum and offering a bitchy wave hello.

Lana waved back the same way a dog perks up when it is called by its owner. Paige rolled her eyes in front of Lana, repulsed at her obedience to the girl who when they were thirteen had nearly gotten Paige arrested for shoplifting by dropping a pet rock into her shopping bag. Part of her repulsion was self-inflicted, for tolerating the friend who was anything but for so long.

It had been a horrible Sunday evening for Barbara Garret, who upon returning from a weekend with her church group, had been berated and mentally abused by her husband. Monday morning had not been much better. Bill had left with the car once she had come out of the shower, and she had been stuck without transportation to the flower shop. The few hours she worked there were critical since Bill was out of work again. She used the neighbor's phone to call the shop and the phone company to tell them her phone couldn't dial out.

Sleeping on the floor made no difference to the pain that filled Max's body. He struggled to his feet, awakened by the light beaming through the basement windows. After looking at his watch, he rushed, frantically grabbing materials from his workbench, which was in shambles.

Counselor Moretz had taken his place in front of the lectern on the stage in the gym and ordered everyone, "OK, quiet down." Harold McCarmick scanned the bleachers, aggressively looking for those who had ignored the counselor's request. Once satisfied, Timothy Moretz droned on about school policy that was being ignored and lectured the audience on wearing ripped jeans and loitering in the hallways.

He was interrupted by the loud sirens of emergency vehicles outside the school parking lot. A woman pulled him away from the microphone and whispered to him.

While the flurry of police and fire sirens sounded at Middleton High, Max was checking and testing his charges before ignition. Barbara Garret thanked her neighbor, who had become familiar with her difficulties that first night when he had heard her screams and pleas across the street. Having already made multiple purchases, Bill Garret was attempting to con a free beer out of the bartender at the Candlelight Tavern while the son he abused regularly was acting out his plan to blow up his school.

The plan had gone accordingly in theory at least.

Before emergency crews could enter the gymnasium, windows shattered and fire erupted out of them, terrorizing all nearby. The earth surrounding the explosion briefly shook with ferocity, and great human injury was inflicted, as Max Garret had expected. A blackened cloud of ash exited the building as anticipated.

Only one major problem plagued him.

Chapter 10:
ERUPTION

The shattered windows were not that of Middleton High's gymnasium—they were in his own home. The earth-shaking tremor was not felt by his tormentors but by his mother and neighbors. The human casualty inflicted was to him and him alone.

A head count was taking place in the school parking lot as emergency workers entered the school. Paige took notice of the sound of even more sirens sounding off in the opposite direction, toward her house. "It's Red Dawn! The Russians are invading," joked Daniel Carinsen. Daniel had started the food fight in the cafeteria junior year and was well versed in distasteful jokes and poor timing. If Paige had known what had happened to her best friend and new boyfriend, part of her might have wished his ill humor accurate.

After seeing her home momentarily lifted from its foundation and pieces of it falling in the center of the street, Barbara Garret ran back to her neighbor's house to call for help. The flames seething out of her basement made her concerns about a malfunctioning phone and missing work a distant memory. Her son lay smothered in a pile of concrete, wood, and ash, clinging to his life.

A day that had begun as a plain Monday that November in 1989 wound up becoming a day that would be remembered by Middleton residents for generations to come. It forever altered the life of Paige Edmundson, who pondered for years to come what could have or might have been on the mind of the boy she loved. She and her parents spent that night in the emergency room waiting area with a distraught Barbara Garret.

The voice of the nightly news anchor simultaneously filled the living room of Katherine Jalorean, the Candlelight Tavern, the emergency room of Hillshire Medical, the kitchen of Ray Gene's, Blackbeard's Seafood, the Middleton Social Club, and countless other locations as far south as Maidens Mist and all the way up north to Hessian's Cliff.

"A Middleton teen's plan to detonate explosives in the school he had been suspended from was discovered by emergency workers who were called to his school and home after he set off an explosion in his basement in a failed test. The seventeen-year-old was pulled from the wreckage and remains in intensive care on life support. Preset explosives at the school were removed without incident, and a disturbing journal was recovered at the home along with hand-drawn diagrams that mapped out the school's auditorium on sheets of graphing paper. A forewarned teacher notified the school…"

That night Paige Edmundson knelt at the foot of her bed and prayed for the first time since she was a little girl. Tears streamed down her clasped hands as she pleaded for Max's life. She left the ER only after receiving assurance from Mrs. Garret that she'd phone the Edmundsons no matter the hour should there be any change in Max's condition.

The following morning any attempts her mother made for Paige to preserve her perfect attendance were futile. She went to Malden's for a get-well card and then selected an arraignment from Flowers II Remember. The purchase was a waste as she was informed by the nurse at the desk that Max's condition was so grave that he had to remain in a sterile environment and could not have flowers.

As she made her way down the hall, Paige noticed a nurse she knew personally. It was Wendy Damon's mother. The sight of Mrs. Damon in her nurse's uniform was not an unfamiliar one to Paige, and although she was no longer friendly with Wendy, she had no ill will toward her mother. Drawing closer in the hallway, Paige broke the silence.

"Hi, Mrs. Damon," she said, wondering just what to follow that up with in the way of conversation. That concern was put at ease as Mrs. Damon said nothing back to her, not even hello.

Wendy's mom saw Paige at the nurse's station, discarding the flowers, and was aware of just whom she had intended to see: the boy who had planned to bring harm to her daughter and her friends. As she walked past Paige, Mrs. Damon thought to herself, *If I could get away with turning off that life support machine, I'd do it in a heartbeat.*

The sight of Barbara Garret exiting one of the rooms on the trauma floor helped Paige forget the smirk she had received from Mrs. Damon, and she picked up the pace in her direction. Once she had caught up with Mrs. Garret, she almost felt wrong asking about Max's condition and instead hugged the distraught woman.

"I don't understand. Maxwell was so quiet and gentle; this is not in his nature at all. He was right about you honey—you are beautiful both inside and out—and he is going to need a friend more than ever to pull out of this! Bless your good heart, Paige!" Barbara Garret said through a continuously cracking voice as she fought back tears.

"Is he going to…" Paige paused and chose her next words carefully. "Is he going to make it? I mean, how bad is he?" Paige regretted her question as it caused Mrs. Garret to break out in uncontrollable tears. Paige comforted her, and once Barbara Garret was able to catch her breath, she requested, "Paige, can you escort me to the cafeteria?" Her throat was like sandpaper, and she was dehydrated. It was only a matter of time before she collapsed and would have to be admitted herself.

As Paige walked with her to the cafeteria and was made privy to Max's condition, Nurse Damon phoned her daughter with the news of Paige's misplaced compassion for the social pariah who was now referred to as Maniac Max.

In the cafeteria Paige explained the torment that Max had met with since the first day he had set foot into Middleton High, in and away from school. When they returned from the cafeteria, Paige could not see Max as he was undergoing surgery once again. The doctor explained Max's narrow chances of survival. When Barbara Garret returned home that evening, she considered swallowing a handful of sleeping pills and chasing it with Bill's whiskey to end her suffering.

She stood in front of the medicine cabinet with the bottle of Leroux Rock & Rye in one hand and a handful of pills in the other. The sound of windows breaking and a car wheeling away outside the Garret home was all that stopped her. A brick had been thrown through the only intact window, in the living room. The faded white aluminum siding was covered in red graffiti that said, "die psycho" and other illegible hostilities. The winter wind sent a chill through her home. Barbara Garret shivered and began cleaning up the glass. The cold didn't bother her; its numbing effect returned her to her senses. She returned the sleeping pills to the cabinet, then assessed the damage in front of her house. A few blocks down the road, Greg Chapman tossed an empty can of red spray paint out of a moving Mustang.

Phil Edmundson helped board up the Garrets' living room window after Bill Garret refused. There was no money to replace the windows, and some weeks later, the boards Phil had put up were graffitied with profanities as well. Discarded beer cans were a constant sight outside the Garrets' home, as well as trash, discarded in retaliation for Max's plan. Even in Middleton City, the Garrets were on shaky ground when it came to social status. Barbara was adored at her job and her church. William brought out the worst in anyone unfortunate enough to cross his path. The explosion set off in the basement was the deciding factor in making them permanent social pariahs.

In school Paige was a pariah as well, and she made a habit of leaving before lunch to join Barbara Garret at Hillshire Medical. Frequently Katherine Jalorean lost focus in the middle of lectures, gazing at the empty desks once occupied by Max and Paige. It wasn't until Max was taken off life support months later that she saw her favorite student in attendance once again. She was happy to have Paige in class but recognized the absence of the sparkle in her eyes, now replaced by sadness.

The *Middleton Observer*'s sports section featured a full-page photo of Harold McCarmick presenting Greg Chapman with the all-conference running back trophy. The games Ross had missed had allowed Greg to shine as he set a school record for yardage. It had been a disappointing season for Harold McCarmick's football team as they had failed to make the playoffs for the first time in his coaching career. The accolade received by his player meant little to him. Jealous over the attention given to his friend, Ross contemplated revealing that Greg was taking steroids. But he quickly came to the realization that he'd be implicating himself as well. Deidre convinced him to run for student government—a suggestion made to her by Timothy Moretz.

Her relationship with the counselor was purely one of manipulation and extortion. He continued to doctor the grades he was tasked with entering into the school's computer. Each time she gave into his advances, a new request had to be adhered to. While most of her classmates needed to beg an older sibling or get a bum to buy them booze, Deidre simply slipped a piece of paper with her liquor order on his desk after one of her frequent visits to the guidance office. She had him by the balls, literally and figuratively. If he ever gave an inkling of refusal, she flashed him the log she kept of each and every sexual encounter she had had with the man many years her senior.

Trips to hotels, out-of-town shopping trips, and dates, times, and detailed accounts of the sexual favors she had performed at his request were all in the log. It was too much for him to refute and too much for him to refuse. The girl he had once preyed upon when he had realized her promiscuity had him on the dangle, and the tables had been turned drastically. Prom was coming up, and Timothy Moretz had another thing coming if he didn't think he was buying Deidre the most extravagant and expensive dress available. She laughed to herself, thinking of the dress as a prelude to a car.

The Edmundsons understood the suffering endured by Max once Paige had explained in detail how he had been tormented. But they were concerned about the fact that all their daughter's social time was spent at the hospital. After constant suggestions from her parents, Paige started hanging around with her old bandmate from Middleton's Crossing, Adam. Max's condition was improving, and she spent less time visiting the hospital and more time with Adam and his friends. Adam introduced her to Ed Darby, who was handsome, good-hearted, and funny. On multiple occasions since their introduction, Paige had had to repeat to Ed that she had a boyfriend when he had come on to her or been overly friendly.

Carrie rejoined Adam and Paige after a fallout with Deidre. According to Carrie, one night after a party at Greg's house, she caught Deidre sloppy drunk in the kitchen hanging all over her boyfriend. Once Carrie confronted and accused Deidre, she was dropped from the clique. Lana, Wendy, and the other girls stopped hanging out with Carrie shortly thereafter.

Happy to have Carrie back, Paige accepted her sincere apology and forgave her. They optimistically anticipated Max's recovery. Adam wasn't happy with his new group, and they figured once Max recovered, they'd form Middleton's Crossing once more. The negative social stigma associated with Maniac Max would have little impact on their band. If anything, it would add a bit of infamous notoriety and mystique, which was never a bad thing for a rock band. The three of them had already decided that once Mrs. Garret provided Paige with an estimate of a release date, they would go to all the clubs they had played last year to arrange future performances.

The trio went to Ray Gene's and was assured by Giorgio that he'd do his best to secure them the clubs previously obtained by Dominic. He inquired about Max's health and was glad to see his former workers and the pretty girl who had accompanied his old friend back in the restaurant. Reuniting with Adam and Carrie did Paige a world of good. She was hated at Middleton for her relationship with Max, and while most girls were looking forward to prom, she was counting down the days until the end of senior year.

Chapter 11:
GRADUATION AND SEPARATION

The king and queen of the Middleton High prom were Greg Chapman and Deidre Lisbon. Ross threw up all over his tux and had to leave early after being physically ejected by chaperone Harold McCarmick. Once outside, McCarmick had a discussion with his coworker and friend Tim Moretz, who had laid down his credit card for the strapless red lace dress Deidre was wearing. She was taking photos with Greg as her distraught boyfriend was thrown out. Moretz confided to McCarmick how his situation with Deidre had put him in severe debt and asked if he had any ideas about how to remedy his woes. Harold McCarmick always thought Deidre was a dimwitted hussy and blamed her for Ross's poor performance on the football field.

The weekend after prom, Harold McCarmick threatened Deidre that if she did not relent from her extortion of his colleague, he'd not only disclose the details of her promiscuity to her father but also discontinue the favorable grades she was receiving from Moretz as well and inform Ross of her cheating on him. Never one to back down, she responded with a threat of her own.

"Oh yeah? If you don't stay outta my business, I'm tellin' your wife about you playin' the field and hitting on Ms. Jalorean! How 'bout you fuck off and go watch some boys takin' a shower or something?" When he grabbed her by the neck and held a closed fist in front of her face, she conceded to his threat for the time being.

Paige's visits to Hillshire Medical decreased in frequency. She felt so helpless in the hospital room, with nothing but the sound of machines and her own voice. Max was mummified in bandages for most of her visits and was heavily sedated; his only responses to her were grunts and moans. In his long slumber, Dominic spoke to him and convinced Max his time had not yet come.

One week after the class of 1990's prom, Max Garret regained consciousness.

The entire left side of his neck and shoulder were covered in scarred tissue. His left testicle needed to be surgically removed, and the scarring traveled from his groin to his shinbone. The surgeon explained when he was thrown from the blast, previous trauma combined with the injuries in the explosion rendered him comatose. At first Max processed none of this because he feared his mother had been injured as well in the blast the man at his bedside kept referring to. He had no memory of it.

The surgeon went out in the hallway and motioned Barbara into Max's room. His mother looked like she had aged ten years since Max had last seen her. She entered the room and gently took hold of his hand; through the bandages and IV, which was itching him profusely, Max squeezed her hand. His thought process immediately shifted to his father once he knew his mom was safe.

"I'm...so sorry, Mom. Did Dad?"

"Your father couldn't make it today, honey. I'm just so glad you're better. We thought we were going to lose you," she said in tears.

The surgeon and additional hospital staff came back into the room and regretfully told her, "I'm sorry, Mrs. Garret, Max needs to rest now. He needs time to adjust." They asked that she return the following day and be present when a detailed description would be provided.

The Edmundsons were preparing dinner in their kitchen as Phil tried to speak to his wife over the sound of her latest musical interest. He escaped the concert going on in his kitchen to summon his daughter to set the table. Paige stood at the top of the stairs with a radiant smile, her face overcome with excitement.

"What's got you so overjoyed? I know it's not your mother's pot roast." Paige stormed down the steps and hugged her father so tightly he found himself short of breath.

"Max's mom just called! He's fully conscious, and I can actually talk to him tomorrow! Mom!" Paige ran into the kitchen to share the good news with her mother. Phil Edmundson remained at the bottom of the steps. He naturally was concerned about his daughter continuing her relationship with a kid who had blown himself up. Once he met Max, he liked him immediately, but concerns for the safety of his daughter caused him to have reservations. Never one to impede on his daughter's joy, Phil took a deep breath and rejoined his ecstatic daughter, who was setting the dinner table with more enthusiasm than ever.

Trying to play it cool, Paige walked swiftly from the parking lot to the hospital entrance. She could hardly contain her excitement once she was given the location of Max's new room. Having been directed to the hall, she sprinted but came to a full stop once in front of the room, which had a temporary paper name placard outside that read, "M. Garret." A nervousness came over her. Paige had been so anxious to see Max recover she hadn't considered what he would be like once he had. She took hold of the metal handle and pulled the wooden door toward her.

Seated in a single chair next to the bed, Barbara Garret got up and offered Paige the seat. She had been there since early in the morning and was anticipating Paige's arrival.

"You two have a lot to discuss. I'll get out of your way." As she headed for the door, she took hold of Paige's arm, hugged her, and continued in a whisper, "No matter what the consequences of this are, I'm certain he would have never lived through this without you." She left Paige alone with the partially bandaged Max.

Paige gave him a narrow smile and grasped the forearm of his outstretched bandaged hand.

"Remember me?" She teased after releasing their special handshake.

"I'd never forget you. Even if I died and was reincarnated as someone else."

His voice was different—a bit hollow and somewhat raspy. Paige's grin widened into a full-fledged smile. They talked for two hours, and Max's mother rejoined them with a special take-out order from Ray Gene's. For the next three days, both Paige and his mother stayed until visiting hours ended. Paige's parents dropped her off in the morning, and Mrs. Garret took her home at night.

On the third night, after they had left, Max struggled with how he was going to break his news to Paige, who expected their lives to return to the way they had been after his release.

When she joined Max and his mother the following day, the mood in the room was different. Mrs. Garret looked at her with regret and couldn't bear to look her in the eye on her way out. Concerned Max's condition may have taken a turn for the worse, Paige called out to her before she could exit. "Is everything OK, Mrs. Garret?" She stood with the door open.

"Max has to tell you something, Paige," Barbara Garret replied with a frown and took leave of them.

Bracing himself for the moment he had been preparing for the last few days, Max summoned his courage and announced to Paige, "I'm not going home, Paige." His voice was overcome with regret.

"What do you mean? You're scheduled to be released tomorrow! I was going to come over to your place right after!" Paige protested.

"I am being released tomorrow, Paige, but I'm not coming home," Max confirmed.

It seemed that Paige had been warped from the hospital room into the parking lot, her head was spinning so rapidly. She gasped for air but felt herself choking on her own tears, unable to respond to the man outside who asked her if she was OK. She held one hand out to him and nodded, unable to speak after the news she had just received.

She felt selfish in her sorrow but was overcome by grief all the same. Hillshire Medical may have been three miles from her house, but she needed a walk all the same. She had to process what Max had told her, which had sent her blasting through the hospital doors, crying the same way she had when her great aunt had died. Making her way through the part of Middleton City her parents forbade her to traverse, she looked at neon lights from a liquor store and thought if she had any money on her, she should like to get good and drunk.

When she got home in the late afternoon, she grabbed a bottle of her mother's wine and did just that. She gulped the wine until she felt dizzy and numb, then hid the bottle in a boot in her closet and passed out. When her mother got home and saw her asleep in bed, she tried to awaken her for dinner but relented, figuring her daughter hadn't gotten a full night's rest.

The next morning was a complete blur. Paige had never been much of a drinker and still felt plastered. After dropping her daughter off, Lynne Edmundson looked on in concern: Paige hardly said a word to her mother that morning on the ride in and looked distressed. Her hair was knotted, and she was wearing an outfit she wouldn't even lounge around the house in, much less go to school in. Once indoors, Paige lumbered from homeroom to her classes and was in a fog until she overheard Wendy talking about her in the cafeteria. "My mom says she visited the freak, like, every day," Wendy said to Deidre just loud enough for Paige, sitting alone at the table behind them, to hear.

Molly Johnson chimed in, "Too bad she wasn't with the psycho when he blew himself up." That brought on a cackle of laughter from all the girls at the lunch table, except for Lana Karrington, who took great offense.

Before Lana could oppose Molly's distasteful comment, Deidre yelled over the laughter. "Totally! Lucky for us the loser only blew himself up," Deidre said in Paige's direction.

"How can you say that? That you wish she had been blown up too? Deidre, you and Paige were friends before any of us even knew each other. Since, like, second grade!"

Deidre held her mouth open, appalled at Lana's protest. She was about to tell her to shut her mouth but was defended by Wendy. "*Were* friends—as in, past tense, before she ditched us for Maniac Max, who wanted to kill us all," she said, speaking the sentiments of her mother, who was disgusted by Paige's sympathy for Max.

The reaction Deidre had been hoping for was not given by Paige. She ignored Deidre, as she normally did, but something was different. Paige looked like shit, which meant she felt like shit. Deidre smelled blood and was not about to relent until she got a reaction.

"Give me your banana," Deidre demanded as she pulled Wendy's lunch away from her without waiting for a response. She cocked her arm back, aiming for the back of Paige's head, which was hung low, buried in a book.

Paige had heard every word they had said about her and Max. She felt her blood boiling and could have kicked herself for not getting new batteries for her Walkman.

A firm hand clenched Deidre's forearm before she could throw the banana at Paige. She swung her head around in surprise and saw the face of Katherine Jalorean, who said, "Ms. Lisbon, I don't think that a potential valedictorian should be behaving like this."

Angered but still composed, Deidre readied her defense.

"I was just stretching," Deidre said, pulling her arm free from the teacher's grip.

"Yeah, besides, according to what my mom said, Paige likes ripe charred bananas," Wendy said, causing an eruption of laughter from the group, save for Allison.

Inspired by Wendy's crack, Deidre felt the need to undermine Ms. Jalorean's attempt to discipline her and yelled back to her minion, "No, no, he blew his nuts off, right? Anybody got grapes?" She was quite pleased with herself and the continuation of laughter that had now gotten Paige's attention, the scene behind her impossible to ignore any further. Deidre stared at the teacher, whom she had always sensed didn't like her; she became sure of it when Ms. Jalorean continued.

"I found some irregularities with the grades I submitted for you the last two terms, Ms. Lisbon. I wonder if you will still be laughing once I have them amended," she said, removing the cocky smile from Deidre's face. Ms. Jalorean stepped away from the laughter, which had died down, and headed off Paige before she could confront her tormentors. "Paige, look, I don't have a class for fifth period. If you don't want to deal with this the rest of the year, you are more than welcome to have a later lunch in my room if you—"

Her solution was interrupted by Paige, who was no longer in a fog of a hangover but instead in a fit of anger. She was listening to her teacher but was locked in on Deidre. Ms. Jalorean was talking to her, but she had a ringing in her ear that made her inaudible.

"Paige? How is Max?" Ms. Jalorean asked a third time, finally being heard.

"He's recovered just fine, and in spite of what these nitwits say, his male equipment is just fine. It's just—"

Ms. Jalorean looked at her with a mixture of curiosity and sincerity. "Just what? Paige, what?" she asked.

"It's just, he can never have kids, and he's moving away forever to North Dakota with his aunt," Paige answered in anger, as if hearing herself say it aloud had confirmed the reality she had so desperately drowned out after she had lost her senses over hearing the words yesterday.

She felt her heart beating in her throat, her composure gone; as she continued, her emotions got the better of her, so much so that she was no longer talking to her teacher but screaming at Deidre, who smiled and stared back at her, looking as cocky as ever while Paige shouted over her. "Because of tramps that have to fuck people other than their boyfriends," Paige yelled in Deidre's face, prompting her to get up from her seat. The two girls stood face-to-face like boxers who were being given directions from a referee. Paige's comment was damaging to Deidre, but she couldn't lose face, so she gave an unfazed smile and whispered in her ear a little something to make her seem crazy.

"Go ahead, Pagey, see what happens. I will fuck you up, bitch. I'll make you scream and howl worse than Elvis did when I let go of the match."

Deidre calmly admitted to Paige what she had already suspected. Prior to Max's accident, it had been her turn to wear Dominic's ring around her necklace. When she had been at Max's bedside, hoping for his recovery, she had made a habit of holding the ring, and it had provided her with a sense of security and comfort. She had not realized this, but the moment Deidre had sprung up and gotten in her face, she had taken hold of it wither left hand. Once she let go of the ring and it tugged on the chain and the back of her neck, everything moved in slow motion.

With both hands she took hold of Deidre's head and bashed her own skull into the center of Deidre's face, then bit her so hard in her face that she felt Deidre's teeth from the outside of her cheek. Loyal as the girls were to Deidre, they wouldn't dare come to her aid as Paige was locked on her face like a rabid beast on the brink of starvation.

But she was pulled off of Deidre by a sea of hands, and once she could no longer get at her, she clenched the ring on her necklace with both hands, screaming, "This isn't over! You think that's bad! Your day will come! Mark my words, Dee Dee. Mark my words!" Paige repeated hysterically as she was lifted out of the cafeteria with Deidre's blood running from her mouth and pieces of her flesh embedded in her teeth.

That was Paige's last day at Middleton High. The Lisbons filed a lawsuit against the school, pressuring them to expel Paige permanently.

In an odd stroke of luck, Paige was able to finish senior year at nearby Kensintin High Prep. A glowing recommendation from Katherine Jalorean, who had taught there in the past, had aided her late application. Early on she had to take two buses just to get to school but eventually caught a ride with Ed Darby, the same Ed Darby who had been introduced to her by Adam the previous year. The same boy whom she had had to remind repeatedly that she had a boyfriend.

Sinking her teeth into Deidre's face was one of the best things Paige could have done for herself. Max was gone, and other than Ms. Jalorean, she had not a single friend in the entire school. The change of scenery did her good and kept her from dwelling on the love that was lost to her. The phone number in North Dakota was disconnected. She managed to get Barbara Garret on the phone, but when they spoke, nothing Max's mom said made sense. It was obvious his injury and departure to her sister's in North Dakota had been too much for her fragile state of mind to endure. Paige mailed four letters, which went unanswered, and knocked on the Garrets' door, only to be screamed at by Bill Garret.

It was Ed who kept Paige from sinking into a depression over losing Max. He was a bit goofy and irrational, but one quality Ed Darby possessed was persistence. He pulled the sports car his grandparents had bought him up to Paige's driveway every morning before school and dropped her home every day. He came on strong and was determined to make Paige his girl.

Chapter 12:

SALVAGE OR SALVATION?

A substantial settlement was paid out to Deidre Lisbon from Middleton High, especially after she parlayed the case of her injuries due to what she described to her lawyer as rape by the school's guidance counselor. It was agreed that Moretz's indiscretions, as the school board described it, would not be made a public matter so long as Deidre was compensated for pain and suffering. Moretz was forced into early retirement and tutored part-time to make ends meet.

A wave of sympathy was ridden by Deidre Lisbon that year for her injuries, accompanied by hushed whispers that she had been abused by Counselor Moretz. She was more or less appointed class valedictorian, the result of another unspoken agreement, in addition to her receiving hush money from the school board. She needed some stitches in her mouth but after some surgery, was left with a small vanity scar.

Ross was in love with her, but his lack of potential made him unattractive in her eyes, and she dumped him on the last day of school. She brought herself a red convertible and showed up fashionably late to every graduation party that summer. She still kept in touch with her girls and would bestow upon them the occasional blessing of coming with her to hang out with the money crowd she had fallen in with.

Distraught after Deidre dumped him, Ross attacked Dwayne at the final graduation party at Greg's house. After being beaten and humiliated, Dwayne decided to join the police force, where his father was still active; his father also would have his best interests at heart. One evening he returned to the station to see a brick had been thrown through the back window of his car. He couldn't confirm who had done it, but he had a very good idea as to who it may have been. The first few years of patrol, every time he got a call for a body, part of him secretly hoped it was Ross Aberdeen. Dwayne never married, and even as a member of the force, he still felt like an outsider.

After graduating from Middleton, Greg Chapman received a full scholarship to college for his prowess on the football field. He was unable to continue his use of steroids due to the stringent testing imposed at the college level, his performance suffered, and he was cut from the team and lost his scholarship. He settled in Preytin, the next town over from Middleton Township, and found work as a car salesman. He also coached part-time as an assistant to his old coach Harold McCarmick, who was still at the helm for the Middleton Rams.

The years went on, but life did not for many in Middleton City. The kind librarian Ms. Evalum, who provided a terrified young Max Garret with sanctuary in the school library, passed away peacefully. Marilyn McCreery, the secretary to former guidance counselor Tim Moretz, had a much more gruesome passing. She never retired from Middleton; walking to work one morning, she was robbed and murdered, her body stuffed into the abandoned jewelry store, undiscovered for weeks.

Once Adam and Carrie found success in the local music scene, they were signed by a major record label, married one another, and relocated to New York. While their careers spanned the globe, they never forgot their roots, frequently referring to a couple named Max and Paige in their songs and occasionally playing the song "Middleton's Crossing" in live performances.

After Max settled in North Dakota with his aunt, he never graduated. The prospect of starting a new school was one he refused to entertain, and being of age, he did not have to. Ida noticed Max's ability to work with his hands repairing and fixing things for her and suggested the service as an outlet to expand on his talents. She was right to a certain degree, but personality conflicts seemed to follow Max wherever he went.

The prayers of Barbara Garret were never enough to keep her husband from starting his days waiting for the owner to open the door of the Candlelight Tavern. The illness that claimed her mind soon took over her body once she fell ill. In the last coherent letter written to her sister, she asked that her condition be kept secret so as to not worry her son, who, according to Ida, had "managed a nice life for himself there." Barbara Garret died shortly after Max enlisted in the service; he was overseas when he got the news. When she passed away, few took notice outside her church group, and those who did referred to her as the mother of Maniac Max who had blown himself up.

Her funeral was organized by Johnny from J&J produce and the headstone paid for by Paige who, when questioned by Ed Darby as to why she never removed the "gaudy" gold ring with the "obnoxious" red ruby set in it, would simply reply, "It's important to me."

After exhausting all attempts at communication with Max, Paige accepted Ed's request to date her. She accepted that she'd not see Max again until the next life. She remained faithful to Ed and convinced herself to love him as he did her. They married in 1999, the same year Max Garret was declared AWOL from the military.

In need of a career, Max attended trade school in the evenings at a local community college, where he met Carolyn Pastrel. She was smart, self-sufficient, and good-humored, qualities that reminded him of Paige, whom he never stopped thinking of. He told Carolyn on their third date of his inability to have children, and unlike girls he had dated before, she had no problem whatsoever with it. They were in complete agreement that once married, they would adopt. Max requested that if it was a boy, he be named Dominic; if a girl, Paige.

News from Middleton was nonexistent in North Dakota. Here and there a story from Hessian's Cliff, Max's grandfather's old town, refreshed his memory about those tumultuous years back East. He thought of Paige often but never Middleton; a major part of him wanted to forget the abuse and torture he had endured there altogether. He figured he'd live and die and never see the town again. After years on a waiting list at the adoption agency, Caroline delivered him the good news. Carolyn and Max were going to have a little girl, who'd have two loving parents and never endure the suffering he had. Yes, Max Garret looked at the bright future that lay ahead, his time with Middleton and the army a distant memory.

Yet, in spite of best efforts, fate can be cruel, and old scars can reopen when one receives a new wound. A new wound lay in wait for Max Garret, one that'd awaken the thirst for revenge he hadn't lusted after since he had lain in that pile of rubble in his basement. Though dormant inside him, vengeance had been given birth, and vengeance would return to Middleton.

PART II:
RECOVERY OF TRAGEDY

You're gonna learn about loss.
—Max Cady in *Cape Fear* (1991)

Chapter 13:
LIFE WORTH LIVING

Thursday, September 4, 2008

The marimba ringtone sounded, causing Carolyn Garret to climb over moving boxes in her kitchen. Seeing his wife hurdling their possessions to get to her cell phone amused Max. He figured it was his mother-in-law calling for the umpteenth time to see how the move had gone and how her granddaughter Paige was doing. The Pastrels didn't like them moving such a distance, but the area had the best customer base Max could establish for his home security company. When he realized it was Ms. Kellan from the adoption agency Carolyn was speaking to, he eavesdropped attentively.

"Words can't express how happy we are that Paige has made a smooth transition into your family," Ms. Kellan said to Carolyn, who smiled as if she could be seen on the other end of the phone.

"Well, Max's business is out here, and she's been so good about it. We love her to pieces, and she's so excited to start the private school we're sending her to out here," Carolyn responded as Max looked on in complete admiration of her sincerity. He thought himself so fortunate to have married such a loving and understanding woman, who was still a knockout in a flannel bathrobe, wool boots, and boxer shorts.

"Excellent, Mrs. Garret, and thank you for keeping us posted with your new address and little Paige's progression."

Carolyn nodded while tussling with the tie to her bathrobe, which had gotten stuck in the refrigerator door, much to Max's amusement. It was an inopportune time for a phone call as she had to get Paige ready and drop her off at school. She was in a rush but made time for the woman responsible for finalizing Paige's placement with the Garrets. Carolyn sought to end the conversation graciously rather than lie and say her mother was on the other line. She turned the phone to her other ear, noticing Max looking at her exposed midsection with humor.

"She's everything we could have ever hoped for and more, Ms. Kellan! You are forever in our graces for helping us with our little angel," Carolyn concluded as she knotted her robe and gave Max a chastising grin.

"I'm just glad to hear things have worked out for you folks. Unfortunately, in my line of work, you come to realize in many cases it does not, especially after the child is over three years old. Best of luck to you and your family, Mrs. Garret. Goodbye," Ms. Kellan concluded, hanging up before Carolyn had a chance to close the conversation. Looking at Max doing his best to prepare breakfast while she was on the phone and talking to her daughter had her caught in a moment. She had no regrets and was as happy as she figured she could be. She hung up her phone, held it to her chest, and smiled.

"Is mama bear going to get in on some of these world-class blueberry pancakes?" Max offered, causing his daughter to giggle. Paige was young but old enough to understand her mother's pancakes were always better than her father's. Cooking responsibilities for Max were relegated to times of emergency. If Carolyn had the flu or was not home, he was on deck.

Humored by her daughter's giggle and her husband, who sounded convincing about his "world-class" breakfast, which looked more like burnt toast than a pancake, Carolyn responded, "No, mama bear is taking over so papa is on time to meet his big-shot client."

After marriage the Garrets had had long discussions about what kind of parents they wanted to be. Prior to Paige's placement, they had agreed infantile baby talk was out of the question. They were adopting a toddler, not an infant. While they stuck to many of their parenting rules, the happy little girl who had brought so much love into their lives caused that rule to fall by the wayside. After Max read the story of Goldilocks and the Three Bears to her, Paige called them mama and papa bear so much they began saying it to one another.

With a parting kiss goodbye for both of his girls, Max headed out the front door, only to return a few seconds later. "Here, Car, your first piece of mail at the new address," Max said, reemerging into the kitchen, where Carolyn was making a fresh batch of pancakes.

Taking the letter, she questioned the use of her maiden name from the sender. "Ms. Carolyn Pastrel?"

"Secret admirer? Someone still think you're a free agent?" Max teased, looking at Paige. "Should your dad be jealous?" he continued, causing Paige to gesture an adorable shrug of confusion to him.

"Secret admirer!" Carolyn scoffed after inspecting the letter, then patted Max's arm playfully and explained, "It's for my class reunion, jerk!"

"Well, in that case, you are single because I'm not going."

"Before you know it, she's going to be in high school and you won't be able to avoid school functions so easily, Mr. Garret."

After kissing Paige goodbye once more, he hugged Carolyn, smiled at her, and said, "Well, for today it's a good thing for me she's only starting second grade, Mrs. Pastrel-Garret." He kissed her and headed for the door, already missing his family the moment he got into his van and drove off for work.

In the kitchen Carolyn continued speaking to her daughter. "Your father sure hates school," she said, pinching her nose playfully, then poured her orange juice and continued, "I bet if he could, he would have us homeschool you."

"I like school," Paige announced.

"I know you do, and you know we named you after one of your dad's best friends from school. Did he ever tell you that?"

"A thousand times," Paige responded as Carolyn observed she was playing with her food more than eating it.

"OK, well, let's get you dressed. I have the uniform shirt for you, honey, but there were no skirts at the school store, so I got you pants for the time being."

"All the other girls will have dresses?" Paige questioned with concern.

"Just wait until tomorrow, honey. If the teacher or anyone says anything, tell her we just moved. Besides, Katherine Hepburn wore slacks, and it worked out all right for her."

"Who's that?" Paige questioned, leaving Carolyn unable to answer, overcome by the sound of the precious little girl she and Max were so fortunate to be blessed with. For a moment she wondered if those who had given birth to her had any idea as to what they had missed out on. The moment passed quickly as Paige questioned her again.

"Mommy, who's Katerine Heps-ber-n?" she said, freezing the smile on her mother's face.

Carolyn took a glance at the clock on the stove and panicked. "She was big, sweetheart—trust me; you just need to know she wore pants and get yours on. Come on, angel. I don't want to rush with you in the car."

Carrying his equipment back to his utility van, Max was pleased. The job had gone smoothly and left him ahead of schedule. The couple walked him out to the driveway and, once he packed up, he handed the customer his card. The man took it and said, "Can't thank you enough for coming out on such short notice. Our dog's great, but around the corner, they have a shepherd and got broken into. I mean, it happens, but since my wife's expecting, I wanted to shore the place up, especially with money and jobs scarce all over now," he said, shaking Max's hand in appreciation.

"As I tell all my customers, it's not a bad investment, and you can't put a price on peace of mind. Boy or girl?" Max questioned, looking at the woman, who held her womb in a guarded manner.

"A little girl," the man replied, putting one arm around his wife as Max hopped into his van.

"We have a little woman of our own, and I'd go to the ends of the earth to protect her. Believe me, I understand," Max answered, tossing the metallic clipboard onto the passenger side seat. He heard a hushed discussion and turned to see the man's wife nodding in approval.

"You sure you won't stay for dinner? Don's grilling up a pork roll we ordered. You ever have pork roll?" the woman asked, bringing a reminiscing smile to Max's face.

"Yes, I have, but not for a very long time. If I didn't have another installation scheduled, I'd gladly take you up on that. It's very kind of you. Thank you." Max was ready to head out and wrap up his day as all the talk of dinner had him concerned about what his wife and daughter were having. A lot of the kitchen boxes were still unpacked, and he was not familiar with places in the area. He wanted to finish up the next job and head home and see how work had been for Carolyn and school for Paige.

His familiarity with pork roll sparked Don's interest, though, and before he could put the van in drive, Max heard, "I figured you were from back East! You from Jersey?" Don's question went unanswered as Max ignored it and changed the conversation.

"OK, number is on the unit, along with my personal number and email. Any problems, call me right away. Thanks for the job, and I appreciate any referrals. Take care now," Max said, pulling out of the driveway in a rush. Don and his wife waved goodbye to him.

"Nice guy, huh? I figured he was from tristate; wonder why he wouldn't say where. Hell of a scar on his neck coming out of his collar. You see that?"

"No. Maybe he didn't hear you," his wife suggested.

"Yeah. Little odd, though," Don replied, unsatisfied.

Max phoned the next customer on his hands-free to announce an early arrival. This particular customer had expressed great concern with the security of their home on the preapplication.

"Thank you for calling ahead. Once you're out front, phone me, and I'll buzz you in at the gate."

"All right. I'm just about five or ten minutes away."

The voice over his van's speakers sounded carefree. Max found the low growl of Mr. Grady a bit chilling, almost too calm.

The call ended, and music returned to the van abruptly. It was a song Max was familiar with, a favorite of a girl he had known and loved many years ago. He smiled, reflecting on Paige Edmundson as he listened to "In Your Eyes" by Peter Gabriel, one of her favorite songs then.

The song was cut off by the sound of his phone ringing. Glancing at the name displayed on the phone propped into his dashboard, Max smiled, seeing, "CAROLYN HOUSE PHONE." "Hello, my lovely wife; how was work and school?" he answered.

"Well, I'm stuffed in a little cubicle, and our daughter caught some flack over her pants."

"I'm ahead of schedule, and I'll be home right after this installation. I'll be home as soon as I can; I want to hear all about it."

"Well, hurry up, we miss you! Hang on, somebody wants to talk to you."

"Hi, Daddy," Paige said, bringing enthusiasm to Max's face as he scanned the street for Grady's address.

"Hi, princess! I'm going to be home soon, OK? Everything OK at school?" Max asked.

Carolyn returned to the line, and Max could hear her speaking to Paige in the background.

"You don't want to talk to your dad?" she questioned, then returned to conversing with Max.

"Hey, hurry home. Your daughter and I are having separation anxiety over here," Carolyn explained with a hint of humor in her voice.

"Give her a kiss from me until I get back. Love you," Max said, finally locating the job site, the only home on an otherwise desolate street. "Love you too," Carolyn responded, ending the call. Max pulled into the pitch-black driveway; the only thing visible in his headlights was the slew of political signage leading up the path.

"I hope this guy's not a nut," Max muttered, wondering what good all the signs did in such a remote, unseen area. Before he started working for himself, Max had been to countless homes for the security firm, and when it came to political signs, he and his coworkers had a tried and tested method of estimation. It wasn't very scientific, but it was effective nonetheless. Three to five signs were safe but suspicious. Anything over five was the danger zone, and more than ten indicated they were either the candidate running for office or they were off the yelzabob. A full-on nutter, buck-fucking crazy, all the way wacked.

He counted fifteen, all with similar slogans: "COUNTRY FIRST," "McCain Palin 08," "McCain for president in 08," and a handwritten poster with black print on white board that read, "Senator Obama Bin Laden, Be Lyin," with an image depicting the Democratic nominee in a turban.

"Of course he's a nut. Great," Max mumbled. As rainfall pelted the roof of his van, he rolled down his window and spoke into an outside speaker planted in the ground.

"Mr. Grady? Max Garret with Garret Securities," he announced. The voice coming back over the speaker crackled and was inaudible to him as it shorted in and out. The pace of the rain increased as Max pulled his phone from the dash to notify the customer he could not hear him. The downpour rattled on the roof. Just as he was about to redial Grady's number, the iron gates before him swung open, revealing Mr. Grady, who had opened them manually.

He waved Max forward onto the property, his other hand gripping an umbrella. Walking along the van slowly, unbothered by the downpour, Grady grinned at Max and pointed him to the entrance. Once indoors, Max wondered just what it was that Mr. Grady wished to protect as his home was virtually empty of any belongings. Just a few pieces of covered furniture were scattered in the large mansion, which could have been mistaken for a small gothic cathedral.

"Part of it was once a wine cellar, heh. Should have seen the pussy I got the place from. Got no use for wine. I'm a scotch man myself," Grady said, leading Max down the steps. He told him where he wanted the system in-stalled. Max preferred to be left alone when working. He couldn't stand to be hovered over by customers like Mr. Grady, who watched his every move. Accustomed to this type of behavior, Max said nothing of the interruptions and questions posed to him by Mr. Grady.

After an hour and a half of labor and multiple trips back out to his van for materials, the job was finished. Max conducted a test run of the system and provided Mr. Grady with directions.

"So I just put my hand flat against here, and I'm in, right?" Grady asked Max.

"Yes, sir. I know you were concerned about a prolonged entry."

"You're goddamned right! What good is it having an arsenal if I have to dial a safe just to get to it?"

"Well, you have here one of the finest packages I install. It's top-of-the-line," Max stated with pride, his description interrupted by the sight of the assault rifle and military-grade equipment Grady was getting prepped to load behind the secured door.

"I know, right? It's a bit overwhelming. Bitch of a wife makes me keep the bulk of it down here. We only live here for a season, which is why I want this vaulted. This one comes with me, though." Grady cackled with pride. Max was uneasy with his customer's casual demeanor, as well as with the cavalier way he was handling the weapon.

"Check this out!" Grady said, motioning for Max to take the gun from him. Max shook his head in refusal.

"Hey, chill out, man! I'm no gun nut or anything! I'm an old vet who became a collector is all," protested Grady, who was a bit perturbed by Max's prudence.

"I'm fine, thank you."

"No rounds in it. Don't be scared."

"Oh, I'm not; it's just, I haven't held or even seen one since I was discharged."

"Oh, honorable?" Grady questioned, his interest in Max piqued.

Packing up his drill and equipment, Max responded in the least offensive way he could think of after being asked about such a personal matter. He smiled at his customer and replied to him dismissively, "Doesn't really matter, now does it? You're all set here, Mr. Grady." Max concluded speaking with his tools in hand, waiting for Grady to usher him out.

Instead Grady peered at the overlapping flesh that ran down the left side of Max's neck. He had become wildly curious about it while watching Max work.

"I'm sorry. I certainly didn't intend to pry. See you were injured." Grady stated a false apology.

Max laughed, initially confused by his observation, and responded, "Oh, this?" motioning his shoulder to the left side of his neck. "No offense taken. Besides I got this from school, not the service."

"You betcha. Well, I'm out of here for the season once I lock up, but when I get back, I could sure use a range partner if you want—if you're up for it."

"Sure, why not? Here's my card. Give me a call, and of course you can contact me or operate the system via wireless app as well." Max made his way back up the steps, positive he'd never wind up shooting with Mr. Grady, as well as ensuring he had not offended his customer.

"Sounds good, Maximillian Garret. We need to stick together! 'Specially since they want to put a goddamned Arab jungle bunny in the White House, he-he," Grady called out from the garage. Max stopped dead in his tracks, ignoring the teeming rain. It'd been decades since he'd been referred to by that name, and he found it unpleasing to his old friend's memory to hear Mr. Grady speak it.

Lifting his head, Max continued to his van and opened the double doors in the rear, still feeling the eyes of Mr. Grady boring into his back directly behind him. He thanked Mr. Grady for his business and attempted to leave, but it'd be another two hours before he left the company of Mr. Ivan Grady, whose address was, ironically, 89 Middleton Street.

The teeming downpour he had encountered at Grady's gate resumed as Max headed into the house. He smiled at the note from Carolyn under the stove light. After warming the dinner she had left wrapped for him, he peeked into Paige's room. Her angelic face peeking out from the covers provided him with an inner warmth. He quietly tossed his wet uniform in the hamper and tried to sneak into the bedroom without waking Carolyn.

"If this is what getting home early means, I'm worried about when you're late," she said, facing the window. Max jumped back, surprised by his wide-awake wife's voice. He joined her in bed and told her about his day. Carolyn enjoyed hearing about Max's clients. Some of the descriptions he gave her were far more exciting than anything she saw on reality TV.

Normally an eccentric like Ivan Grady, who lived in an imposing, heavily armed mansion would have sparked her interest, but she had missed Max terribly. Carolyn aggressively massaged his shoulders as Max went on explaining his delay.

"Then I'm ready to go. I'm out the door, and he starts pulling crates of grenades and all other kinds of shit from his garage. It was awkward; he was a whack-out, but he had purchased my most expensive product, Car, and the economy is so bad. I'm so sorry I missed our first dinner here."

Max apologized as Carolyn kissed him gently on his back shoulder. "Scary wondering what a guy like that wants all that firepower for."

Having heard enough, Carolyn shoved Max on his back and rolled atop of him playfully and continued kneading his skin with her fingers. She cautiously ran her fingertips over the scarred left side of his body. She knew the overlapping skin brought him no pain, but it always made her hesitant. The sight of Max unclothed could likely horrify someone who didn't know him, but she enjoyed the uniqueness of his body and always told him that scars spoke volumes over tattoos every time he suggested masking them in ink.

"Oh, I don't mind you standing me up for dinner; it's your daughter you need to worry about," she said. Her delicate aggressiveness was always such a turn-on to him.

Unable to relax, Max spoke his thoughts once Carolyn brought up Paige. "You said they gave her trouble about not having the dress?"

"She just said one of the kids called her a boy and some of them giggled is all," Carolyn replied nonchalantly, continuing to gyrate seductively. Max took hold of her waist, alarmed.

"Called her a boy? And they all laughed at her? What do you mean?" Max asked, grabbing Carolyn's wrist to get her attention.

"Honey, calm down. New kid always gets ragged on a bit on the first day, right?" Carolyn asked, naïve of the severity of the insult in Max's eyes. "It wasn't anything major. Besides, she said she really likes it there, OK? OK?" she asked a second time of her husband, whose mind seemed elsewhere.

Snapping out of his brief daze, Max replied, "Yeah, sure. Just make sure you get her the right uniform as soon as possible."

"Picking it up tomorrow; I'm on it," Carolyn whispered in his ear, her reassuring tone a comfort.

In a mischievous voice, he said back to her, "Oh, you're on it all right."

Carolyn giggled as he returned his hands to her waist, wrestled her aside, and positioned himself on top of her. She rolled over and wiggled her backside against his groin. Aroused, he entered her slowly, then his thrusts sped up and became rampant. As he lost himself, Max's mind drifted as his body reacted to the flashbacks occurring in his head. A vision of him clapping the erasers after his detention at Middleton High was followed by him hitting his father with the ice skate. Dominic's voice repeated, "Everything's gonna be all right, Maximillian." It echoed and was accompanied by a vision of Dwayne and Deidre under the bleachers. Sweat beaded up on his brow as he pounded into Carolyn violently and images of Ross, Greg, Dwayne beating him caused him to take hold of his wife by her hair with his left hand, his right with a firm grip on her throat as he slammed into her even harder.

Once he had climaxed, he released her, flung himself backward, and struggled for air. The final visions of his mother's smile on the first day of school and Paige Edmundson kissing him on his forehead in the hospital brought him out of his trance.

"What are you trying to do, drive nails with that hammer back there, Max? Christ!" Carolyn exclaimed, joking about Max's overwhelming aggression.

"I'm sorry, Car. I just—" Before he could finish, she kissed him on his sweat-covered forehead and went to the bathroom attached to their bedroom.

"I'm not complaining. Just let your wife know when you might crush her pelvis out of nowhere, Dirk Diggler," she said, continuing her humor while Max sat up at the foot of the bed, still winded.

"I'm sorry. It's just when I get into it, sometimes I just…" he explained as Carolyn put on her robe and completed his sentence.

"You just really get into it. I know." The conversation was cut off by the sound of movement outside their bedroom door. Carolyn hushed Max as a nervous voice spoke from the darkened hallway.

"Daddy? Mom? I heard noises in my room. I'm scared," Paige called out to them.

"OK, honey, come in here. You want to stay in our bed tonight?" Carolyn called out in the same comforting tone she had used to whisper to Max.

"Yes, please," Paige said, running up to the foot of the bed and into her father's arms.

"How about I do you one better? Who wants a story read to them?" Max asked, causing excitement to overcome any fear his daughter had had seconds ago.

"All her stories are still packed up, Max," Carolyn said.

"Then I'll just have to tell you a new one while you show me your fabulous new room! Come on." Max encouraged the excited little girl, who was already pulling him by the hand.

Looking back at Carolyn, Max grinned while playfully exaggerating the force he was being pulled away with.

"Not too late, you two. Give me a hug and kiss good night first, sweetheart," Carolyn said, stopping them at the bedroom door. Her instructions prompted Max to shove his face in front of her playfully and pucker his lips with his eyes closed.

"Not you—my daughter, you goof!" Carolyn teased as Paige rushed up to her and ran back to the door.

It was no wonder Paige was scared in the bedroom, Max thought, as the only thing in it was furniture and large moving boxes. He handed her the stuffed animal giraffe, tucked her in, and started the first story that came to mind. Within minutes she was half-asleep but still listening.

"Then he was made head of the knights' watch." Max spoke softly in an attempt to conclude his story.

"Did he ever see his sister again?" Paige questioned, notifying her father she was still awake. Before he could respond to her inquiry she yawned and delivered a follow-up question. "What happened to the dragon queen?"

"Well, we have to save some for next time, don't we, honey?"

"Can you stay until I'm asleep completely?"

"Of course, my angel. I'd sing you a lullaby if I knew any."

"Sing anything to me, please."

"I'll try, princess, but I'm just a novice, and I don't remember many songs either."

Wide awake, Carolyn listened to the sound of Max singing Poison's "Every Rose Has Its Thorn" to Paige through the vent in the master bedroom. His strong but gentle voice overwhelmed her with love for him. If her heart had eyes, it'd be weeping tears of joy, she thought. She tightly gripped the pillow Max was not using and fell fast asleep; Paige did as well.

Quietly unpacking the bedroom while Paige slept, Max unboxed all of her things, then fell asleep beside her bed just before daybreak. The combination of Carolyn opening the door to Paige's room and the daylight creeping in the window made Max groan. Carolyn sat beside him on the floor Indian style and kissed him softly as he came to.

"Coffee, Lord Stark," she said to him, smiling.

"Why yes. Good morning, m'lady."

"She's going to grow up thinking her father's a literary genius, baffled as to why he installs alarms for a living, if you keep up your copyright infringement."

"Well, in my defense, she's too young for that story anyway. Think of it as edited CliffsNotes, by me,"

"Oh, I enjoyed every word of it from the vent in our room."

"Speaking of, I think I know what noises she heard. This house is brand-new, and sound travels like it is a tunnel."

"I swear I heard an eighties power ballad coming out of the vent in our room as well. You hear anything like that?" Carolyn teased.

"I don't know what you are talking about," Max replied, trying to keep a straight face.

"Sure, you heard it the same way every cowboy sings his sad, sad song, though, right?" Carolyn continued, causing Max to set down the coffee and wrestle her. Max tickled her, and she erupted in laughter, waking Paige.

"Good morning, angel," Carolyn called up to her, still laughing from Max pawing at her.

"Get off me! Come on, Paige, let's get you some breakfast so your dad can get ready for rehearsal with the band today." Carolyn rose to her feet and led Paige out of her bedroom.

"Hey, I used to be in a band," Max joked, still on the floor in Paige's room. "Yeah, I used to be," he repeated to himself more seriously as he got up and prepared for his day.

Chapter 14:
SNAKES

The ball rattled the chain fence next to Paige as a little boy with a big head ran to retrieve it. She hardly noticed him as she was focused on a small frog in a clump of weed rooted up from the fence's foundation. The boy grabbed the ball as it ricocheted back to him and walked closer to see what had Paige Garret in such a state of amazement.

"What is that?" he asked of the peculiar new girl who was wearing pants instead of a dress.

"Shh, don't scare him. It's a tiny frog," Paige whispered.

"Throw it in! What are you doing?" a second boy called out to the big-headed boy impatiently. Receiving no response, he ran to where Paige and the other boy were standing and slapped the ball from his hands; once the ball was freed from his hands, the first boy pointed at the bottom of the fence in excitement, getting the attention of the boy who was content to have the ball back in his hands.

"She found a tiny frog," the boy announced to the other, sharing a fraction of Paige's excitement over the creature, which he had expected to be bright green.

"So? Frogs just get eaten by snakes. They're gross and stupid," the second boy replied, dribbling the ball to himself, hoping to entice the first boy to resume playing with him.

"No, they are not," Paige protested. "Frogs have been alive as long as the dinosaurs. My dad told me a story about a frog that was a prince," she continued, much to the annoyance of the boy, who was pounding the ball against the blacktop with both hands.

"Well, your dad's an idiot!" he responded.

"Yeah, that's so stupid!" the big-headed boy added.

"He is not!" Paige yelled back.

"Yes, he is. Your dad's stupid, and your mom's fat!" the boy continued, pleased that he had gotten such a reaction from Paige, while his friend laughed, encouraging him.

The frog leaped out from the pile of weeds, stirred by the commotion of the ball being bounced close to it. The dribbling boy hoisted the ball over his head and announced with pleasure, "I'm gonna peg it!"

"No! Don't! Stop," Paige cried as he hurled the ball with an overhead toss at the creature below him, missing it badly due to the force he had tried to crush it with. The ball careened as he attempted to stomp on the frog as it retreated back to the clump of grass by the fence. But he failed in that as well.

A bell sounded, signaling the end of the recess period. The two boys sprinted back to the door. The big-headed boy kicked the ball as hard as he could at Paige, before they rejoined the rest of the class in line. Paige shuddered as the ball went past her and hit the fence. She saw the frog on the other side, unharmed from the attempts to hurt it, and smiled. She picked up the ball and began to bounce it herself as an adult walked up to her.

"What's your name, honey?" the woman asked.

"I'm Paige, Paige Garret," she answered cautiously to the inquisitive stranger.

"Well, Paige Garret, when the bell rings, we go back inside." Paige hugged the ball with both arms and looked at the boys from her class roughhousing on the way back into the school.

"OK, I'm coming," she responded in defeated hesitation.

The lighting in the Bismark Bar was so poor Max needed a headlamp to finish the install. Privately he suspected what the place needed for security was lighting, rather than an alarm. He tinkered with wiring in the darkened corner, got down from his ladder, and tested the system. Then he collapsed his ladder and started cleaning up. He was happy to be finished but concerned about the absent owner. Ivan Grady's check had been returned, and he was away for the season.

The only other person in the closed tavern with him was a barmaid restocking the cooler. After going outside to pack up the van, he walked back in with the metallic clipboard and the triplicate copy of the work order he needed signed.

The jukebox randomly kicked on, playing "Nothing Else Matters" by Metallica.

"Hey, alarm guy! How's about a hand over here?" the barmaid called out to him as she balanced a hand truck overstacked with cases of beer. Max hustled over to her and took hold of the toppling cases and steadied the hand truck, then placed a case gently on top of the wooden bar.

"So, is, uh, Stan here?" Max asked once the woman had walked behind the bar.

"No. He's paying me time and a half to let you do your thing and restock and reorder all the stuff that got stolen along with the till," she explained, crouching down to pick up the case on the floor. As she leaned away, Max couldn't avoid noticing her lower-back tattoo. It had a heart with a dagger through it and something else he couldn't make out. The rest of it was covered by her lace panties, which cinched up her backside when she bent over.

"Which I don't mind," she continued, facing him and putting bottles into the cooler. "I need a break. Should have seen what a mess those thieving pricks left this place in." The barmaid took a look at Max and decided he looked like a whiskey man, so she took hold of a bottle behind her and placed two rocks glasses on the bar. She poured two shots into each glass and slid one across the bar to Max.

"We'll drink to security," she announced cheerfully.

Max wondered if the glitter flakes on her cleavage were from her top or had been put there on purpose.

"No thank you. Is there anyone who can sign the work order for here for me?"

"Uh, uh, what you see is what you get," she answered, giving Max a playful shimmy of her shoulders. "Come on, a chivalrous gent like you isn't the type to make a woman drink alone so early in the day, are you?"

"Oh, it's not you, ma'am."

"Janine." She corrected him.

"It's not you, Janine; it's just that I come from a long line of bad genetic history when it comes to the firewater."

She shrugged in a carefree manner, drank both glasses, and lifted the partition of the bar.

"I'll sign what needs signing for you," she said, taking hold of his clipboard, ending the friendly charade.

"Here on the x?" she asked, whipping her hair around and tying it in a ponytail.

"Yes, ma—I mean, Janine," Max answered. She bit the cap off the pen and smiled at him flirtatiously. When she got close to him, Max picked up the scent of her fragrance—a soft cinnamon overpowered by what smelled just like cotton candy overwhelmed him.

"Sooo if you won't drink with me, security man Max…" she began while forcing the clipboard back into his hands "Maybe you want to do something else with me, huh?" she offered, placing both her arms on his shoulders. The smell of whiskey still bubbling on her lips permeated the air magically, mixing with the scent of her perfume. For a split second, Max imagined how amazing it'd be to discover what lay beneath the bleeding-heart tattoo on her backside.

He stumbled backward and returned to his senses. They told him that as damn beautiful as this woman was, she paled in comparison to his wife. Flustered, he held up his ring finger as if to shield himself from Janine's seduction. Her hands dropped to her sides as she shook her head in error while Max found his voice.

"I'm sorry, Janine. You're a beautiful girl, but I'm married. Happily married with a daughter," he explained, his tone sincere and apologetic.

"Shit! I'm sorry. It's so damn dark in here. Them gray eyes of yours had me entranced. I didn't see. I'm so embarrassed"

"Please don't be. Honest mistake."

"Well, if you don't want my booze or my body, maybe some business, if you're interested?" she said, making her way back behind the bar. "The guy in the place next store from here. Tito at the tattoo parlor. He had a break-in, same as us," she continued as she resumed stocking her inventory. "He should be open by now. Tell him I sent you, and maybe he'll give me a break on the rest of my ink."

Max nodded in agreement at the prospect of a new client. "Greatly appreciated. I'm new to the area and need new customers. I'll stop over there now."

"You do that, Max, and take care of that beautiful family of yours, and, uh, should anything change for better or worse…" Janine said, pouring herself another drink. She added with a wink, "First one's on the house."

"You got it! A pleasure meeting you, and thank Stan for me," Max said, then took leave of the Bismark and went next door to see about the prospect of a new customer.

The children were in a single-file line, making their way into the classroom. In the back of the line stood Paige, her every movement spelling out anxiety and hesitation.

"All right, before you take your seats, leave yesterday's worksheet on my desk," the teacher instructed. One by one the children left the work and took their seats as the teacher inspected each sheet laid down beside her. Paige was confident with the worksheet, which her mother had helped her complete, and moved forward in the line. Her right leg bumped into her left, and she fell forward.

She had thought she was at the end of the line, but as she had inspected her work, Zachary had joined the line behind her—Zachary who told her that her dad was an idiot and tried to kill the frog on the playground. He had just tripped her and was grinning in amusement. Paige quickly got up and filled in the vacancy in the line ahead of her, then placed the sheet on the teacher's desk.

After dropping the work off, Paige turned around to make sure Zachary was not behind her. She made her way to her seat but was interrupted when the teacher addressed her.

"Oh, I see someone did both extra credit sections on the back. Very good, Paige. It's good to see you finally have a complete uniform as well," the teacher said, her compliment bringing a bit of comfort to the distressed child.

"Yes, thank you," Paige replied in a meek voice, only to have her words mimicked by an unseen classmate, removing the small smile the teacher's praise had put there. Paige took her seat as the teacher hushed the class, which was still laughing and carrying on. She nearly fell getting into her seat as the big-headed boy from the playground, Ronnie, tried to pull her chair out from under her, from his desk, which was behind hers.

Paige ignored him and settled into her desk. She took the puppy-dog pencil case from the Little Pony backpack, which her mom had surprised her with. She smiled, looking at the puppy's image on the case, and removed her pencil.

The teacher was handing out books to the class as Ronnie whispered behind her, "Oh, baby had to put her pants away and get a dress?" He taunted her in a whiny voice as a crumpled-up piece of paper was thrown at her by Zachary who was at her back, alongside Ronnie. The boys giggled as Paige's eyes watered. The paper didn't hurt, but her feelings were devastated.

In the subsequent days and weeks, Paige Garret was subjected to ridicule, torment, and hostility previously unknown to her. The upright, wide-eyed, happy little girl who had been so excited to start school became a slumped, teary-eyed, defeated child who grew accustomed to her hair being yanked and things being thrown at her.

Chapter 15:
PROACTIVE APPROACH

Seeing Carolyn getting dressed made Max want to reconsider not attending her class reunion. He couldn't recall the last time she had looked so incredible. His workdays started early, so he never saw Carolyn in work clothes. When he arrived home, his wife was in her sweats making dinner. She saw him behind her in the mirror as she put on her earrings and smiled. Max kissed her on the neck and handed her the dark-blue silk wrap that matched her dress.

After hearing her parents make their way down the stairs, Paige exited her room and eavesdropped from the top of the stairs. They were discussing how quiet and withdrawn Paige had become. She took hold of the wooden spindles on the staircase and listened.

"Maybe the move has affected her. I mean, she didn't have much time to settle in with us, then we moved," Max estimated.

"I don't know, Max, when I try talking to her, she just kind of clams up," Carolyn explained, picking up her overnight bag.

"I mean, her grades are great, but shouldn't she have made at least one friend by now?" Max responded, getting Carolyn's coat from the closet for her.

"I agree with you. All she does is complete projects and study. She already read her textbooks, and when I press her about it, she tells me that you and I are her best friends. I mean, what do I say to that?"

"Well, I'll talk to her during our father-daughter weekend. Maybe she can open up to me. Is Donna on her way yet?"

"Yeah, texted me a few minutes ago. I wish it were you taking me and I were meeting Donna there."

"Uh-uh, no high school reunions for me. Besides, who else is going to watch the princess? You look so damn beautiful, though."

"I feel guilty going. I'm going to make sure she's OK with me going," Carolyn said, making a pouty frown.

"Don't. She's taking a nap. I just checked in on her, so go and have a good time. Let me have her to myself for once," Max said, guiding Carolyn away from the staircase and toward the door.

"You think I look OK?" Carolyn asked, standing in the foyer. Max smiled and nodded, answering one of the most ridiculous questions he had ever heard. A car horn sounded in the driveway, followed by the sound of Carolyn's phone vibrating.

"OK. If for any reason you can't reach my cell, you have my parents' house number, right? Or you can call Donna's, right?"

"Yes. I'll phone the Pastrel residence tomorrow and let your mom and dad talk to their granddaughter."

The horn sounded again, and Carolyn nodded in hesitant agreement. She gave Max a quick hug, opened the door, and waved to Donna, then turned back to Max as if she had forgotten something.

"Max?"

"What?"

"No horror movies," Carolyn said, making her way to Donna's car.

"But it's October. OK. We can just watch one of those exciting debates you recorded on the DVR."

"Max, I'm serious!" she continued. Once she had loaded her bag into Donna's car, she blew him a kiss and shouted, "I love you!" out the passenger window. Max closed the door, overcome with gratitude for his wife, then went to wake Paige, who greeted him from the top of the steps. He let her pick a cartoon to watch and ordered takeout as Carolyn had insisted. The doorbell sounded twenty-five minutes later, and Max answered the door with Paige holding on to his leg. Her curiosity brought a smile to the upbeat delivery man's face as he handed Max the pizza box.

"OK, munchkin, you take this so I can pay him," Max said as Paige carefully balanced the box.

"It's twenty-two-thirty. Adorable little girl you got there."

"Here you go. There was supposed to be a two-liter as well?"

"Shit! I knew I forgot something."

"Don't worry about it; keep the change."

"Thanks a lot, mister."

"Thank you, pizza man," Paige said, peeking out from the side of the door, humoring the delivery guy as he left.

They finished Paige's *Madagascar* cartoon and finished the pizza. Max discarded the empty box and called out to her from the kitchen, "I hope you left room for dessert." Max had made Paige a bargain: he would allow her to watch a scary movie so long as she did not tell her mom. They sealed the pact with the forearm-gripping handshake introduced to Max by Paige Edmundson so many years ago. Paige finished her ice cream with haste as she was drawn in by the movie.

"Daddy, the ice cream made me cold. Can I get my Nemo blanket?" Bundled up, Paige settled into her father's arms until the film concluded. Max had anticipated her falling fast asleep and needing to transport her back to her room, but she was wide awake when the credits ran. She turned to him, her expression ignited by curiosity. Max smiled as her every movement tugged at his heartstrings.

"So, what did you think of *Invasion of the Body Snatchers*, Paige?"

"The doctor and woman were the only ones who weren't bad, and all those people wanted to get them."

"Correct, my smart girl," Max said, playfully pinching her little nose.

She then turned around in her father's arms to face him, her facial expression the most serious a child could possess.

"Daddy? Is it bad sometimes to be smart?"

"You mean too smart for your own good, honey?" Max redirected the conversation, confused by her general question.

"No." She sighed, looking down in search of how to voice her concern. "No, like, bad that no one likes you because of it?"

Max repositioned himself from the corner of the sofa and sat upright, realizing his little girl wanted to tell him something. "What do you mean, honey?"

"I heard you and mommy talking about why I don't have friends," she explained, unable to look at her father, her head down as she played with her fingers.

Max sprung up and did his best to mask the tense emotions he was overcome by.

"Honey, please tell me what's going on."

Paige did her best to explain but then burst into tears and spoke through them. "When school started, if I knew the answer, the other kids started teasing me when I got it right. So then I stopped raising my hand, but they teased me anyway." She started speaking rapidly, and she cried harder, exclaiming, "They push me and trip me and say you and mommy are fat idiots. They throw stuff at me all the time and pull my hair, and I don't know why, Daddy. Why?" She trembled, unable to speak any longer, and let out a long cry.

Reacting to Paige's description of what had been happening to her, Max went from disheartened to devastated. He held the trembling child tightly and comforted her. He cradled her and rocked her to sleep as he sobbed steadily to himself. Heartbroken at the realization that his daughter was the subject of what they today described as bullying, what he had experienced long before there was a defining term.

Her cries echoed in his head, accompanied by disturbing images of his little girl being tormented in his mind. Max brought her into his and Carolyn's room as he did not want to leave her out of his sight. He lay awake the entire night reflecting on the abuse he had endured in his teens and came to the decision that he'd be damned if his daughter would suffer as he had. The following day Max took Paige to the KB Toys store and denied her nothing, spending beyond his budget. He decided not to inform Carolyn of this or Paige's troubles until she returned from her parents that Sunday.

Monday, October 20, 2008

Outside the principal's office, a secretary typed nervously, trying to ignore the intense argument occurring in front of her. The participants were visible to her through the office's glass windows. She could see the principal's hands motioning downward to ease the tension, to no avail.

Max's voice boomed through the administrative office's corridors. "I want her withdrawn from this uptight, shithole school and transferred," he said, leaning forward, pressing his index finger down on the principal's desk. Carolyn felt Max's rage and may have expressed it as well had she not been stunned by the sight of her husband's anger. They had had minor arguments and disagreements in the past, but Max had never lost his temper like this.

The administrator stood beside the principal, then stepped forward and addressed Max in a calming tone. "Mr. Garret," he began with a smile that Max took as condescending, "I, Principal Venerbeen, and Ms. Clausen, Paige's teacher, understand your concern. We sincerely do, and we apologize for any anguish caused to Paige that went unnoticed by our staff here," he said, staring at Ms. Clausen.

"In spite of these conflicts with a few other children, your child is performing academically at a fourth-grade level. Switching the learning environment may have a negative impact on her education," Principal Venerbeen added.

Carolyn watched as Max shook his head in disagreement. Seated beside him, she consoled him by rubbing his back. Her touch seemed to prompt him to respond, "I don't care. Boys hitting her, taunting and teasing her, throwing things at her. I paid the extra money for your private school here to avoid this. I should have sent her to public school," Max said, voicing his regrets.

The administrator gave Ms. Clausen a second glaring look. This time there was more scorn coming from his eyes. "Ms. Clausen?" He said, expecting a solution to put the Garrets at ease.

The teacher stammered a bit, and Carolyn decided to talk to her to get to the bottom of what was occurring to her daughter in the classroom.

"Ms. Clausen, Paige is so obedient and considerate for her age. I mean, for her to be bullied at this age, I don't understand. I mean, sometimes she's so well behaved I forget she's a little girl and not an adult," Carolyn said, mimicking Max's emotion.

Ms. Clausen composed herself, ignoring the administrator's threatening body language.

She lowered her head like a pet that was expressing shame for soiling its owner's rug and explained, "I do not disagree with you at all, Mrs. Garret. Your daughter is an incredible child and student, as her grades demonstrate. In addition, she requires little additional instruction and is self-sufficient, which is the only explanation I can offer you for neglecting to notice her being harassed by her classmates," Ms. Clausen stated apologetically.

While Carolyn nodded, understanding the teacher's reasoning, Max would have none of it. "So you're telling me because my daughter is a good student, you ignore her? Is that what you're trying to tell me here? I'm supposed to be OK with this?" he said, looking to the principal and administrator.

"What I believe Ms. Claussen is trying to say is that the unacceptable behavior that went unnoticed will be given priority in and out of the classroom so long as your child is in our care here," the principal stated as the administrator nodded in agreement.

Principal Venerbeen saw the Garrets out. In an attempt to make an impression, he told the nervous secretary, "I want Ronald's and Zachary's parents contacted for a conference."

"Who?" The secretary asked, dumbfounded.

"The parents of the boys Rebecca Claussen identified as harassing Paige in her class," he said, raising his voice as if he'd made past mention of this. Carolyn saw this as a step in the right direction, but Max was unconvinced. He picked up Paige, who was seated outside the office, while Carolyn spoke to Ms. Claussen, who provided Paige's assignments for the upcoming week.

On the ride home, Carolyn tried to talk to Max, who was beside himself. She knew it was bad when he asked her to drive—something he never did. He hardly spoke a word except to answer Paige from the back seat. She figured Max wanted to discuss the school's response with her in private, when Paige was occupied, but was wrong. Max took advantage of his scheduled day off and started helping Paige with her schoolwork. While Paige explained her science work to Max, he heard Carolyn in the living room speaking to her mother.

"I don't know, Mom. Well, they swore up and down to us that they wouldn't let her out of their sight…yeah, OK, hold on." Carolyn made her way back to Max and Paige at the dining room table and handed Paige her phone.

"Say hello to Grandma real fast, honey."

"I guess you told your mom?" Max asked, acting like himself once more, providing a smile to the exhausted face Carolyn was displaying.

"She's driving me up a wall. My dad's almost as mad about this as you are," Carolyn replied as she stood behind Max and massaged his shoulders. "So what do you want to do?" Her question was well-timed as Paige was explaining her schoolwork to her grandmother in specific detail.

"Not a lot of options. I mean, we can hold her back a year, but I know she's against it. The prospect of starting another school has her petrified, and I can't say I blame her there. Devil you know and all that," he answered in disgust as Carolyn stopped rubbing his shoulders and leaned in front of him so he could see her speaking to him.

"Speaking of petrified, I thought you were going to flip over Principal Venerbeen's desk for a minute there. I've never seen you so heated. I mean, justifiably so."

"Well, the way that admin guy was looking at Ms. Claussen, I think he had her petrified for her job." Max stopped as Paige brought the phone back around the table and handed it to her mother, a big grin on her face after speaking to her grandmother.

"Yeah, Mom. Yeah, next week she goes back. I'm going to be home with her. I put in for family leave…OK, I'll talk to you tomorrow…Mom, I need to feed her and Max. It's been a long day…OK, love you too, bye-bye."

Max assisted Carolyn with dinner while Paige drew a picture of them on construction paper. After dinner Paige fell asleep on the couch with them while watching *Dancing with the Stars*, and Max carried her off to bed.

When he returned downstairs, he was relaxed. Carolyn felt comfortable enough to ask him what had made him lash out earlier, to which he
responded only, "It just hits a little close to home with me when it comes to
what happened to her. I don't want it to escalate, for her sake." He looked
away, then changed the channel. It occurred to Carolyn in that moment that
Max always became uncomfortable when discussing his past and dropped
the subject as soon as it came up.

The following week Paige returned to school, and the Garrets were happy
to hear her report that the boys who had picked on her before had let her be.

Chapter 16:
DEATH OF INNOCENCE

The country was in economic turmoil, and more people focused on protecting what they did have. Max's business was gaining momentum. Carolyn's company had downsized but retained her to pick up the slack. Her small promotion provided a surplus budget for Paige's birthday, which they celebrated that entire Halloween weekend.

The first Monday in November, Paige returned to school with a Nintendo DS portable game device, much to the displeasure of Ronnie and Zachary, who saw her playing it in the morning.

While eating her sandwich, Ms. Claussen looked out the teachers' lounge window on the first floor with a blank expression. Principal Venerbeen came in and greeted her while retrieving his lunch from the refrigerator. "Rebecca?" the principal asked, removing the container as he gazed out the window and frowned at the overcast day.

"Yes, Will," Ms. Claussen replied, setting down her drink.

"I forgot to tell you—I got a most pleasant phone call from Paige Garret's father this morning," the principal said, observing children engaged in clap song games on the playground at recess. Rebecca was the only one in there. He sought to strike up a conversation to liven up the gloomy day as his meal warmed in the microwave.

Rebecca Claussen was taken aback by the rare praise being sent her way by her boss and the rancid smell of the fish he was reheating. She set her sandwich down to respond, "Well, I meant what I told them. Her first day back, one of the girls yanked at her hair, and I removed her from class..." Her speech stopped as the microwave timer went off, and she looked on the playground to see what the principal was gazing at as he rambled on. "Well, I'm just glad that father of hers is back on the reservation. Last month I thought that big bastard was going to really go batshit craz—say, Will, who is proctoring the recess period today? I don't see anyone out there with them!"

"Uh, Cynthia Blarznik; she has recess the whole week," he responded, holding his rancid container of trout, looking for the absent Ms. Blarznik on the playground.

His answer caused Rebecca Claussen to rise from her seat and grab her coat as he studied her movements with a blank stare. "Will, Cynthia called in sick with the flu this morning. Didn't your secretary tell you?

"No, but she must have gotten one of the room mothers to sub in her place," he replied, taking a second look out the window before covering his lunch and following the concerned teacher toward the exit.

The birthday present had Paige eagerly anticipating recess for the first time. She perched herself out of sight at the top of the jungle gym playset and turned on her game. Her enjoyment was short-lived as she was pelted with wood chips from the unsupervised children at the bottom of the playset. She covered her face and ran across the bridge toward the slide and was pursued by Zack and Ronnie, who had been punished due to Paige reporting them. Zack nudged Ronnie, notifying him of the opportunity to get even with her.

Clumps of dirt and bark were heaved in Paige's face. She dropped her game and bent down to retrieve it. Ronnie took the basketball he had tried to flatten the frog with and aimed it at the back of the distressed Paige. She picked up her game and ran toward the slide as Ronnie aimed at her head and heaved the ball with all his might directly into the back of her head.

Principal Venerbeen and Ms. Clausen came out to the schoolyard and heard the children who were throwing debris at Paige still chanting the clap song:

One twenty was the time when he spent his last dime.

He dropped it in the phone so he could call home. "No, no, no," the operator said, "in this phone you must insert more bread."

One twenty-two was the time when he found another nickel.

Put it in the phone to get out of a pickle.

"No, no, no," the operator said, "the call can't connect because the line's gone dead."

At one twenty-four no more would be said

Ronnie's throw caught Paige in the back of her head. The singing came to an abrupt halt as Paige descended from the highest point of the playset into a free fall. The impact of the ball sent her careening off the side of the sliding board. Rebecca Claussen and Will Venerbeen looked on in horror as her leg hit one of the playset attachments and the forward momentum slammed Paige's body to the ground face first. Ronnie's face turned from elation to fear. Zachary and he ran back inside the school, frightened from the sound of Ms. Claussen screaming, which brought on the screams of the frightened children.

She frisked her coat pockets for a cell phone that was not there. "Call an ambulance!" she shouted, holding Paige's lifeless little body in her arms, attempting to revive the child in vain.

Emergency workers called to the scene were traumatized at the sight of the grounded little body; its legs and pleated skirt could not be covered by Ms. Claussen's parka. The paramedic checked for a pulse and shook his head to his coworker, confirming what was already known by Rebecca Claussen as she sobbed into the chest of Will Venerbeen.

Officer Van Alden and his partner had just concluded a discussion about how their salaries did not nearly equate to the task they were charged with performing. They entered the office complex and spoke to the receptionist seated behind the main desk. She had had her head down, looking at her phone, until she was alarmed at the sight of the uniformed officers.

"Hello, ma'am. We need to speak to a Carolyn Garret," Van Alden said, his voice overcome with regret.

"We have a Carolyn in customer service," she responded, setting down her cell phone to point the officers to where Carolyn sat. The secretary emerged from her desk and watched the officers walk down the narrow pathway and instructed them further, getting the attention of the other workers, who stood up in their cubicles.

"Third desk from the window," she called out. The officer nodded to her in response as he followed behind Van Alden, who had stopped at the entrance of Carolyn's cube.

"Yes. Yes, ma'am. No, you are all up to date. You can discard that notice, and we will send you an updated statement," Carolyn said with a smile on her face. "Very good. Well, you have a pleasant evening as well, Ms. Sheean. Goodbye." Carolyn concluded the call, removed her headset, and grabbed her purse to go to the ladies' room.

Before Carolyn had gotten off the line, Van Alden had been looking at the two photographs tacked up on her desk and he grimaced. She turned to face the two men with downcast faces and knew a catastrophe had struck. They had sent there to tell her that the happy little girl in the photos, Paige, was dead. Carolyn collapsed to the ground as Van Alden and his partner embraced her, then escorted her outside as she could not breathe or walk.

Working ahead of schedule, Max anticipated getting home early and was looking forward to it. He was singing in his car and tapping the steering wheel as the song was interrupted by the incoming call. He looked over at his phone on the dashboard and smiled, seeing Carolyn's name. He answered, excited to give her the good news he would be finishing up early.

He needed Carolyn to repeat herself three times to comprehend what she was telling him. Max pulled the van over, and once the news of his daughter's death became evident, he ended the call and slumped his head over the steering wheel. He then beat the van's roof and interior until his fists and arms would no longer allow him to do so. He tried to recall a time when he had felt worse in his entire life, and his mind was vacant.

Chapter 17:
GONE

Fearing a crippling lawsuit, the school made several attempts to contact the Garrets, but the calls went unanswered. Both Max and Carolyn were near catatonic throughout the funeral service. Against their wishes, those who attended came to the house afterward, invited by Carolyn's parents, who had already worn out their welcome. The guests chose to ignore the grim reality of the little girl's death by discussing the newly elected president.

In the hallway of the Garrets' home, the receptionist from Carolyn's work stood behind the secretary from Paige's school. The secretary turned to Carolyn's colleague, who was in a rush to use the bathroom.

"They should be out soon; they've been in there a good while. Are you a relative?"

"No. Carolyn and I work together," she responded, stomping back and forth to subside her urge to go.

"Me neither. I work at the school," she whispered in a ridiculously low tone as if it were her intention to gossip.

"School wanted someone to express condolences, and I drew the short straw. Such a tragedy."

"Oh, absolutely terrible."

The toilet flushed as the school secretary leaned close and continued whispering.

"Did you know that they adopted her?"

"I heard that. I mean, not that it's any consolation, but to lose your own flesh and blood would be just...how long did they have her?"

"No, I agree. I mean, if anything were to happen to my daughter, I'd…"
Her voice was interrupted by the bathroom door being flung open by Max,
who looked more distressed than he had at the service. The undone black
necktie had vomit on it, as did his pants, and his hair was a combination of
combed and undone. He studied the strangers in his hallway with bloodshot
eyes irritated by the saturation of tears and a pale face.

"Are you OK, Mr. Garret?" The receptionist spoke up.

"Is there anything we can get you?" added the secretary, to whom Max
nodded aggressively.

"Yes, as a matter of fact, there is. The two of you can get your flesh and
your blood and get the fuck out of my house!" He brushed past them and
staggered off in the direction of his kitchen. Carolyn stepped away from her
mother and joined him. She hugged him tight as he observed the crowded
living room.

"Oh, Max," Carolyn said tearfully.

"I want everyone out, Car."

"OK. I do too." Max nudged her aside and clapped his hands, getting
the attention of those gathered.

"Hey, hey. Thank you all for your sympathy and support, but Carolyn
and I just want to be alone. OK, good night," he announced, distracted by
Paige's portrait on the mantle above the fireplace. Beside the mantle was his
father-in-law, whose face showed blame, resentment, and disapproval. The
crowd was slowly dispersing but not making for the exit. Max clapped his
hands together once more.

"Again, thank you, and we would really appreciate it if we could call it
a night." Max paused his announcement and looked directly into his father-
in-law's continuing scowl. "Of course, my in-laws are welcome to stay, even
longer," Max continued, only to have Carolyn's mother interrupt him.

"We booked a hotel, honey," Ms. Pastrel told her daughter as Max
pointed to her husband.

"But if my father-in-law keeps looking at me the way he's been since
the service began, we're going to have to have another burial. Get out!
Yeah, right here, Dennis," Max said, making a fist, then giving the finger
to Carolyn's father.

Carolyn saw the guests and her parents to the door and returned to Max, who was busying himself in the kitchen discarding food he knew neither of them would be able to keep down. Carolyn took hold of him from behind. They embraced one another and fell to the kitchen floor, wallowing in anguish.

The sound of Max's van starting up in the driveway awoke Carolyn in a fright. She turned on the lamp, knocking over medications and clumped-up tissues from the nightstand. She then raced to the bedroom window, only to see the van speed off. Carolyn headed to the top of the stairwell to get her phone off the charger to call him but was distracted by the light coming from Paige's bedroom. She entered the room and gasped at the erratically written note on Paige's bed, which read:

SELL THE HOUSE

MOVE BACK NORTH WITH YOUR PARENTS

TAKE BACK YOUR MAIDEN NAME

IM SORRY I FAILED YOU BOTH

INTO ETERNAL FIRE I WHO AM

CURSED SHALL DEPART

LIVE ON LOVE MAX

The medley of prescriptions in her system had her uncertain as to how to act. Carolyn contemplated going out in her car and looking for him. Besides work and home, Max went nowhere else she could find him.

Carolyn dialed her parents, numb from medication and petrified for Max. Meanwhile the Garret Securities van drove to Ivan Grady's residence at 89 Middleton Lane.

Chapter 18:

89 MIDDLETON LANE

After performing a manual override of the primary alarm system, Max made his way into the cellar. He attached a device to disable the palm-print entry.

While waiting, he examined his phone, which revealed seven missed calls from Carolyn. Images of Paige pleading and crying to him replayed in his head as he looked at the image of her face on the wallpaper of his phone's screen saver.

He put the phone away when the device signaled it had gained access. Once inside Grady's war chest, he began stacking weaponry on the hand truck. Initially put off by the outrageous arsenal amassed in his client's basement, he now marveled at it. He grabbed boxes of ammunition, handguns, a long-range rifle, as well as the assault rifle Grady was so proud of.

Max flung open the back doors of the security van and tossed all his work materials onto Grady's driveway. He packed everything from the hand truck and headed back inside. He looked at the samurai sword hanging over the entrance and contemplated taking it. He then dismissed the notion as he decided there'd be nothing noble in the deaths of his targets. They were going to die in a swift, painful fashion, the same way Paige had.

A case of hand grenades in the corner got his attention, but he was redirected to a tactical baton and gloves next to the case. He took the baton and gloves, as well as a black mask that wrapped around the face, from the nose down with Velcro fasteners. The skeletal teeth design on the front of the mask would give him away in the dark, he thought, but he took it anyway. It didn't matter if he was seen, and he didn't give a damn about being subtle.

Exiting Grady's weapons vault, he saw a pair of jungle knives on the shelf and figured they should come in handy should he get in close. He looked at the device attached to the security system he had installed and felt the need to feel something through pain as well as provide his customer with an explanation. Max unsheathed a knife and cut into his left hand. As the blade's teeth tore into his palm, he thought about the lies he had been told by the school that had promised not to let his little girl out of their sight. He pressed his right index finger into the bloody gash on his left hand.

Above the security system, Max provided an answer to Mr. Ivan Grady's question. One that he had denied him in their previous conversation. He wrote it in a bloody smear on a smooth gray slab of brick above the palm-print identification system. Max packed up the grenades in the van, which was now filled with tools for murder instead of tools for security. Blood streamed down Ivan Grady's wall; the writing left for him read, "AWOL."

Max drove into town and parked out front of the Bismarck Bar, where he had met Janine. The pretty barmaid had told him to stop in if anything changed for better or worse. Things had changed indeed, Max thought, wrapping a bandage from the first aid kit around his palm. The ointment he put over the gash wasn't holding, and blood-soaked gauze protruded from the covering. Max covered his wounded hand with one of the tactical gloves and exited the van.

The phone vibrated in his pocket, and he saw a preview text from Carolyn, as well as an alert from his security contractor seeking confirmation for his override at Grady's residence. He slammed the phone on the sidewalk like a football player spiking the ball after a touchdown. A patron exiting the bar stood motionless, about to light up a cigarette when he saw a guy stomping out a cell phone.

"Say, you all right, dude?" the man said in a panic, concerned the unstable character might choose to focus his rage on him rather than the phone.

"Yep. No more calls to make," Max replied, looking at the phone, which had been shattered to his satisfaction.

"Say, I know you!" The stranger spoke up in excitement. He immediately regretted it when Max turned to him with a scowl. It may have been the same man he remembered, but the temperament was way off from the first encounter.

"Three sixteen Layebert Lane," the man continued, not helping matters by adding Max's home address to him.

"SD's Pizza and Packaged Goods? Delivery guy from before Christmas?" The man persisted, and Max nodded in recognition.

"Oh yeah," Max responded without concern.

"Say, man, how's that cute little girl of yours? She had a good Christmas and all?" he asked Max, taking a long drag from his cigarette.

"Yes, she did have a very good Christmas, but now she's dead," Max said, looking down at his black Timberland work boots to spare himself from the stranger's reaction. "You spare one of those?" Max continued, motioning to the astonished man's cigarette. He quickly handed Max his pack and lighter and looked him over while taking an even deeper drag.

"The private school thing? Oh damn! That was her? Shit! Now that I think of it—oh man, I'm so sorry, man. That shit is fucked. Some accident on the jungle gym or something, right? I read about it."

"No, that was no fucking accident. The school was trying to cover their ass so I wouldn't sue them." Max coughed from inhaling the cigarette. "Like I even give a shit after they killed my little girl!" His voice broke, partially because of the smoke he was unaccustomed to but primarily because of sadness. It hurt too much to speak. Speaking about it made it real.

The delivery man looked to his right and left for someone else or any consolable words he could offer, but nothing came to mind. He decided to just start talking once he noticed Max wearing a single glove and a long line of blood streaming onto his forearm.

"Shit, man. I don't know. I was heading out, but fuck it. Let me buy you a drink. Come on," he said to Max, who was hunched over weeping. Max straightened himself, took in a deep breath, and looked at the man who was trying to comfort him.

"We're going to make it right, though; yes, we are," Max affirmed with conviction, puzzling the nervous stranger.

"Look, I'm Gerry. It's getting cold as hell out here, and I don't think you should be alone in your state. Come on in; warm up a moment and relax."

"I'm fucking Maximillian, Paige's papa bear."

"Uh, OK, sure. Come on in," Gerry said, holding the door open.

The bar looked different from when Max had been there to install the alarm. The light above the pool table and neon beer signs surrounding the jukebox in the corner lit up the place. He glided in the door as if walking on air.

"Hey, Gerry, tell your asshole friend he can't smoke in here. It's not two-thousand-fucking-five anymore," Janine yelled from the bar. Max flicked the cigarette to the floor. Gerry hustled up to the bar and whispered an explanation to Janine. Max walked up to the counter and looked into Janine's face.

"If worse should occur, the first one's on the house, right?" he asked of the woman who was still trying to place him.

"Security man Max! What has got you in such rare form? You don't look so good, sugar," Janine responded. Her question caused Gerry to shake his head, signaling no to her.

"Shot for him on me, Janine," Gerry interjected before Max could respond.

"I don't know what's got you on the backslide, darling, and I'd hate to add to any regression, but I'm a woman of my word. So what'll it be?" Her question led Max to scan the bottles behind her.

"Grab me a pint glass with a little ice and give me a shot of everything clear in it."

"Tequila as well?" Janine asked, a bit put off by his request.

"Uh-huh. I want it to burn."

"I'm driving, so no great white pint for me. Just a SoCo and lime," Gerry said.

Janine placed the glass in front of Max.

"All right, you got your rum, vodka, gin, sambuca, and tequila. There you go, killer; it's on me."

Max stared at the two of them and raised the glass as if to toast.

"We don't have to drink to nothing, man. I know you're hurting and all," Gerry began.

Max interrupted; he raised the glass higher and tilted his head upward as if speaking to it. "To vodka and vengeance and a trail of forensics." Max toasted, then finished the pint glass in three long gulps, to the bewilderment of Gerry and Janine, who had not even brought their glasses to their lips.

Janine mouthed the words "What the fuck?" to Gerry.

Max placed the glass on the bar, staggered off, and exited the bar, muttering to himself. "I have to go. Paige is waiting for me," he repeated on the way out the door.

Back inside his van, Max felt the dizzying effects of the stiff drink he had just downed and saw the neon lights go out from Tito's tattoo parlor next door to the bar. He crept out of the front seat into the back of the van and opened up one of the cases from Grady's arsenal. He flipped open the lid of the case, which contained matching .45s, took one, and disregarded the holster. The weight of the gun told him it was loaded, but Max checked it anyway and loaded the chamber.

He set his sights on Tito, who was still in his shop, with the front door wide open. Tito was arming the alarm system he had yet to pay a dime for. While Max had been unconcerned about his delinquency before, small things like Grady's rubber check were starting to add up. He exited the van and crept up behind Tito, who was locking up the entrance.

Thinking he heard footsteps, Tito looked over to the bar, assuming it was the source of foot traffic he heard behind him. The steel from the pistol pressed into the back of his head as he dropped some sketches he had drawn.

"You owe me money, asshole," the voice behind him said.

"Say what? What's your problem, man?" Tito said, buying time to distract whoever the person was who had a gun to his head.

"Alarm installation months ago?"

"Yo, I pay that shit every month, cuz!"

"Sure, you pay the company for the service, but you stiffed me for five months on the installation, and I'm here to collect."

Whether the stranger knew it or not, this was not the first time Tito had had a gun pointed at him. He dealt with his fair share of rough customers, and every now and again, a dispute would arise. Once Max told him this was about money, he relaxed. Tito knew it made no sense to shoot him if this guy wanted to recover the cash. Tito took a deep breath and began to bargain.

"Chill, OK? I had all credit transactions today. You come back tomorrow, and I'll square up with you, OK?" he suggested with confidence but became worried when no reply was given. The gun was removed from the back of his head as Max had decided to let the iron give his reply. He tapped the handle into the right side of Tito's face twice, pistol-whipping him to the ground.

"Fuck tomorrow! I spent a day here working for you that I could have spent with my daughter, who's dead now. Grab them keys, and open it the fuck up," Max said, pointing to the parlor's door with the gun. Staggering, Tito picked up the keys on the sidewalk and stepped over his scattered drawings and leaned into the door to open it. The description of his daughter being dead made Tito realize bargaining was not a priority to Max but could very well be a means to his own execution.

Rubbing the side of his face, Tito flipped on the fluorescent lighting. Max trained the pistol on him with his left hand and pressed standby on the alarm with his right.

Max motioned to the register on top of the counter and pointed at it with the gun. "Hurry up and open it!"

"It's turned off, man. Give it a second." Once the register powered on, the drawer slid open, and Tito took out the bills inside it and placed them on the clear counter. "I told you, it's just enough to make change."

Looking at the small pile of bills on the counter, Max trained the gun on Tito's head, unsatisfied.

"You're light. Way light."

"I don't know what the fuck you want from me, man! I moved the safe out after the last time I got jacked, before you did the work. Take my tattoo gun. I got nothing else of value here!" Tito exclaimed in distress.

Above Tito's head, on the wall behind the register, was a template for a tattoo that caught Max's attention. It was a skeletal robed and hooded reaper with a sickle meshed with the hands of a clock with Roman numerals that read, "Time the Avenger."

"That. I want that," Max said, motioning to the drawing, causing Tito to look at the wall.

"Shit. Fine. Let me take it down for you," Tito said in relief.

"Uh-uh," Max said, shaking his head no.

"I performed a service for you; now you are going to perform a service for me."

Tito frowned at the ridiculous request. He didn't want to spend another moment with this unstable lunatic with a gun on him, much less work on him. "There's no way I can do that design in one sitting. Shit would take hours," he protested.

"Scale down what you have to, and just make sure you finish by daybreak."

"And I'm supposed to work on you under the gun? I can't work like that."

"No, no, this was just cleaner than killing you with my bare hands, but I will if you get any ideas," Max said, placing the gun on the counter.

Once Max was positioned in his chair, Tito planned to run over to the gun. When Max came out of his shirt and revealed the scarring on the entire left side of his body, he decided against it. Max pointed to his heart, displaying where he wanted the avenger to be placed. The scarring was a challenge to ink over, and Tito always enjoyed a challenge.

As the tattoo gun whirred, Max was completely still. A lot of his customers engaged in small talk or every so often wanted to have a peek at the work in progress. Tito looked at Max for a moment before resetting and felt more distress from the blank gaze in his eyes than he had when the gun had been pointed at him. While the ink pricked into his skin, Max's mind drifted back to the Garrets' basement in Middleton.

The last time he had attempted to right a wrong done to him, it had blown up in his face. But thanks to Mr. Grady and past training, he'd be more precise and methodically dismantle those responsible for Paige's death. Gazing up at the ceiling, Max planned how he was going to take revenge. It wouldn't bring Paige back, but they'd pay a great price for their negligence. Perhaps if the school had been more upfront with him, he would have dismissed the extremity of his acts to come—probably not, but the lies were the icing on the cake he was ready to cut into.

The more time he spent inside his head, the more Max thought about Middleton. He pictured his enemies from the past living happy lives and raising children like them who'd go on to torment kids like Paige. He gritted his teeth and clenched his fists so much that Tito had to stop working.

"You're tensing up, man. I'm almost done, but I need a break." Tito rose to his feet and looked at the design over Max's heart. He thought it some of the best work he had done in some time. The lunatic in his chair had made him focus and use the skills he had thought diminished. He had grown complacent in his work and was sick of painting flowers and hearts on teenage girls' legs.

Returning from the bathroom, he looked at the avenger, seeing work he took actual pride in doing for the first time in a long time. "OK, now how do you want the lettering anchored at the bottom to read?"

"'For Paige, now and forever.'"

"OK, so you want me to replace the original lettering?"

"No, keep it. Just put that in the beginning. That's Paige with an *i*."

"'Time the Avenger. For Paige, now and forever.' All right." Tito nodded.

Inside the Bismark Janine turned off the lights and bolted the doors after closing hours. She and Gerry played pool and got plastered into the early morning. Once outside, she noticed Max's van and saw lights on inside Tito's shop. She was about to comment on the van, but Gerry hugged her and slurred, "Breakfast is on me, Janinny." Janine decided she was the less drunk between the two of them, so they headed across the street to her car.

"You said scale it down, but I pretty much was able to fit it all in there," Tito said. Max marveled at the design in the full-length mirror on the wall. "I mean, I could add color to it, but—"

"No. It's perfect. Besides, I don't think I'll be needing this skin suit much longer anyway."

Stepping away from the mirror, Max reached into his pocket and placed the money from the register back on the counter and buttoned up his shirt and exited. The door started to close as Tito walked to it, holding a tube of anti-irritant ointment. "Hey. You got to put this cream on! Shit crazy mother…" he said, recovering his cash from the counter. Overwhelmed by what had just transpired, Tito took a breath and shook his head in disbelief. He went to put the cash back in the register, then his ears were pierced as the alarm sounded off, rattling his skull.

Max came back in the door and picked up the .45 off the counter and screamed to Tito over the blaring alarm, "See, good security system!" then headed back out the door.

Across the street, waiting for her car to warm up, Janine slapped Gerry's arm to get his attention. "Look, look!" she said. Once alerted, Gerry looked at what was being pointed out to him by Janine. They looked at Max in shock as he walked out of the tattoo parlor, gun in single gloved hand, as the alarm blared.

"'Avenger' my ass. Sub-Mariner's an Avenger. You're just a crazy motherfucker," Tito muttered to himself, disarming the alarm. Tito turned off the lights, exited his shop, and joined Janine and Gerry across the street as Max pulled away.

"Where's that guy going, Tito?" Janine asked out the window of her Buick.

"Damned if I know. Damned if I care. I just hope he don't come back ever!" Tito replied.

"Wanna go to brekkie with us?" Gerry slurred.

"Yeah, but you two are all banged up; let's take my truck. Wherever he's going, it's gonna be bad for him or whoever he's looking for. I can tell you that much." Tito said in reflection, looking in the direction in which Max had driven away.

Chapter 19:

SCENE OF THE CRIME

In the school parking lot, Max sat in his van and stared at the playground where Paige had died until cars began to pull in. Rebecca Clausen and the school secretary who had been gossiping about Paige in his house parked and entered the side entrance of the school. The jungle gym that she had fallen from was being dismantled by two workers as he made his way inside. The school was silent as a church, and some of the lights were still on in the halls.

The secretary sat at her desk across from where the administrators and Principal Venerbeen had made false reassurances to Max and Carolyn. Promises he sought to make them regret. The secretary took off her coat and powered on her computer. Once she had taken her seat, Max lunged out of the principal's office, placed the .45 on the side of her temple, and covered her mouth with his gloved hand.

She froze. Max hadn't killed anyone in decades. He had only taken someone's life when it was sanctioned and had never killed a civilian, but if she was stubborn, he knew he'd have no problem snapping her neck. "Give me the home addresses for the boys named Ronnie and Zachary from Rebecca Claussen's second-grade class—fast," Max said with his left palm steadying her head. She wanted to scream but knew there was no one in the office to hear her. She directed her nervous energy to her keyboard and proceeded to print the information.

Satisfied, Max grabbed the printout, then bound her to the chair with the computer's ethernet wire and adapter cables and gagged her with her own scarf. He rolled her into the principal's office and sighed with regret, thinking about the fact that the last time he had been in this room, his little girl had been alive. He shoved her into a small wardrobe closet, closed the door, and kicked off the round bronze doorknob. Exiting the office, he stared at the bench where Paige had sat with her legs swinging, waiting to go home. He holstered the .45 and summoned rage with memories of the grit of sand between his teeth, with a foreign sun beating upon his scarred neck. His body was in South Dakota, but his mind was in the desert, and Max was once again at war.

"I mean, we are in a world of shit over this, Bill," the administrator said to the principal, who was balancing his metal thermos and briefcase in the parking lot.

"You think I don't know that? Bad enough I'm the first principal in the school's history to have a student die! They're probably going to shitcan me. Have you spoken to the superintendent? Do you know something?"

The administrator shook his head in refusal. "To make matters worse, your own damned teacher's saying you made a false report. If I were you, I'd let her fall on the sword here, shoulder some of this blame. Why the fuck haven't you fired her? Did you see this?" he asked, holding out the newspaper in front of the principal, who looked to the ground, nodding in acknowledgment.

"If I fire her, she has a discrimination case as a whistleblower. I mean, the fucking kid fell and…arrgh!"

Venerbeen squealed in pain as the tactical baton slammed into the back of his leg. As he stumbled, the administrator stepped backward. On the ground, clutching his leg, Venerbeen turned and saw his attacker. The figure in the skeletal mask held the baton up high to deliver another blow.

The administrator grabbed Max's arm and attempted to wrestle the baton away from him. Thrown off balance, Max surrendered the baton and picked up the metal thermos dropped by the principal and thrust it into the administrator's head. Multiple blows from the metal container dropped him alongside the principal, who was trying to use a parked car to regain his balance. Venerbeen, halfway to his feet, took his cell phone out of the interior pocket of his coat. He unlocked the screen while the masked attacker was still slamming the thermos into the administrator's skull. His palm shook as he pulled up the dial menu and pressed 9, then 1. "Ahhh!" he screamed as

Max poured the contents of the thermos on his hands, scalding his fingers. The black tactical glove took hold of his hand and phone, then twisted his wrist backward. Max pressed his right elbow against the fold of Principal Venerbeen's bent arm and snapped it backward.

If it hadn't been for the crazy note Max had left behind, Carolyn might have been able to get some sleep. She talked to her parents, and both of them agreed she should give him some space. When she told them about the disturbing letter, her mother said she'd still have to wait a day to report him missing. Her father said, "He's bound to get tired and come back home." Carolyn wished she could believe that.

She called and texted and even drove around aimlessly looking for his van, hoping to see it parked in the driveway when she returned. She felt stir-crazy by the time she returned home and dialed him again. The same voicemail greeting she had heard all night sounded after the eighth unanswered ring: "You've reached Max Garret of Garret Securities. I'm not able to come to the phone, so leave a message, and I will address your concerns right away."

Hearing the voice on the machine caused Carolyn to hang up. The devastation of Paige's death had begun to set in after the service, and now Max was missing. She decided to leave a voice message as she paced in the living room. She'd hung up on the voicemail in all her other calls, but she was desperate. The more time passed, the more her instincts told her Max didn't need space—he was going to hurt someone or himself.

"Honey, it's Car. Come home, please. I love you so much, and I need you. We need each other if we're going to get through th—" *Beep.*

In the exact moment the recording cut off Carolyn's plea to her husband, his arms dropped in exhaustion from pulverizing the bodies of the men who had sworn to protect and watch over his child. They had most likely already been dead after the fifth overhead blow from the baton and thermos, but rage had kept him from stopping. If his arms had not betrayed him, he might have never stopped.

The two maintenance workers from the playground ran over when they heard the men's cries coming from the opposite end of the parking lot. Max retracted the baton as they drew closer. They were both sprinting at him with a full head of steam, then both came to an abrupt stop after Max fired two shots into the ground in front of them. They ran off in opposite directions. Max jumped back into the van and sped for Zack and Ronnie.

In the driveway of the Chestnuts' home, Max opened up the throat of Zachary's father and gutted his mother with the jungle knife. The big-headed boy, who liked to hurt animals, terrorize little girls, and throw things, trembled as the skeleton masked man approached him. Max grabbed his hand and put the jungle knife in it.

"You keep this, and remember what happened here. I took your mommy and daddy away from you for what you did to Paige, and if I'm alive when you grow up, you're going to need this when I come for you," the skeleton-faced man said and left them.

The child ran to his mother, who lay on the pavement bleeding out, paralyzed with terror for the rest of his days.

The Gibsons were at a traffic light a block from home when a car rear-ended them. It was just a fender bender. The other driver got out and apologized, admitting complete fault. He told them he was going to report the accident and went back to his vehicle to get his insurance information. After exiting the car, Neil Gibson inspected the damage to his car and got back in the driver's seat, waiting for the other driver to return.

When the other driver walked back to the Gibsons' car, he pulled their son Ronnie out of the back seat. He set Ronnie down then threw a grenade into the car and closed the door shut. He put the pin in Ronnie's hand and said to him, "Stop crying. Shut the fuck up, and take this! Your parents just blew up because of what you did to Paige Garret." Then he pulled away from the Gibsons' burning car.

In a booth at the Longshank Diner, eggs dropped out of Tito's mouth as the local news report came over the television behind the counter. Janine and Gerry looked on in disbelief as the reporter described the murder of two men in the parking lot of a prestigious private school. They had been bludgeoned to death by a man driving a van. The secretary, a surviving witness, described him as a large, hulking man wearing a navy-colored Dickie's uniform. The composite sketch over the television sent Tito running to the bathroom, where the rest of his breakfast exited his body through his mouth.

Janine and Gerry froze in the booth at the television image of the killer they had shared a toast with last night.

"We should call somebody, right, Ger?" Janine asked in a panic. Gerry looked up from his omelet and shrugged while he resumed chewing.

"What's that mean?" Janine asked, appalled at his carefree reaction.

Once he got his food down, Gerry explained himself. "I don't know...I mean, according to him, somebody killed his daughter, Jene. He had his reasons, didn't he?" Gerry said as Tito returned to the booth.

"We have a moral responsibility to report this, Gerry! He's killed people!"

"Oh no, fuck that. We aren't having shit to do with this crazy son of a bitch. Believe me, nothing good can come from this. Come on. I'm taking you two home, and I'm going to sleep until I forget this shit. I suggest you two do the same."

Chapter 20:

FUELING THE FIRE

After swapping the van's license plate with one from a car in a strip-mall parking lot, Max returned to Grady's house. In Grady's garage, he found materials to paint over the Garret Security logo. The paint streaked down the sides of the van, and he contemplated hanging himself or shooting himself, but he wasn't sure just yet.

Inside the garage he looked for a rope or cable and came across some unopened mail: a bill from *Field and Stream* magazine as well as some letters and other pieces of junk mail. After rifling through all the mail addressed to 89 Middleton Lane, Max Garret decided to finish what he set out to do decades ago and failed to accomplish.

Hours driving on the highway had Max continually envisioning all his past tormentors living happy lives. Scheming and bullying as they always had, at the cost of others. When he had left Middleton and moved in with his aunt Ida, he had learned structure and self-discipline in the armed services. If it hadn't been for his crooked commanding officer, who pegged him and the rest of his unit as murderers and thieves for what he had ordered them to do, he might have stayed the course until retirement. Instead he had walked out of the stockade and met Carolyn months later at trade school. She and Paige had helped him let go of past trauma, but Paige was gone, and Carolyn would never be the same again, and neither would he. Max Garret decided it was time for a long-overdue trip back to Middleton.

He passed through Minnesota on I-94. The needle on the odometer never went below eighty as Max heard news of his retribution over the radio. Hours later, as he came to Illinois, fatigue crept in. The tattoo on his chest was itching the bejeezus out of him, and he had to pull in somewhere for the night. He tried checking into an economy inn, but when the desk clerk asked him for identification, he protested. "I'm paying in cash. I just need a room for the night."

"I'm sorry, sir, it's hotel policy even for cash customers," the check-in clerk explained. Max had already withdrawn all the cash from his business account back home to avoid detection, but this was unexpected. He thanked the clerk and drove to a fleabag truck stop hotel he spotted down the road. Barry the desk clerk at the off-pike inn, was devouring Cheetos while holding *People* magazine and enjoying the copy of *Swank* he had hidden between the fold.

"You're in number nine," Barry said, sliding the key across the counter without lifting his head. However, the large roll of bills in Max's hand stood out in Barry's peripheral.

"The movie's on channel four," he yelled to the door as Max left the office. Barry set down his magazine, smeared some Cheetos crumbs into his shirt, and picked up the desk phone.

After cleaning up and applying some ointment to his chest, Max examined in the cracked mirror of the bathroom the first tattoo he had ever marked his body with. He patted himself down with a towel that was half the size of a normal one. He sat on the bed and put on the movie on channel four the Cheeto man from the desk had told him about and grinned at the casual description he was given for "the movie." His thoughts for revenge escaped him for a moment as the screen displayed two women aggressively massaging each other's vaginas. The brunette vaguely resembled Carolyn, and the blonde could have passed for an adult version of his lost love from Middleton, Paige Edmundson.

Just before he fell asleep, he thought about Paige and wondered why she had never responded to the email he had sent her the night his daughter had told him about the torment she was facing in school. Max collapsed in exhaustion. As Max slept, a fantasy played out in his dreams.

He dreamed he was at a barbecue and Dominic was working the grill with his mother assisting. His daughter was on Carolyn's lap, applauding him and his old band, Middleton's Crossing, as they jammed out in the backyard of Grady's mansion, for some reason. Then out of the woods came Rebecca Claussen, who repeated what she had said to Carolyn the day of Paige's death: "She didn't fall; she was forced over. They hit her in the head and knocked her over. They pushed her; they pushed her."

The picnic was covered by a rain shower, and the sound equipment began to short out. Paige Edmundson displayed a guitar case with her dog Elvis inside of it. The dog looked at him and spoke in Ross Aberdeen's voice. "I'm not even closed to finished with you, Garret!"

Then the dream shifted from the barbecue to a hospital bed. Max's mother and Paige were standing over his bandaged body as Paige explained his actions to his mother.

"He would have never done it. They pushed him; they pushed him." Paige's voice blended with the voice of Rebecca Claussen, and they echoed in unison. Dominic's spirit then approached the hospital bed next to Paige, and his mother placed a hand on his. A voice joined in with the echoes of Paige Edmundson and Rebecca Claussen. "They pushed him. They pushed her…"

"Don't worry about anything, Maximillian. Mommies and daddies are going to the cemetery for good," Dominic's spirit said as his face morphed into a disturbing version of Ivan Grady, who repeated Dominic's words, only faster.

"Look what you did! Left me here to die alone with him," Barbara Garret yelled, pointing to his father, who was in the corner of the hospital room snapping his belt. Max tried to get out of the hospital bed but was in a state of paralysis as his daughter's voice boomed over all the other hostile spirits, screaming at him, "Why, Daddy? Why?"

A banging sound filled the small hotel room Max was in. He awoke and thought himself still in the nightmare. Someone was pounding on room number nine's door. He looked outside the sliding doors on the other side of the bed and saw a pair of motorcycles parked next to his van in the near-vacant lot. The banging at the door continued as Max, relieved it wasn't the authorities, threw on his boots and made his way around to the front of the motel. Once in the interior hallway, Max heard the voice of Barry the motel clerk. "I'm tellin' you he had a wad of cash on him. Fucker's probably passed out in there. I'll just open it up for ya."

"Well, he's a long ways from Dakota; only fair he should pay a tax," said the man who was leaning on the outside of his door, with a husky guy in his late thirties and a beat-up-looking woman behind him. They all had matching denim and black leather jackets with patches on them that read, "Devil's Disciples." Their hair was greasy, and they were all breathing heavily. Max went back out to the van once he saw Barry unlock his room from the corridor.

He thought about the shotgun but decided it'd be no good in a closed-in space. He cackled to himself, thinking what a bad decision these slobs had made in picking him as a victim. None of them appeared to be armed, that he could see, so they must have figured on robbing him by intimidation. He closed up the van and kicked over the cycles on his way back inside.

"Hey there, amigo." The one who was pressed up against the door addressed Max as he entered through the open door.

"Our buddy Barry here said you had a decent amount of walking-around money on you. We figured since he helped you out with the room, you can help us out as well." The speaker of the group pointed to Barry, whose shirt was covered in Cheetos orange.

"I hear you, and I suspect a grimy, dirty piece of motor trash such as yourselves would like to add the cost of those two bikes I just kicked over into your figuring," Max said, pacing farther into the room. "There's just one problem though, amigo—you're not Hell's Angel; I am. But that's where I'm going to send you," Max calmly explained, raising the machete from his side. He shoved it into Barry's Cheetos-covered chest as he tried to run out of the room. The woman dug into a small pouch purse and produced a small Saturday night special. She aimed it at Max, who shielded himself with Barry, using him as a human shield, steering him by his head and the handle of the machete still jammed in his midsection toward the gunfire.

A last gasp was given by Barry as she shot at Max, who deflected the bullets with Barry's back. He then drove Barry's body forward, aiming the machete handle toward the man who had referred to him as amigo. The woman drew back and fumbled around for another cartridge of rounds. The biker got around Barry and lunged for Max at the waist. Using the wall behind him for leverage, Max slammed his right elbow into the back of his shoulder blade, then grabbed him by the face. Max closed two fingers into the back of his Adam's apple while he flung wild punches, some hitting Max, some hitting the wall.

The flurry ceased once he gave a crushing squeeze to his larynx and pulled the machete from the grounded body of Barry. The fat one scared once the leader dropped, and he bolted for the sliding glass doors. The woman took aim at Max once again and fired blindly as Max crept toward her in tiger style. Then she blew the light bulb out of the only lamp, blacking out the room. She paced backward toward the open door the fat kid had already run out. Max placed a closed fist over her trigger hand, snapped her elbow backward, and once she was grounded, dropped the full weight of his body into her face with his kneecap. She moved on nerve impulse alone, like an ant smeared across concrete.

Max grabbed the gun and gave chase to the fat kid, who was lifting the bike off the ground. When he saw Max in pursuit, he gave up on it and started toward the road on foot. Max started up the van and ran him down before he could reach the guardrail at the motor lodge entrance.

Feeling the van's undercarriage rattle, he revved it harder in reverse over the screams of the fat one, burning from the exhaust pipe. Exiting the van, Max kicked in his face until the kill had been confirmed. Returning to the hotel room, he took two grenades and tossed them inside the small room.

The explosion burst out of the room, and he nodded to himself with confirmation. "Happy to help you out. Just the warm-up I needed." The adrenaline coursing through his veins made the rest of the ride through the Ohio turnpike a breeze. A car in front of him hit a trailer and spun into a 360. Max calmly entered the opposite lane in a split second and floored the accelerator.

He was highballing it. At the breakneck pace, he estimated he was mere hours from Middleton as he cut through Ohio into Pittsburgh like a wraith. Nothing alive was going to impede his path or stop his will. He needed to get rid of the van. The out-of-state plates had already made him a target of the devil's disciples and diverted him from his plan.

Chapter 21:
WARPATH INTERRUPTED

A combination of fatigue, anticipation, and glaring sunlight behind the mountains past Pittsburgh had caused Max to miss an exit, and he'd gotten turned around. He came across a broken-down, abandoned sedan in a remote lot and affixed the Pennsylvania plates to the van. After getting back on the road and taking the plates, he felt so tired he thought he might collapse. Once back on the turnpike, Max pulled into a small rest stop and parked between two 18-wheelers and slept over half a day. He awoke in the late afternoon of Tuesday, November 11. A half mile from the rest stop, he pulled into a gas station with a store behind it.

The entrance tone sounded as Max entered the mini-mart. A cashier studied him with curiosity while scratching underneath his turban. Connecting to any GPS was risky. It'd been some time since Max had had to resort to using a map, but the stop was welcome. His legs were cramping up, and it felt good to stretch them; plus, he was the hungriest he had been in a long time. What he did eat after Paige's, funeral he vomited up soon after.

After walking through the four small aisles, Max approached the clerk, who was watching his every move. "Do you sell any road maps here?" Max asked.

The clerk was cut off before he could answer by a frat boy behind Max, who blurted out, "Just get a GPS, Pops, and get on with it. Yo!" swaying from side to side in his flip-flops, laughing to his friend beside him.

"Shut the fuck up, Brett. Where the fuck is Chetty, yo?" the friend said, play-punching at Brett's arm. "Yo! Chetty, grab me a fuckin' Red Bull, bitch!" he bellowed out to the back of the store.

"Fuck you, Chris! Get your own shit," Chetty yelled back.

"Chetty, you don't get my man his drink, we're gonna tag team your girl when we get back," Brett said, tilting his visor.

"That's my word, yo!" Chris agreed, laughing while leaning into Brett.

"We used to have behind register, but nobody buy anymore," the clerk explained to Max, showing him a black metal road atlas display stand that was stocked with packets of synthetic marijuana tablets and cell phone chargers. This did not remedy the absence of maps for Max.

"Hey, Hapu! If I'm done with this trail mix before this tool's, done, I'm not paying for it," Chris said, tearing open the wrapper. As he tilted the bag upward, sliding its contents into his mouth, Max watched Chris in his peripheral vision.

"OK. Could you direct me toward Route One from here?" Max asked as Chetty joined his friends, his boat shoes squeaking as he handed the energy drink to Chris.

"Yo, Chetty, what the fuck, bro? You didn't grab me sugar-free, dick!" Chris said as Chetty ignored him and saw Max still in line.

"Get the fuck out of here...this doucher is seriously still in line? I told Brooke we'd be right back," Chetty yelled, ignoring the beratement he had received over the Red Bull selection.

"Trail mix is finished, Hapu," Chris said, throwing the wrapper on the floor and cracking open the energy drink. As he tilted his head back to gulp from the can, Max removed the sleeve knife from its sheath and slammed it into Chris's neck. In the blink of an eye, he retracted the blade and pounded into the neck of Brett. Chris was on the floor with both hands on his neck, spouting a mini geyser of blood.

The cashier retreated into the back of the store as Chetty dropped his Slurpee on the floor, where his friends' opened veins were flooding the white tile red at his feet. Max grabbed him with his left hand, the sleeve blade held over his head with his right.

"Whose convertible's out there, Chetty?" Max asked, motioning toward the parking lot with the small steel pointed blade.

"It's...it's Chris's car. He drove. Please!" Chetty responded, frantically shielding his face.

"Get me the keys, and unlock your cell phone, and give it to me, you plaid-madras motherfucker, and fast!"

Chetty attempted to take Chris's keys from his cargo shorts but fell out of his boat shoes, slipping in the pool of blood around Chris's body; his wild kicking gradually slowed to a twitch.

The in-store radio commercials stopped as "(Don't Fear) the Reaper" by Blue Oyster Cult played. The entry bell sounded once more as a man turned around and quickly walked out as he viewed the mayhem unfolding in the store. Crying, Chetty pulled Chris's keys from his pocket after a second attempt. Trembling, he handed them over. When Max reached for the keys, he felt a shotgun press up against his head.

"State police are coming! You fucking kilt dese guyz."

Max casually sighed and raised his hands to his head in a surrendering pose. The cashier got the drop on him, and he cursed himself for ignoring him. Fortunately for Max, he was standing way to close to him to get off a clean shot.

Pulling his head back from the twelve-gauge, Max dropped his right arm and took hold of the barrel. With all his might, he yanked the gun toward himself and slammed his elbow into the clerk's head, using his forward momentum to assist the impact. The clerk was out cold. Max made his way over to Chetty, who was sniveling and sobbing, hiding behind an ice cream cooler.

"Sorry, Chetty, it's a fear the reaper kind of day, and this doucher's the last thing you're ever going to see," Max said, unloading the shotgun into his chest. The thunderclap in the back of the store brought the clerk out of his daze, but he was still too lightheaded to get to his feet. From the ground he observed Max grabbing some items from behind the counter.

"You muthafucka, you fucked my head, mutter bitch." He groaned from the floor.

"So, uh, you get some maps for next time, probably, huh? Sorry about the damage," Max said, leaving a bundle of bills beside him.

As Max neared the exit, he took a hooded dark zipper coat and put it on, concealing the blood from the encounter that saturated his torso.

The outdoor gas attendant ran in the opposite direction of the shotgun-wielding figure exiting the store. The convertible was black with dark-red racing stripes on the sides that matched the dark-red interior. Max dumped the cases from Grady into the back seat and turned the engine over. The car powered on, Drowning Pools' "Let the Bodies Hit the Floor" blasting from the speakers. Max shrugged his shoulders and pulled back onto the turnpike.

He took the next exit and got on the other side of the turnpike. On the opposite side of the road, a fleet of state police cars raced past him. Three miles down the road, he pulled under an overpass and plugged an adapter into the cigarette lighter and powered on the portable GPS device he had taken from behind the counter. The sun went down on the day during which Max had killed seven more people. He had not intended to, but they had been most deserving, and he figured the world better without them, regardless.

The GPS screen displayed the exit he had missed, and Max tossed it out of the car. After another hour of driving, he looked up at the highway sign. The green background with white lettering announced, "Route 1, Middleton Exit, 15 miles."

Stirring the cup of tea she had prepared for her distraught daughter, Deena Pastrel stepped into the Garrets' living room. Carolyn was curled up in the fetal position on her couch with Paige's Nemo blanket barely covering her. "Drink this, honey—help you relax," her mother directed in the most soothing voice she could manage.

"I want him back here, Mom," Carolyn managed to say. Her voice was an indication of the sedatives that had her in such a fog.

"Your father went down to the police station to take care of that for you. I want you to rest," Deena Pastrel replied, pulling a larger cover over Carolyn. She caught a glimpse of the local news at her daughter's back. The broadcast was on, and although the volume was turned down, her mother took notice of the red banner anchored at the bottom of the screen, which read, "LOCAL PREP SCHOOL DOUBLE MURDER."

Deena snatched the remote and turned off the television; she helped Carolyn up the stairs and into her bed. Once Carolyn was settled, she rushed back downstairs to see what had happened at the school where her granddaughter had died. Before she could turn the TV back on, the front door was flung open. She dropped the remote as her husband, Dennis, walked in with a look of bewilderment on his face.

"Two of the people from that school are dead, Deena," he announced, removing his hat, clenching it tightly with both hands.

"Shush. I know. I just got her in bed. I just saw it."

"They think it was Max. Hell, let's be honest—it was," Dennis said, looking down at the floor.

"Don't be ridiculous! That man doesn't have a mean bone in his body, for God's sake. What makes them think he did it?" Deena asked, ignoring intuition, which told every fiber of her being that her son-in-law was either dead or in trouble.

Continuing to look at the floor, Dennis continued, "The secretary they found tied up and locked up in the closet confirmed his description and…" he paused.

"And what?"

"On one of the bodies in the parking lot—there was a note that said this was an accident as well. Police want to question Carolyn, but I refused, told them she was heavily medicated and that I'd bring her there once I got back here. To fuck with that. After all she's been through! Pack her up—she's coming home with us."

Deena saw it as a moot point to question whether Dennis had made a missing persons report for Max and nodded in agreement.

They headed to the staircase, then ran upstairs to the sounds of their shrieking daughter.

PART III:
TIME THE AVENGER

Farewell to all the sentiments which rejoice the heart. I have played the part of providence in recompensing the good. May the god of vengeance now permit me to punish the wicked!
—Edmond Dantès in *The Count of Monte Cristo*

Chapter 22:
SCORES TO SETTLE

November 13, 2008

Technically proficient almost to a fault, Max still needed the help of Jules at the donut shop, who got the burner phone's browser working. The teenager with the lip ring and blue streaks in his blond hair was helpful and polite. It was late afternoon, and Max was the only customer. Once he handed a hundred bucks to Jules to help him out, he went above and beyond.

Logging into Jules's social media account, Max was able to look up all his old "friends" in Middleton. At least that's what he had told Jules so he could make sure all the little hogs were still living in the same pigpen. Once on the social media account, Max sought privacy but didn't want to be rude to his helper, who in addition to letting Max log on to his account had also provided the store's free Wi-Fi password.

As Jules leaned over Max's shoulder looking at the profiles he was scanning through, he commented, "Man, that chick is a MILF for real. You hit that, Preston?" he asked Max, calling him by the name he had given during the account setup.

"No, but I'm going to; I'm gonna hit it till I split it. Here, partner, you were a big help to me getting this set up. This is a bonus for your troubles. You mind if I stay on your account here? I really don't have time to set up my own, and I'm in a bit of a hurry."

"No sweat, Preston. Good luck."

As Max had suspected, what went around hadn't ended up coming around for the Middleton High class of 1990. The only one who lived outside of town was Greg Chapman, whom Max was not inclined to forget about. An issue of traveling a few miles out of the way was no issue at all.

"Say, Preston, some dudes are looking in your car out there!" Jules said from behind the counter, figuring the sole car in the parking lot was his. Max ran out the door and approached the two men looming over the recently deceased Chris Martin's gaudily painted convertible.

"This yours?" an elderly man asked Max, who was about to unsheathe his knife once more.

"We're classic car enthusiasts." The old-timer's companion spoke up, handing Max a business card.

"What year is this one? A seventy-three, right?" the elderly man asked Max, who was thrown off by the men, who he had thought were interested in the contents of the convertible's back seat, not the car itself.

"How much you want for it?" the other man pressed before Max could provide his estimated guess.

"I'm not paying top dollar for it. We'd have to repaint it, Andy," the old man said, walking around to the driver's side and inspecting the mileage. "It's a 1973 Buick Convertible. What the hell possessed you to deviate from the original color scheme? And cover up the chrome with this racing stripe shit?" Max was irritated and actually considered defending the racing stripe and color of the car of the mouthy little cunt whose throat he had punctured open.

"They must not have taught you too well at that college," the old man continued, eyeing the automobile.

"What college?" Max asked.

"The one from the bumper sticker you put on the back, bumper genius," the old man complained, ready to seize the moment and really make a lowball offer. Max couldn't help but admire his passion.

"Take it easy, Dad. What's with all the equipment in the back—these cases and all? Are you a photographer or something?" Andy asked.

"Yes, something like that. Tell you gentlemen what, I only need the car another day or so. I finish what I need to do without complication, I'll call you guys up, leave it in the same lot, and you can have it free of charge. I have to run; sooner I get done, the sooner it's yours," Max said, climbing into the driver's seat.

Andy and his father walked off ecstatic as Max looked up the lot and block number for one Greg Chapman, resident of Maidens Mist, just outside of Middleton, and drove off. The car was a classic, and the growl of the engine mimicked the fire burning inside Max. The last thing he wanted was a conversation piece and school spirit sticker bringing unwanted attention. He parked it down the street from his destination. The buzz from the overhead streetlamp flickering on and off was the only sound Max could hear on the quiet suburban street.

The colonial two-story rancher that voter registration and tax records confirmed to be the residence of his target stood in front of Max. He chose not to get up close and personal with Greg. While he wanted to, there was still much work to be done. There were plenty of windows, he deduced, performing his initial reconnaissance. He walked back to the car and took hold of one of Grady's cases.

The light of a television upstairs helped Max decide where to set up. He climbed the trellis of the house next door and had eyes inside. A flabby, overweight adult version of Greg Chapman was seated in a recliner drinking a can of beer and laughing hysterically at the television set with his back to the window.

There was still a good number of grenades, and the glass on the window didn't appear to be double pane, but Max had to be sure. It was difficult assembling Grady's rifle from the neighbor's roof, especially in the dark. The back porch light was on at the house he was stalking his prey from. With the mini mag light, Max was set. It took him only a second to direct the rifle's scope toward the light beaming out of Greg's window. The chucklehead was laughing so hard his head kept moving forward, but at this distance, Max figured he couldn't miss. He took a deep breath from his sprawled-out position and placed his finger on the trigger.

Grrrr...grrrr. the growling sound caused Max to back off the rifle, and when he peered out over the roof, he saw a Rottweiler. Once the massive beast put his paws on the foot of the trellis ladder, he and Max were face-to-face.

Grrrr. the beast directed his suspicious, low growl toward Max, showing his teeth.

"Shit!" Max exclaimed to himself. Quickly he pulled the half-eaten sausage, egg, and cheese sandwich from his pocket and dropped it down to the Rottie, whose black coat was shining from the overhead moonlight. After devouring the sandwich, the dog looked up in the direction of the dart that had just pierced his hide.

The dog became more aggressive and started howling, confused. Max blew three more tranquilizers from the blow dart gun and connected with two that finally slowed the beast as the first dart took effect on him. By the time Max returned to his rifle, the damage had been done: Greg was gone, and the first-floor lights were on.

He shoved the rifle and the blowgun in the case without putting everything in place and made his way down the makeshift ladder. He heard the screen door open across the way and knew it was Greg. The pear-shaped shadow showed up on the lit-up concrete below the small porch. Then he heard a loud belch, accompanied by the sound of cans crushing. Max unlatched the entrance to the fence of the backyard. The sound got Greg's attention. As Greg leaned over the railing, Max crept below him.

He jumped back, surprised by the figure who rose from the side of the porch. Max aimed for his neck and stabbed a dart into Greg's cheek. Max pierced another dart into his neck by hand after scaling the porch. He was wobbly but not out. Then Greg stumbled; Max ran to keep him from toppling over. He braced him and dragged him into the house after propping open the screen door.

"There you are! Sorry about all the duct tape, but you didn't have any rope around here, Greg!" Max said in jubilation. Bulging eyes were looking back at him. Greg was nude and bound to a wooden rolling chair from his office. His concern was further heightened as he felt the forced air from a central air vent, which brushed against the hairs of his ass, exposed through a hole in the seat of the chair. Goosebumps caused him to clench up, and his eyes widened further.

It was a real pain in the ass chipping out the seat with the drill in the basement. The arms made it impossible to use the circular saw, but Max had to do something while Greg was knocked out. The look on Greg's face made it worth every second.

"Mmmph, errhhh, mmph." Greg rocked from side to side, struggling in vain to speak through the silver tape gag. The only thing in his line of sight was the man who had put him in the chair, covered in a hood and skeleton mask. He rocked furiously from side to side while Max paced his office.

"Oh, McCarmick—I mean, Mr. M. Yeah, I'll see him next, but I remember that one, Greg. You were in the paper, and I was in the ICU," Max said, taking hold of the wooden placard, adorned with brass and a picture of Greg and Coach McCarmick presenting him with the trophy. Max held out the plaque and looked at it once more, reflecting on it.

"Good times," he said. Then he smashed it over Greg's head, increasing the muffled screaming, before rolling over to his desktop computer.

"I'm so glad you're still in touch with the old gang. Nice! Nice pictures. Everybody having a good time, doing real fucking good, huh? Barbecues and bullshit. Thanks for the blueprint."

Blood trickled from Greg's head, mingling with slobber and saliva, loosening up the duct tape covering his mouth. Max patted him on the shoulder, shaking his head, indicating no.

"Oh, fuck it. Why not!" Max then removed the tape from his mouth with the sidearm trained at Greg's head should he start screaming again.

"I don't know who the hell you are or what you want, but…" Greg stammered to catch his breath.

Max removed the half mask and hood, revealing his face. "Yeah," Max said, nodding with a disappointed frown. "You're probably going to tell me you're sorry, right?"

"I am! I'm fucking sorry. OK!" Greg shouted in desperation as Max crouched before him and pulled another length of tape.

"Hmm, yeah. I know you are," Max said, calmly covering his mouth once more.

Max took hold of Greg's chin to keep his head from moving from side to side and zoned in on the black of Greg's pupils before giving his final reply. "Sorry's no good now, Greg. Shit wasn't good then either. You can put sorry right up your ass, which is exactly where this trophy is going. You know how it is these days—everybody gets a trophy."

Relaxed on his sofa, Harold McCarmick was watching the early evening edition of SportsCenter. He was relieved his wife was out and he didn't have to hear her bitch about how he had already watched this.

If she came back late, he didn't have to watch the Country Music Awards. He hoped to catch a half of an NBA game in peace. An email alert sounded from his cell phone, and he muted the broadcast to check his phone.

"What the hell is he sending me now?" McCarmick said aloud. He had already had communication with Greg earlier. He normally received links via text message from Greg, and it was a hassle to open up the attachment. The email in the subject line read in all caps, "MY BEST RECEPTION."

"What the fuck is this?" McCarmick uttered in annoyance, expecting to see a VCR to DVD transfer of some of Greg's highlights on his phone. There were no football highlights in Greg's email, and McCarmick thought it was a half-ass joke message until he lunged back at the sight of Greg taped up and bleeding from his head.

"Behold Greg's final reception. Technically, I suppose, it's a flaming enema, but anyways," the hooded figure in the skeleton mask said, presenting the trophy to the webcam. He then doused Greg in gasoline, heated up the squared marble base of the trophy with a torch, took hold of the camera, and placed it on the floor in front of Greg's swollen, beet-red face. Enormous blue veins pulsated with a life of their own, nearly bursting through his temples as he was penetrated with the base of the trophy first.

"What the fuck!" McCarmick yelled back at his phone; as the video played on, a match was struck. The sound of Greg's continuous dying screams was heard as he was set ablaze.

Closing the video out, McCarmick attempted to call Greg but was jolted by the sound of the grandfather clock chiming. He composed himself once the clock's chime had ceased and put the phone to his ear, only to pull it away when he heard his whistle being blown inside the house. For a moment McCarmick thought he was hearing things, until the whistle sounded again.

When he saw the masked intruder dangling his whistle on the other side of his sofa, he knew he had heard correctly.

"Hey Mr. M. Jughead's back, and he's making the calls tonight," Max said, enjoying fear in the face of the man who was so tough when browbeating eleventh-graders.

"Motherfucker!" McCarmick leaped from the couch to tackle Max, who backed up, causing McCarmick's leap at him to fall short at his waist. Max took a firm hold of him and unleashed a trio of ferocious headbutts into his face, the third hitting the lower part of the nose and some teeth. As McCarmick's head slumped, Max paused, then continued with back-to-back pistol-whips until he dropped the limp body.

"It's going to be closed casket, coach." Max gasped, out of breath, and extended the baton. McCarmick's body went into a half-dead crawl of desperation. A key sounded in the lock in the front door.

"Harold, help me unload the car. Whose convertible is that down the street?" A woman's voice called out as the light in the foyer came on and revealed McCarmick's bleeding hamburger-meat face to Max.

"Fuck it!" Max said, raising the .45 as the pace of high heel shoes drew closer.

Blam. The sound echoed in the blackened living room, with a flash of light followed by another shot. *Blam.* Max grabbed the phone off the floor and a set of keys from an end table and exited through the back door he had come in. Moments later Mrs. McCarmick's blood-curdling screams filled the sleepy suburban street. Before exiting the McCarmicks' residence, Max moved broken teeth out of the way in Harold McCarmick's mouth and shot a hole in his head that was still seeping smoke when the police and paramedics discovered him.

A status update chimed on McCarmick's phone as Max packed his arsenal into McCarmick's maroon Chevy Blazer. After adjusting the seat,

Max pulled off and looked at the cracked phone screen, which showed a profile picture of Deidre Lisbon and a message that read, "I'm going shopping bitches…Tharington's woot woot!"

"I bet you are. Looks like I'm going shopping too," Max said to himself and headed for the Middleton Pines Mall.

Chapter 23:

VOICES OF THE PAST

Friday, November 14, 2008

News of Deidre's murder at the Middleton Pines Shopping Mall had Paige Edmundson-Darby in a fog the entire day. She had a consultation with a divorce attorney scheduled, but the news of her onetime friend's death had left her in no shape for that kind of meeting. She spent the morning remembering those long-ago years she had suppressed in the far corners of her memory. After transferring from Middleton High and getting no return correspondence from Max, she had hidden that hurt and pain in her past.

A part of her past was now dead. Whether she wanted to admit it or not, Deidre Lisbon was a big part of it. While her effect had been negative, the impacts on her existence had been monumental. If it hadn't been for Deidre, it would have been Max who had taken her to prom that year. He'd have never blown up his basement and moved away, and she might very well have been happily married to him instead of having gotten involved with Eddie.

She had conned herself into loving him to get over the hurt of Max being gone. It worked for a long time, too. He was sweet and sincere. A few months turned into a few years, and he was all she ever knew. But red flags popped up left and right six months after the marriage. Drinking, gambling, and losing led to more drinking, then drugs. Paige thought having Olivia would change him, and it did, for a bit, but not for the better—just more of the same.

Sitting on the floor in her closet, Paige flipped through the 1988 Middleton High yearbook. There were only two signatures in the entire book: one from her favorite teacher, Katherine Jalorean, and the other from the only person she was ever truly in love with—Max Garret. A fast-running tear streamed down her cheek and fell on the glossy black-and-white photo of Max in the yearbook. She smiled, seeing the heart she had drawn over his photo. The ink made her recall the purple pen that had been her favorite when she was seventeen.

The photos were in alphabetical order, and the yearbook automatically opened to the most viewed page. Months after Max had moved away, she had spent a good amount of time gazing at his yearbook photo and the photo-booth pictures they had taken together. She had cried herself to sleep listening to the cassette tape of the band's practice sessions in Dominic's garage. She had played it so much the tape was inaudible, and she cursed herself for never making a copy. There was one other item of remembrance from those times, and its weight shifted from one side of Paige's memory box to the other.

Last year she and Eddie had been at a holiday party with friends of his and she had gotten into a heated argument. Normally she would have had a few drinks and kept to herself while Eddie went on about how great he was. Somehow the dinner conversation had shifted from politics and sports to betting and bookmakers. Then the talk around the table had turned to who was the most criminally infamous person in Middleton's history.

The first name mentioned was Artemis Kane, formerly on the FBI's most-wanted list and a never-caught bank heist man. Then one of the older guys in the crowd had protested that Kane had learned everything he knew from his mentor, Ice Cold Carmine Infantrino. It had been boring, and Paige had poked at her salad and taken no notice of the discussion in progress until a name was spoken that made her ears perk up.

"None of them guys would have been shit if it hadn't been for Dom Gladgem Gervallo! He just wasn't as public about his," one of them had spouted. Without realizing it, Paige had taken hold of the gold ring dangling from her neck inside of her sweater.

"That dude was a piece of shit! He extorted my great-uncle's liquor store back when!" another had added.

"Well, maybe your great-uncle wasn't really that great!" Paige had said, snapping one of her nails. Clasping the ruby stone, she had felt the ring she was holding defensively. The fact that these deadbeats Eddie hung out with had even mentioned Dom had gotten her heated. When one of them had had the gall to insult him, she had hurled a drink in his face and then flung her salad dish at him.

She and Eddie had fought the whole way home. He had claimed she had embarrassed him and been disrespectful. When they had gotten home, she had thrown another drink in Eddie's face while she was getting changed. He had slapped her and snapped the necklace and ring from her neck; it had not been removed since she was a teenager.

Now the sound of the heavy ring sliding against the base of the memory box caused her to pick it up.

She still had photos of Max out. After gazing into the ruby centered inside the large ring, she looked at Max's photo and said aloud, "You never came to take it, but something tells me you're back now." While Max's photo did not answer back, a voice barked at Paige, sitting on the floor of her closet reminiscing.

"Are you cooking, or am I ordering food tonight?" Eddie shouted up the stairs. Packing up her things, she turned off the closet light and headed downstairs. Olivia was with her parents, and she felt little to no urgency to prepare dinner. She only did so out of obligation. Stirring the pot on the stove, Paige dreaded having to talk to him. In a sad way, her little girl was a buffer that made dinner more manageable than having an adult conversation with the man she had fooled herself into marrying but had come to loathe.

There was nothing for them to talk about, so current events it was—the morning's events, to be exact. For the first time, Eddie expressed interest in her past. This was attributable, by and large, to Deidre's murder. Still, Eddie had to share his great deed of the day. The look on his wife's face was one of insincere joy when he told her, "The job cost about a buck fifty. When I saw this goofy bastard, I elbowed Johnny and told him we're hitting him for another three hundred in parts and service." Minor victories, overcharging people—it was all he had, and normally she humored him with false interest for her daughter's sake. Today she just didn't have it in her.

"Then I bled him for another couple hundred and told him it took me four hours to fix the door," he said in excitement, seeking to up the ante in response to her unimpressed expression.

"You're just a regular Lex Luthor, aren't you, Ed?" Paige replied dryly. This forced him to change the subject. Dipping his bread into his gravy, he decided to question Paige about the, in his words, "sexy dead girl."

For once Eddie listened to her as she explained her onetime friendship and how and why it had ended. She was never as certain that she wanted to divorce Eddie as she was when she heard his reply when she got to the part about Deidre killing Elvis.

"Good thing! You know I can't have no pets in the house," he replied in humor. Before Paige could tell Eddie just how much she truly had come to despise him, he dipped a piece of bread into what was left on his plate and asked through unchewed bread. "So he was the one who was going to blow up your old school? I can't believe you knew Maniac Max! How come you never told me?"

"I did, Ed, a long time ago. You were ignoring me as usual. But yeah, we were friends, and that's why he told me not to go in that day," Paige replied, downplaying the nature of the relationship between Max and her. *The moron doesn't even remember hitting on me when Max was in the hospital*, Paige thought to herself, overwhelmed.

"Well? Is it him?" Eddie asked, slurping what was left of his soup. Paige looked at him, befuddled. "Was it him that killed her? Do you think he did it?" The color drained from her face as her dopey husband asked the question she had asked herself since learning of Deidre's murder.

"No, he moved to Dakota after he got out of the hospital. I talked to him once before he moved, then his number wasn't in service. I tried writing him, but..." Paige's reflective response was cut off by the obnoxious ring tone from her cell phone. She looked at the screen of her phone in confusion.

"It's a six-o-five area code. South Dakota?"

"It's probably him. Maybe he heard what happened to her"

"How could he have my cell number?" Paige replied in doubt, telling herself the location of the caller was nothing more than sheer coincidence.

"Well, answer it and see!" Eddie ordered in his usual impatient tone.

"Hello. Is this Paige?" a nervous, tearful, feminine voice said when she answered.

"Yes, this is. Who, may I ask, is calling?" Paige replied, hushing Eddie, who was badgering her, asking who it was.

"I hope you don't mind my calling. Your parents' number was listed, and I got your cell number from them once I explained the emergency." The voice sounded regretful and teary.

"Who is this? What emergency?"

"I'm Carolyn Garret. Max, who you went to school with? His wife?"

In shock, Paige stood up from the table. The dizzy feeling she had had earlier that day was affecting her once more.

"Is he OK?"

Carolyn let out a big sob before being able to continue. Once composed, she spoke up. "We recently had a family tragedy, and I don't know where he is. He sent you an email last month, and I was hoping you had heard from him. In the message he reached out to you about problems with our little girl, Paige." The mention of her deceased daughter's name caused Carolyn to choke up once more. "We lost her this M-Mo—I mean, last Monday—due to the negligence of her school," Carolyn continued, holding back tears.

"Oh, my goodness. No. I'm so sorry! I never got any message from Max. As a matter of fact, I have not heard from him since I was nineteen. It was months ago?" Paige asked, scanning unread emails in her inbox at her desk. She began opening any unread messages until she came across one that had Max's last name in the address.

"Garret Securities?"

"Yes, that's it," Carolyn confirmed as Paige began to read the message's content aloud:

> To my old knight in arms. I hope my getting in touch with
> you doesn't freak you out or anything. I still regret the way
> things ended but as your online info shows you have a lovely

family of your own, as do I. On the way home from work after one of my first jobs out here, I heard a song you used to turn up on the radio and sing all the time. IN YOUR EYES by Peter Gabriel was always one of your favorites, but it's not what prompted me to reach out to you. Tonight, I had a discussion with my daughter Paige (yes you read correctly) the most noble name I could think of. Tonight, little Paige told me about how she was being picked on and bullied in her second-grade class and it broke my heart to hear it.

What are the chances right? I feel like I passed on my curse to my adopted daughter. My wife is for the most part oblivious to my pre-Dakota past. She is actually attending her reunion tonight and has no idea how bad something like this can be. You were there for me in some of my darkest times and I know you understand. You were my one and only when no one else was and again I'm sorry for how things ended. In the hospital you and my mom were the only things that kept me from despising humanity altogether. I thank you for being your wonderful self and enabling me to give life a second chance. I thank you for giving me the confidence to go on. I truly believe if not for you I would have never wanted the beautiful family I am blessed with today. I see you have a girl close to my daughter's age and would appreciate any advice or suggestion of how to go about handling this.

Love Max

P.S. I've attached a picture of Carolyn, me and our little Paige. No pressure to respond but it'd be great to hear from you.

Once Paige finished the message, she asked Carolyn if she had tried Max's aunt.

"Yes, I called them. He never went there, and now the principal and administrator from her school, well, they're dead. They were murdered…oh God!" Carolyn said, causing Paige to place a palm over her head as she felt like Carolyn's news was going to cause it to roll off her shoulders.

"I'm so sorry. I don't know how to tell you this, but somebody who made a lot of trouble for Max years ago—she was…"

"She was murdered too?"

"Beaten to death in a parking lot."

"Can I please call you back?" Carolyn questioned anxiously.

"Of course. Anything I can do to help."

"I'm coming there," Carolyn said, then the phone disconnected. Eddie stood in front of Paige, arms folded, expecting an explanation for the call. *Saved by the bell!* Paige thought, seeing her parents' phone number show up on the caller ID.

Chapter 24:

REST FOR THE WICKED

Due to the media coverage, Deidre's service included mourners who knew her and a good many who did not. They had felt compelled to show support due to the way her life ended. The complete cost of the burial was paid for by Matt Bergman, or as Deidre and Lana knew him, Let-Me-Get-That-Matt. Bergman escorted her mother, and Lana was watching him with interest; she sought to fill the vacancy left by Deidre's death. Why wear Deidre's clothes from last season? Now that the sugar daddy was sugarless, he could spoil her instead, Lana thought.

Matt knew Deidre had only loved him for his money, but they had spent enough time together that he would have liked to think she thought of him as a friend too. He found himself more bereaved than her mother, who had been clinging to him inappropriately since the service ended. While he had ensured Deidre received a proper burial, he wanted this day to be over fast. He was questioned by multiple representatives from Middleton's finest, and in spite of his airtight alibi, they had their doubts about his innocence.

As Matt Bergman sat under the tent at the burial site, he looked over Deidre's friends from high school. They were talking among themselves and not even listening to the burial rites being said by the pastor. If anyone should be questioned about her death, it should be this clump of disrespectful assholes across from me, Bergman thought as he stared over at Ross Aberdeen in annoyance.

Deidre had dropped Ross as her boyfriend but always kept in touch with him. She had made it clear to him that he was her throwback guy. Whenever she felt down, she fit in a confidence quickie with her old boy, who wasn't doing so well himself and always jumped at the chance to lift her spirits.

"This is fucked, man! This is so fucked! She deserved better than this! I bet that wrinkled-up old ball bag over there killed her," Ross said loud enough to be heard by Matt Bergman. His comment caused the pastor to stop, then regain his place and resume.

"That's the guy she was dating, Ross. Did you talk to Greg?" Lana asked in a much lower voice.

"Look at Paige, the phony bitch. You know she's probably glad Dee got killed." Allison added to the gossip.

"Yeah. Say, where is Greg?" Ross asked, nudging Dwayne.

"My dad was at his place with the shorthanded fire department in Maidens Mist, dude. Greg's house burned to the fucking ground," Dwayne explained.

"Was he in it when it happened?" Ross responded back to him.

"Don't think so; they said his car was gone," Dwayne replied.

"Well, fuck his house! He should have come. He should have shown up!" Ross exclaimed, earning another stare from the pastor and Bergman.

Lana leaned in and tugged at the sleeve of Dwayne's jacket, then whispered loud enough for all nearby to hear, "Did you or your dad get called to Mr. M's, Dwayne?"

"No, neither one of us were, but when they got back to the station, the guys who were there said his face looked like it had been beaten with a—"

Twipt.

Suddenly Dwayne's knees buckled and skull fragments fell out the side of his face.

From a rooftop of a mausoleum crypt, blackbirds scattered as Max shifted the crosshairs of the long-range rifle's scope off Dwayne and set his sights on Ross. "No, no. Not that way for you," Max said, giving another squeeze of the trigger. The shot let off an echoing thunderclap into the cemetery trees, vibrations giving sound to the bullet that had just ripped through Wendy's neck as she fell to the ground.

"His head's bleeding!" Ross said, crouching over Dwayne.

Twipt. "Arrgh. Ahh!" Ross fell back, shrieking with both hands covering his shattered kneecap. Once the funeral-goers had grasped what was occurring, they panicked and ran for the safety of their vehicles. Paige was off to the far side of the service, away from the main road, so she took shelter behind the largest gravestone available.

Mollie Johnson, Allison Kyle, and Cindy Lawton were crying and running hand in hand with no sense of direction. Cars were crashing into one another as people tried to drive away from the grounds. The three girls stood in front of the chauffeur who was pulling away in the hearse.

"Cindy," Max said, then saw his next shot hit Mollie Johnson in the back, causing the driver to climb into the back of the hearse for cover as the car, still in drive, rolled forward. Allison and Cindy abandoned Mollie and ran from the cover of the hearse, opening them up to a flurry of bullets sent their way and through their flesh.

"Class dismissed," Max said as he saw the hearse roll over Mollie, who was clutching with both hands the point where the bullet had cut through her chest. Max descended the side of the mausoleum wall.

"Help! Help!" Ross cried as Harold McCarmick's Chevy Blazer pulled up in front of him.

Reeling in pain, Ross clutched his knee and went into a sideways crawl to the car he thought was coming to his aid. The hooded figure stepped out of the car with his jawline covered in a skeletal mask. Ross knew his assumptions had betrayed him. The man in the hood walked past Deidre's casket and over to Ross.

"Remember when you told me you weren't even close to finished with me, Ross?" he asked, removing the sidearm from its holster.

"What the fuck do you want? Who the fuck are you?" Ross screamed before receiving a second gunshot from the handgun into his other kneecap.

"I'm your Frankenstein, Ross. A fucked-up villain you helped create. I always meant to kill you, just took some time. So…" Pulling a jungle knife out from its sheath, Max leaned toward Ross to finish him. As he brought the blade near his head, Ross grabbed at it, causing Max to reset.

"No, Ross. No Greg or Dwayne to back you up. No homeboys to help you out. Oh. Wait a minute," Max said, pulling down his hood, his focus distracted by Deidre's casket behind him.

The pleas for help and mercy would continue to spout from Ross as Max flung open the top of the closed casket and reached inside it. Making his way back over to Ross, Max screamed at him.

"Look, dead Deidre's panties! You were always so worried that I took them, right? By the way, so nice of you to show up here. Trying to help Dwayne after I opened his melon up and all. 'Specially since the dead skank you're here to see hated me cuz she was fucking him. You die knowing that! You fucked-up piece of human garbage! Not a crusty jockstrap, but it'll do."

Max forced white lace and silk into Ross's mouth, then carelessly dropped the underwear on Ross's slobbering red face after the initial shove. "Favor returned! Keep the hellfire stoked for me, Ross! I'll be seeing you soon!" Max said, raising the pistol, aimed at Ross's head at point-blank range.

"Max!" Paige screamed as she made herself visible from behind the tombstone, overcome by the sight of the dead bodies surrounding Ross.

"Why did you even come here, Paige?" Max asked, identifying Paige's voice without turning his head away from Ross, who crossed his arms in front of his face to shield the kill shot to come.

"Wait, Garret! Don't. *Stop.* I'm sorry so-suh-suh. Ahhh. Oh God. No, no!" Before Paige could answer, *blam.* Max pulled the trigger, ending the life of Ross Aberdeen, who had had the nerve to beg him before he took it. Ross who lived every day with his chest puffed out, only to die on his back a sniveling, whining coward.

"Couldn't hear you over that. Sorry, Paige, you were saying?"

"This isn't you, Max! I wanted to see you for so long, but this isn't the Max who wrote me, who I loved," Paige exclaimed in tears.

Max held the gun upward, and for a moment, Paige feared he was going to shoot himself. She held her breath as he looked at her and removed the mask and holstered the gun.

"One day from now, the old spot at noon. Love you. I got to go," he said, turning away from her and kicking over Deidre's casket on the way back to McCarmick's Chevy as sirens blared. Before entering the car, Max passed by Allison, still struggling from the shot through her neck. He unloaded a shot in her face in stride, ending her agony. Reentering the Blazer, Max drove over a wounded Cindy Lawton, then sped off.

Paige fainted from the carnage that surrounded her.

Chapter 25:

SOMETHING HAS DIED

Middleton Township had drastically changed since Max had shipped off to live with his aunt. There were superstores and chain restaurants everywhere. Flowers II Remember, where his mother had once worked, no longer showcased a beautiful display out front, only boarded-up windows. In the city, Malden's Pharmacy was a tax preparation location. The J&J Produce Market across the street from Middleton Social was now a "pawn your gold for cash" shop.

While so much had changed, there was much that remained the same. Zerilli's Funeral Home, where Middleton's departed were laid to rest, was thriving, as it had in the past. A closed-casket viewing was underway for one Harold McCarmick. The *Middleton Observer*'s headline had read, "Beloved Teacher and Coach Slaughtered in Home Invasion." Local authorities would not confirm if the Lisbon and McCarmick murders were connected. After the deaths of five more at the cemetery, the press came to their own conclusions.

The remains of Greg Chapman were discovered in a pile of soot and rubble the night after Harold McCarmick was pronounced dead on the scene. A crowd shuffled into Zerilli's for the wake; an eight-by-ten framed yearbook photo sat atop the closed casket. Rising from the kneeler in front of the casket was former guidance counselor Timothy Moretz; he placed a palm on the casket of his former colleague and embraced his widow a bit longer than she would have liked.

If it had not been for Deidre's lawsuit after graduation, Moretz and Harold McCarmick would have still been working together. The school parted ways with him once Katherine Jalorean had Deidre Lisbon's academic records amended and he was of no use to her. She sued him and the school for a litany of offenses, and they were eager to settle out of court. The school decided Timothy Moretz was more of a liability than an asset and fired him. When he read about the murder of the girl who had ended his career in education, he had been elated, but not so when he discovered his old buddy Harold had been beaten, then shot to death.

Distraught over the loss of Coach McCarmick, he exited the funeral parlor. Max studied him, amused at the sight of the same navy blazer, wire-rim glasses, and greasy hair.

Outside, Moretz composed himself, took a deep breath, then was shoved down a flight of concrete steps. At the bottom of the embalming entrance, Timothy Moretz lay, his neck broken and twisted like the lies he had fashioned for his own benefit. Max Garret not only avenged the wrong done to him but also that done to countless other Middleton students who had been mentally and sexually harassed, browbeaten, and intimidated by the demoted teacher turned misguided counselor.

Ending Tim Moretz's life gave Max a momentary satisfaction similar to that given to him by killing those who had allowed his daughters to be tormented and who had lied about their intentions to protect her. The guidance counselor, far more responsible for hindering than helping students, was equally deserving of his wrath. His lie had fueled Deidre's hatred of Max and made his life in Middleton a living hell.

After taking her statement as a surviving witness, the detectives drove Paige to her parents' house. They were hesitant, but she assured them she had only fainted from the shock; they couldn't force her to go to Hillshire Medical. Paige didn't lie to them, but she also didn't tell them it had been Max. She thought about the question Max had posed to her before finishing off Ross. He had asked her what she was doing there, and in her head, she was still searching for an answer. Why had she gone to the funeral of her onetime friend turned hated enemy, whom she hadn't seen in years?

The tone of his voice when he had asked her had sounded like one of concern and not anger. The detectives had dropped her off and told her they would speak to her tomorrow to see if there were any details she may have neglected due to shock. Paige had explained once the first few shots were fired, she had taken cover behind a tombstone and left it at that. Once she got in, Phil and Lynne comforted her and counted their blessings she was not hurt.

"Cup of tea, Paige, or something stronger?" Lynne Edmundson asked, feeling the need to calm her nerves with a glass of wine herself. Paige opted for black coffee instead. Once she had settled into the comfort of her parents' home, she privately wished she had never left. She told her parents everything. They liked Max, even after his plot decades ago to blow up the gymnasium was discovered.

"This is different, Paige. He's murdered someone, then killed more people at the funeral. It's a miracle you weren't hurt," Phil Edmundson said. With tears streaming down his cheeks, he hugged Paige, nearly spilling the coffee her mother had just made in her lap. While she knew she could trust her parents with her secret, she didn't want to burden them with the worry of her seeing Max again. She decided not to tell them about his request to meet with her.

Once she calmed down, she told her folks, who were in greater shock than she was, that she was heading out. Her dad's vision wasn't what it had been; all those years of looking at screens and monitors had taken a toll on Phil's eyesight. Still he insisted on driving her home. In the car he questioned her about her marriage. His eyes were bad, but he wasn't blind. Her parents loved Olivia but tolerated Eddie for the sake of Paige and their granddaughter. He knew something had been wrong.

This was the kind of question Paige typically would have responded to with a generic "good" or "fine" as an answer. She didn't know if it was seeing Max or seeing five people die earlier that made her give her father the answer he already knew. She felt no need to mask her feelings.

"I love my daughter, but I'm miserable, Dad. I thought having Olivia would bring Eddie and me closer together, but instead we're further apart.

The way he treats her makes me so angry at him. It's like he never wanted her in the first place." They parked outside her house with the engine running.

As usual Phil said just the right thing to put her at ease. "I'll support your decision no matter what you do."

Paige waved goodbye to her dad as he pulled away and watched him from the front porch until his car was out of sight. When she opened the door, Paige nearly tripped over the two suitcases, which toppled over.

The sound alerted Eddie. He walked out of the kitchen and stopped. Paige stood in the doorway with his suitcases at her feet. Eddie remained in the arch of the kitchen. They looked at one another without speaking, and for the first time in a very long time, they understood each other. Typically, when one of them walked in the door they nonchalantly greeted one another with a lifeless hug. But here they stood in one of those moments in which time stood still, confronted with reality, no matter how badly they wanted the moment to end.

A lump in her throat prevented Paige from speaking. Desperate to break the silence, Eddie spoke up.

"I'm glad you're not hurt," he started, then looked down at his shoes as if he could find more to say on the floor.

"Ed, I…" She began to explain.

"It's OK, Paige. Look I, uh, fed her, and I put her to bed. I was just waiting for you to…" He paused, now looking up at the ceiling. "I got to go," he finished, then stormed over to collect the suitcases. Paige made room for his momentum, which carried him out the front door. From the porch, he turned back before taking the first step off and said, "I always loved you more than you loved me, and I knew it. I guess that's what made me such a lousy husband. I was never cut out for a kid either, but I thought it would help you tolerate me more. I'm sorry."

The dizzying feeling that had overcome Paige earlier in the cemetery was beginning to take hold of her. She fought to say something back. She felt she could do that, but all she managed to say, in a whimpering voice, was "So am I. I'm sorry too, Eddie." He gave a nod that was more like a bow of submission and took off down the front steps. He loaded his car, and she watched him drive off until he was out of sight, in the same direction she had seen her father go in minutes earlier. After checking in on Olivia, who was sound asleep, Paige looked out her window from her bed. She was physically and mentally exhausted. She'd remember the sadness of this day until her last.

She lay awake in bed, unable to sleep and after spending too much time with her thoughts, took her phone and called the one person she was certain was going through a tougher time than she was.

Chapter 26:
REUNION IN DESPAIR

They talked until Carolyn had to turn off her phone as her flight was departing. Paige left at daybreak to pick her up at the airport. There was a crowd of at least thirty people exiting, but Paige was able to put a face to the voice she had heard on the other side of the phone well into the night. There could have been a thousand people there, but only one had the face of a mother who had lost her child and was trying to save her husband. Paige double-parked her car and approached Carolyn Garret.

"I know you just got off a plane and you're most likely in more shock than I am, but would you mind driving? I almost hit a bus on the way here."

"Yes. Thank you for getting me. Just tell me where I'm going. I could use the distraction." Paige directed Carolyn through the city to a residential area.

"I thought you said you lived in the city?" Carolyn asked in confusion.

"I do, but my folks still live here. Don't worry—we're not going in," Paige replied, understanding the fewer people Carolyn Garret had to explain her presence to, the better. They exited the car, and Paige led her through the fence to her parents' backyard. One in front of the other, they walked down the trail into the wooded area behind the Edmundsons' home.

After sending Moretz down his last flight of stairs, Max left Harold McCarmick's car a few blocks from Zerilli's funeral home and walked, taking the back way into the woods behind the Edmundsons' house, then fell asleep in the wooded area where he had spent some of the best days of his life.

A twig snapping, followed by a rustling of leaves, caused him to jump down from the broken-down picnic table in the clearing. Someone was there; he just didn't know who it was.

The multicolored picnic table was now a mossy-green warped wood color. More forest than outdoor furniture. Only a few chips of the paint a teenage Paige Edmundson had marked it with remained. After Elvis had gone missing and Max had followed, she had no longer hung out in the quiet woods behind her house. Instead of being a sanctuary, it had become a monument to lost love.

But back she was, running through piles of dead leaves from the fallen trees in the wooded area, once so full of life. She saw Max sitting atop the old table through the trees. He was surrounded by crabgrass that had overtaken the flowers she had once planted. The wild plants and shrubs were untended clumps of weeds too. Instinctively he jumped from the table and unsheathed the knife, then dropped it immediately at the sight of the girl he loved so much that he had killed a multitude of people for taking him away from her.

"Look at you!" Paige said, running to Max and hugging him, the embrace bringing them both to tears. "Max, you have to turn yourself in. I talked to my parents last night. We can get a lawyer to arrange your surrender. It's the only way to…"

He paused her speech by placing a gentle finger to her lips while shaking his head no back and forth. "My daughter's dead. Most of whoever I was died along with her. I just wanted to make them pay and say goodbye to you. I have no one and nothing left."

The leaves thrashed once more as Carolyn emerged from behind a tree; Paige had told her to wait there until she knew it was OK. Max let go of his embrace of Paige in a panic. The alert reaction turned to shock at the sight of his wife crying.

"You have no one left? Are you sure about that?" Carolyn asked, speaking through her tears. Stunned, Max looked back at Paige, only to be taken aback by Carolyn, who clung to him in a bear hug. Max reciprocated his distressed wife's embrace while looking at Paige in confusion.

"Paige, how did you…" he started, before Carolyn interrupted him.

"What did you do, Max? Did you really think I would just forget you?" she said, crying and half-heartedly pounding his chest. Part of Paige wanted to make herself scarce and give the Garrets a moment, but another part of her felt she had to speak to the regretful look of surprise on Max's face.

"I'm so sorry for dragging you both into this. Twice for you, Paige. I'm so sorry. When she died, honey, I snapped like I did when I lived back here and had to do something," Max explained as Carolyn held on to him as if it were the last time she'd be able to. Seeing Carolyn was unable to find words, Paige spoke up.

"I know you're not supposed to blow people up or kill people, Max. It's basic right or wrong, but that doesn't mean that I don't understand. I don't think Carolyn would be here if she didn't either. But shit, Max, what are you going to do?" Paige asked, feeling the need to stress the urgency of the situation.

"I honestly didn't plan on making it this far. There's one more score I have to settle. Paige, if you're keeping track, you know who that is."

"Max, please, no!" Carolyn protested.

"I don't even know if you're aware of this, Max, but Dwayne was a cop. If you don't surrender, they will kill you without a shadow of a doubt. You may never see the light of day, but wouldn't you at least like to explain yourself for your family's sake?" Paige asked. Both her hands were out, a far cry from the pointed-finger-in-the-air questioning technique of Max from her youth.

Before Max could respond to Paige, a megaphone sounded from the woods toward the clearing. "Step away from the women. Get on your knees, and put your hands over your head!" the voice on the megaphone ordered. Max shoved Carolyn in Paige's direction once he heard the helicopter overhead. Paige gripped her with both hands to prevent her from running back in Max's direction. She saw infrared beams from weapons trained on Max's black hood.

"Max, please, they will kill you!" Carolyn cried out. A police tactical unit crept into the clearing and aimed at Max's head as he raised his hands. Carolyn eventually gave into Paige, pulling her in the opposite direction once she regained her footing. Max turned, facing the swarm of armed men in black coming through every opening into the clearing toward him.

The unit commander farthest back from Max fired a shot in the direction of his head. "Max, we will be there for you no matter what!" Paige's voice rang out, turning Max's head away from the bullet, causing the kill shot fired at his head to rip through his left shoulder instead.

He fell backward as authorities surrounded him and rushed Carolyn and Paige away from the scene. Max returned to Hillshire Hospital under armed guard. He underwent surgery for the gunshot to his shoulder. While he lay sedated, handcuffed to the hospital bed, a nurse cautiously pulled his gown away. She took out her phone and snapped photos of the alleged mass murderer, as well as the reaper and hourglass tattoo embedded over Max's heart.

"Has he regained consciousness yet?" the surgeon asked, forcing her to shove her phone in her smock.

"No, doctor."

"Notify me when he wakes. Legal counsel is waiting to speak to him. They have to move him for a preliminary hearing tomorrow. Also, I need not remind you of this institution's privacy laws regarding patients, do I?"

The Edmundsons opened up their home to Carolyn Garret, who stayed with them for the duration of the trial.

Chapter 27:
EXECUTIVE DECISION

The President of The United States stared at the copy of *Time* magazine, disgusted. An enlargement of the photo taken by the nurse at Hillshire Medical was plastered across the cover. He scoffed at the image of the sickle-wielding reaper and hourglass. Anchored at the bottom of the cover in bold yellow letters was a question posed to the reader: "What could make you murder?" Practically the entire issue covered all aspects of Max's many crimes and motivations, as well as the difference in opinion over the killer who had encapsulated the minds of the nation.

The death penalty debate. Points of view of supporters and detractors. A separate article painting Max as a vigilante and the face of a nation amid turmoil and recession.

"Get me the attorney general." He spoke into the speaker phone on his desk and stood up, staring out the center window of the Oval Office out into the patio.

In a few short months, his second term would be over and he'd give way to his successor. For the past eight years, he had dominated the news and minds of the American people. He expected a celebration of his legacy for his final days in office. Instead he was overwhelmed with a financial crisis and a serial killer the media was treating like the second coming of Jack the Ripper.

"Yes, Mr. President," the attorney general answered.

"I want you to have the state attorneys coordinate with South Dakota, Minnesota, Pennsylvania, and wherever the hell else this son of a bitch killed someone and tell them to pull resources."

"For what, sir?"

"I've already spoken to the justices, and they stand with me on this. The Middleton City Courthouse is on the Pennsylvania side. That's where I want him tried and convicted. I do not want this coverage carrying on from Christmas into the New Year. Pennsylvania has the death penalty, and this will be a capital case. We will try it all there."

"He needs to be tried separately in each state. We can't..."

"We most certainly can. He is going to be tried for all crimes in one trial. The American people will appreciate tax dollars not having to be spread from state to state for what should be an open-and-shut case."

"Sir, the House would have to put it to a vote; it could take time to..."

"Just put on yer goddamned C-SPAN, AG; there's about to be a land-mark decision in about an hour. I want this done and over with before every American sits down for their turkey dinner."

"Very good, Mr. President. One other item. It's gone public that the banking CEOs paid themselves bonuses with the bailout funds the government provided. Justice may have to step in."

"I heard. Unbelievable. Maybe we should have Garret kill them next. You're a good man, AG. It's been an honor serving with you. It can be a thankless job, I tell ya," the president concluded and hung up.

Chapter 28:

BLACK FRIDAY

In the national coverage of the case, the media dubbed it the "Max Garret Massacre." Defense attorney Dean "The Shield" Stapleton represented the defendant. Stapleton was renowned for securing not-guilty pleas in most cases; in Max's case, the goal was to keep him off death row.

The prosecution called Rebecca Claussen as a witness, along with the secretary who Max had locked in Principal Venerbeen's wardrobe closet.

Sheila Darvo's testimony was damaging to the defense as she identified Max to the jury as the man who had put a gun to her head and locked her up before the deaths in the prep school parking lot. The next witness proved to be a major setback for the prosecution. Once the prosecution used her testimony to establish motive, Rebecca Claussen broke down on the stand under intense cross-examination by Stapleton.

In tears she admitted she had been coached by the principal to tell the paramedics that Paige Garret's death had been an accident. A gasp was let out in the courtroom when Stapleton revealed Rebecca Claussen's interview in the local newspaper, which cited negligence on the school's part. An article brought to his attention by Carolyn Garret. The prosecution was blindsided, and had the two murders at the school been the only counts Max had been tried for, Stapleton would have felt confident of a deadlocked jury.

But this was not the case. Max was being charged with the murders of Principal William Venerbeen and administrator Jacobs, who had been bludgeoned to death, and for the kidnapping and assault of Sheila Darvo, the stabbing deaths of Zachary Chestnut's parents, as well as the double murder of Ronald Gibson's parents by explosive.

The hotel room with the duo of dead bikers and desk clerk Barry would have been difficult to tie him to if only he hadn't run Gary Simmons over with his security van. The tread marks embedded in his stomach matched the Garret Security van to a T, connecting Max to the corpses inside the off-pike inn. Additional forensic evidence from the soles of Max's Timberlands matched DNA from Simmons's face.

Stapleton thought he had caught a break when the clerk from the convenience store went back to his country due to the duress caused to his psyche by the murders. But the owner provided security footage of his client poking away at frat boys like pinatas, as he explained it to Carolyn and Paige in one of their many strategy sessions. Then the classic car collectors came forward to connect Max to the deceased Chris Martin's Buick convertible, if the security footage was not damning enough.

Then there was the matter of the revenge killings. Deidre Lisbon was portrayed by the defense as an all-American homecoming queen; video was recovered of the tortured burning murder of Greg Chapman, which added a charge of arson to boot. Harold McCarmick's widow was too shaken to testify, and with so many things going for them, the prosecution decided they didn't need to factor in the disappearance of Tim Moretz—not with all the surviving mourners who had seen Dwayne Bishop, Ross Aberdeen, Lana Karrington, and others cut down at Deidre's burial.

After a week of testimony, Carolyn and Paige had perfected the art of dodging reporters outside the courthouse steps. A cameraman pointed out to Middleton News 12 reporter Astra O'Donnel that the wife of the accused had just run behind her as she looked into the mirror of her compact and vented.

"We fucking live here, and we can't even get a good location outside the courthouse? What's that about. It should be first come, first served; all these douchebags from national get to go have breakfast while I'm freezing out here. Wait. What? Shit, that was them? Did you get anything? Never mind. You ready? I look good, right? OK, go.

"This Thanksgiving Eve marks the final day of testimony in the case dubbed the 'Murderton Massacre.' Prosecutors called in experts to nullify the credibility of a temporary insanity plea on the part of the defense and are aggressively seeking the death penalty for thirty-four-year-old Max Garret, whose murder spree after the death of his daughter crossed state lines and took lives every step of the way. The jury will break for the Thanksgiving holiday and return to hear closing arguments, then deliberate on Friday the twenty-eighth for a verdict. This is Astra O' Donnel reporting live for Middleton News Twelve."

The local report was repackaged and sold to other news outlets across America. It aired in the Bismark Bar in South Dakota and was seen by the barmaid Janine, Gerry, and Tito from Tito's Tattoos. Katherine Jalorean turned off her television set in disgust after seeing the report.

The bailiff instructed, "All rise," and Stapleton waited for his client to be led into the courtroom.

Two sheriff's officers led Max, in a prison jumper and hand and leg restraints, through a narrow gray corridor. An entourage of four more met him at the entrance to the courtroom.

If Dean "Shield" Stapleton thought twenty counts of first-degree murder was going to make avoiding the death penalty impossible, there was one mitigating factor that practically made it a guarantee. Putting Max on the witness stand destroyed the insanity plea, and he had countered Max's insistence that he speak.

"Your Honor, I killed them all. I admit it," Max said before being forced back into his seat by his attorney and one of the many sheriff's officers stationed nearby him.

"Defense requests a continuance, Your Honor," Stapleton said as Judge Grizer slammed his gavel to quiet the uproar Max's admission had caused.

"No, counselor, no. I'm not having this trial take any longer. Continuance denied. Proceed with your closing argument."

Stapleton nodded. He elected to use the shorter version of the closing statements he had prepared after seeing one of the jurors he thought might rule in his favor gasp at the idea of a further delay and began, "Ladies and gentlemen of the jury, Mr. Garret was lied to by the very people who were negligent, as Ms. Claussen, the prosecution's own witness, pointed out. Her testimony demonstrated who was truly responsible for his daughter's death. How would any of us react if our child were killed on a playground where she was bullied and tormented day in and day out? Unsupervised children throwing objects at her sent her careening to her death. I'm not saying that Mr. Garret's actions were justifiable. I am saying his actions were not premeditated as he was not of sound mind."

Stapleton led with the best hand he had to play, and he strived to drive home the circumstance that had driven Max to murder. He returned to the defense table, took a sip of water, and proceeded to address the Middleton murders.

"Katherine Jalorean sat on that very stand!" He pointed demonstratively. "And she told you that Max Garret himself was beaten within an inch of his life by his former classmates at Middleton High! That as a youth she had taken him to the Hillshire emergency room, where records confirm trauma to his head and concussions. It is not inconceivable that in his state over the death of his daughter, coupled with the violent abuse he suffered in the past, Mr. Garret went ballistic and, in a shock-induced episode of post-traumatic stress disorder, was driven to murder?" Stapleton asked the jury rhetorically with his arms open.

"Was Mr. Garret insane? No. Is he following the tragedy that befell his family and caused him to act out on these post-traumatic impulses? Yes. I firmly believe this beyond a reasonable doubt. Thank you. Defense rests, Your Honor."

Stapleton fought the case harder than he had any prior case. He felt his best was still not enough to keep Max from getting the needle. Throughout the trial Max was attentive and at times remorseful, especially when he looked behind him and saw Paige and Carolyn pulling for him day in and day out. The testimony by Ms. Jalorean on his behalf reduced him to tears. Seeing her made him recall the good in an otherwise miserable existence in his teenage years.

The jury did not have an immediate verdict, and Max's attorney told him, "This is a good thing." When the foreman returned a second time, he instructed the judge they had come to a decision. As the foreman read the ruling, Max zoned out. The foreman's voice was a blurred echo in his head. He turned and gave a regretful smile to Carolyn and Paige. The expressions on their faces told him all he needed to know. They rushed out of the courtroom as Stapleton made room at the defense table for his client to be taken back into custody.

Chapter 29:
CONCLUSIVE TERMS

It had been a comfort for Paige, Carolyn, and Olivia to spend the past two weeks at the Edmundsons'. Carolyn joined them for Thanksgiving. Having anticipated the worst, Phil warmed up leftovers for the girls to have some comfort food after the verdict. Carolyn was having a glass of wine with Lynn while Phil cleaned up the kitchen. Paige went upstairs to her childhood room and opened her old high-school diary, which she started making entries in once again after spending so much time at her parents'.

"Paige, are you coming down for dessert?" her father called up to her, yelling over the sound of vibrating bass from Lynn Edmundson's EDM music.

"Be right down, Dad!" Paige yelled back and smiled, thinking her mom was just the distraction Carolyn needed. She looked at pictures of her and Max that she was using as bookmarks in her diary and thought about the first time she brought him home from school—when her mom was in her aerobics gear and they hung out in the same room she was in now. Her eyes welled up as she stopped writing and looked over to the dusty video game cartridges that were still neatly stacked under her TV stand.

She heard Carolyn coming up the stairs to use the bathroom and continued her journal entry in haste. "Paige, please hurry down. Your mom's gotten me drunk and is trying to get me to dance the cha-cha," Carolyn called into her room. The tone of her voice indicated spirits had reversed her feelings of sadness, if only for the moment.

None of it mattered—guilty on all counts. Carolyn's bringing charges against the school for covering up Paige's death, which was exposed by Rebecca Claussen. It's little consolation for her. Losing Max and her daughter in an instant. I share a small part of her grief having lost him not once but twice and my own marriage dissolving as well. She's going to stay until sentencing next week. I know it's selfish of me to wish her to stay; Olivia loves her being around and so do I. I guess I'm the social pariah of Middleton once again. I still have my folks and besides I'm used to it.

Judge Chester Grizer had been on the bench for twenty years. The reputation his previous rulings had garnered him was that he was a tough judge. Grizer was firm but fair and above all followed the law to the letter. He acknowledged flaws in the system but also maintained that the justice system was, in his words, "as good as we can be until we are better."

Throughout the trial of Max Garret, attorney Dean Stapleton had found it impossible to get a read on him. Usually a judge's facial expressions and reactions indicated their personal feeling toward the case, no matter how well the judge tried to mask them. He'd brought defendants before Grizer before, and this time he had been an oak throughout.

"Do you wish to make a statement on your behalf before I give my recommendation for sentencing, Mr. Garret?" Judge Grizer asked. He privately always wished for the defendants to say no. Not because he didn't want to hear anything they had to say but because in his mind he followed the guidelines laid out to the best of his ability and he didn't like to give the impression that this was an opportunity for the defendant to plead their final case. The time for pleading had passed. The appeal would follow.

"Go on, Mr. Garret. The court is listening."

"I exercised poor judgment with the men at the rest stop, Your Honor. I was in a bad place mentally, and they were quite rude to me and the man working there. That alone did not deserve my vengeance." Max's explanation caused his attorney to wince in pain. It was obvious Max was deviating from the planned statement.

"Noted, Mr. Garret. Noted. Just the three from the rest stop?"

"Yes, just them."

"Well, Mr. Garret, I have to ask, what about the other souls who perished due to your hands alone? No regret for them?"

"No, sir. World's better off without them. They made choices that sealed their fate. Hell, most of them made those decisions long ago." Stapleton just looked down at his new pair of Johnston & Murphys and saw the leather had creased and braced for Judge Grizer's reply.

"So I am to understand that you have no apathy whatsoever with regard to the other seventeen victims? While your statement may give merit to the defense with regard to your mental capacity, I myself find it tragic and unsettling. Having said that, I wish mercy on your soul, Mr. Garret. I truly do."

When he spoke of mercy, it struck a nerve with Max. He thought of his little girl crying to him. He thought of all those times he had covered his head to prevent being punched or kicked. He thought of his mother being beaten and begging his father to stop to no avail. Max Garret knew no mercy. He had never been shown any, and he did not wish to receive it at this stage in his life.

"*Mercy?*" he asked in amazement. "I mean, no offense, but mercy wasn't doing me any good when my little girl was killed or when I was getting my head kicked in to the point of blowing myself the hell up," Max said, his voice growing fiercer as he cocked his head to the left to reveal the mangled flesh on his neck to the judge. "You just offer that mercy to someone who can use it. Perhaps to my departed mother and my little girl, both dead too soon. Or maybe to my wife. Send some mercy their way because it's not worth a damn to me."

Stapleton lifted his head, looking at the justice in true anticipation of his response to his client's suggestion. Judge Grizer grimaced; he leaned back in his chair and let out a deep breath, removed his glasses, and sighed.

"I've sat in this chair, Mr. Garret, and heard testimony for days of your reasoning as well as your undeniable guilt in these proceedings. I understand and certainly realize that society has failed you and failed your family. We are here today, though, sir, because you, Mr. Garret, have failed society at large yourself. I hereby sentence you to life imprisonment with no possibility of parole. The sentences are to be served concurrently for each of the homicides you were found guilty of."

"Th-thank you, judge," Stapleton said in disbelief as Max shrugged defiantly.

Avoiding the death penalty was a feather in Stapleton's cap, but it meant little to Max. In his mind he had died with his daughter. If he was going to be sentenced to death for fighting back, he was fine with that as well.

After sentencing, Paige and Olivia saw Carolyn off to the airport. They made plans to reconnect, and when Paige got back to her parents', she decided to write a final entry and complete the journal she had started in 1988, the year she met Max.

She wrote:

> Judge Grizer and the media afterward concluded that if not for my testimony Max would have been put to death. You can imagine how much of a hit that made me with the locals. My job told me they needed to make economic cutbacks due to recession, sure. Eddie came to the house one day when I was at the trial and took the rest of his belongings. It's just me and Olivia here alone. My folks asked us to stay, but they have their own life. Which is why I'm done writing in this journal and I'm going to start living as best as I can for me and my little girl.

Once Max was ushered into the penitentiary, he was x-rayed for contraband, deloused, and led to the place where he would, in Judge Grizer's words, "spend the rest of his natural life." On the way into his cell, another prisoner scowled at Max. The other inmate stopped mopping the floor and stared him down as he passed. They all knew who he was. Screaming could be heard from the upper tiers. Encouraging shouts of "What the fuck's up, killa?" "Murderton in the muthafuckin' hiz-ouse," and "Maniac Max!" echoed back down the iron and concrete corridors, along with insults: "Fuck you, Garret!" "I'ma make you mah bitch!" You ain't shit," and "I'ma see you, Max!" It was then that Max understood his level of infamy among the condemned men. The prison routine was more stringent than the service but simple to follow. He answered bells, followed orders, and tried to stay off people's minds.

Once the prison population caught wind that he was the Middleton Maniac, they quizzed him about if he ever knew Cold Infantrino, Artie Kane, or Gladgem Gervallo. The name alone brought a wide smile to Max's face as he recalled his friend. He provided an unquestionable account of his old friend, which caused his new friends to call him Maximillian—a name he liked much better than Maniac Max.

By the time the new year rolled in, he had made alliances with old-timers who were in for the long haul, just like him.

Months turned into a year. By the end of 2009, Max found himself making the best of a bad situation. Keeping in constant contact with Carolyn, Paige, and Olivia kept him going.

In a secluded log cabin, Carolyn steadied a cup of hot chocolate and handed it to Olivia to free her hands to knock on the door. Paige was seated behind a desk with the same trapper folder she had had all her life and her diary, which had loose pieces of paper stapled to the back of it. Olivia gave her the steaming cup, then hugged her once she set it down.

"Sorry to interrupt, but I figured you could use a break," Carolyn said, gently rapping on the open door.

"Are you finished yet, Mom?" Olivia asked Paige impatiently. Her mother took a sip of the hot chocolate and pressed a dab of the whipped cream to her nose on purpose. She smiled at her daughter, humoring Carolyn as well.

"Just about. Then your aunt Carolyn has to translate and type out the last chapter of my chicken scratch. You were supposed to help me think of a title," Paige said cheerfully while playfully dabbing a touch of whipped cream on Olivia's nose as well.

"How 'bout *Mommy's Friend*?" the child asked, giggling.

"Not too bad, Olivia, since *Mad Max* is already taken."

"Speaking of which, Carolyn, we need to get a copy to him before we send it to the publisher," Paige said, waving her handwritten manuscript cautiously.

"May have to read it to him over the phone. Pricks are constantly changing what can and can't go in. Mind if I take a look?"

"Be my guest, Mrs. Garret," Paige said, sliding her handwritten work over to Carolyn. She read what she recognized as Paige's final journal entry, which had been added to the diary:

> If you were to say that Max ruined my life, I'd say you were wrong. Dead wrong. I didn't lose nearly as much as I gained. I still have my Olivia, and we moved out West with Carolyn after the trial. One really good friend when the odds are stacked against you; that's exactly what you will need in this world to survive. I'm living proof of that.

A tear fell like a raindrop on the piece of notebook paper Carolyn was reading. She hugged Paige, and Olivia joined them.

"I'm going to grab a tissue," Carolyn said, making her way toward the cabin's living space.

"OK, and you hand me that pile there, angel," Paige instructed Olivia, who was helping her clean off her desk. Carolyn stormed back into the office, her face pale white, as if she had seen a ghost.

"Car, what's wrong? Are you OK?" Paige questioned, fighting to get her arm back from her friend, who was tugging at it. Carolyn pulled her into the living room and pointed to the television and the banner headline anchored to the screen.

"I need you to tell me I'm not seeing things, Paige," Carolyn said with her index finger still out long after Paige had seen what she was pointing at.

"Oh no. They'll kill him for sure, Car. I have to call my parents."

"SERIAL KILLER ESCAPES PRISON EXPLOSION MASSACRE; MAX GARRET REMAINS AT-LARGE" covered the news broadcast on the television.

Chapter 30:

LOOSE ENDS

The bartender gave the bright-red and blue neon open sign a pull of the cord so no one else would come in while he was closing. He grabbed one belligerent drunk from the bar and hustled him toward the exit.

"At least let me get some packaged goods or takeout!" the bent old man yelled as he was forced out the front door.

"Ah, fuck ya's all." He growled as the light over his head went out.

The old man grabbed a bottle off the bar on his way out and was chugging it out front. The outside overhead light came back on, and the door opened once more.

"You can't walk out with an open bottle, you drunk!" the bartender yelled.

The crotchety, staggering inebriate tilted his head back and took a long swig and threw the bottle at the door, yelling, "Keep it, ya cunt!" repeatedly before heading down the street. He almost tripped over a small curb at the mouth of the alleyway in the center of the block he was trudging down. As he regained his balance, a voice called out to him from the shadows.

"Say, mister, you got a dollar to spare? Five would be better."

His balance regained, he straightened his head toward the stranger's direction and without looking slurred, "As a matter of fact, I do. But first you're going to need to lick my hairy ass for it! Ya fuck you!"

"I was hoping you'd say something like that." The stranger spoke back in a calm voice, confusing the drunkard.

"I know you. Yeah, you used to work at that produce store, right?"

"And just who in the fuck are you?" he asked, stumbling toward the alleyway known as Murderer's Row.

"Well, it was a long time ago," the voice started calmly, then continued in rising fury. "I was once your son, William Garret, but now I am the Avenger, and this is your time."

Max yanked his father toward him with both hands. The old man only managed a single shriek before being engulfed by the darkness of the alleyway and the brutality of Max Garret, who continued whaling on him long after he had drawn his last breath.

"You can rest now, Mom. I can rest now," Max said before torching the mangled and broken remains of William Garret in the alley.

Having fulfilled the wish he had made while staring out his bedroom window as a teenager, Max left the flaming corpse and walked to Zerilli's Funeral Home. The funeral director, Davey Burke, had a line on an old acquaintance.

Carmine Tenagia, lifelong friend of Dominic Gervallo, was living in Budd Lake, New Jersey, and expecting him. Max was going to need help and luck if he had any hope of eluding capture and reuniting with Carolyn and Paige. He loaded the back of a hearse with the stashed remains of Grady's arsenal, put on a chauffeur's hat, and left Middleton, never to return again. Thus ending the time of the Avenger.

ABOUT THE AUTHOR

Jason Marinko is an actor, author, poet, and screenwriter who has embarked upon over thirty other careers, providing an abundance of real-world experience. He has been a lifelong resident of the tristate area, incorporating East Coast elements into his stories while fictionalizing locales so as not to make any one place too good or bad as these communities have given so much to him in the way of storytelling. He is a proud member of the Hamilton Township Creative Writing Group, Barnes & Noble of Hamilton Writing Group, and McCarter Theatre's Shakespeare Community Reading Group. If it had not been for the guidance and support of these organizations, this work would not have been completed. He currently resides in New Jersey with his girlfriend, Michelle, and his pet and coauthor, Mr. Speedy Catface.

For more visit timetheavenger.com or contact
Jason Marinko Author | Facebook.

Printed in the USA
CPSIA information can be obtained
at www.ICGtesting.com
LVHW022121131023
760975LV00010BA/153